Jonathan Trigell was born in Hertfordshire in 1974. *Boy A*, his first novel, was written as the thesis for an MA in creative writing at Manchester University. It won the Waverton Award for best first novel of 2004, the inaugural World Book Day Prize and the John Llewellyn Rhys Prize. *Boy A* was filmed in 2007 and went on to win a total of four BAFTA awards in 2008. His second novel, *Cham*, shortlisted for the Boardman Tasker Prize, is set in the death-sport capital of the world – Chamonix Mont Blanc, in France – where the author himself now lives, pursuing his passion for the mountains.

D0544475

C333122075

GENUS

JONATHAN TRIGELL

corsair

Constable & Robinson Ltd
55-56 Russell Square
London WC1B 4HP
www.constablerobinson.com

First published in the UK by Corsair,
an imprint of Constable & Robinson Ltd., 2011

Published in this paperback edition by Corsair, 2012

Copyright © Jonathan Trigell 2011

The right of Jonathan Trigell to be identified as the
author of this work has been asserted by him in accordance
with the Copyright, Designs & Patents Act 1988.

Excerpt from *Toulouse-Lautrec: A Life* by Julia Frey © 1994
published by Weidenfeld and Nicolson.
Reprinted by kind permission of the author.

'Fifth Philosopher's Song' from *Leda* by Aldous Huxley,
published by Chatto and Windus.
Reprinted by permission of The Random House Group Ltd.

This is a work of fiction. Names, characters, places and incidents are
either the product of the author's imagination or are used fictitiously, and
any resemblance to actual persons, living or dead, or to actual events or
locales is entirely coincidental.

All rights reserved. This book is sold subject to the condition
that it shall not, by way of trade or otherwise, be lent, re-sold,
hired out or otherwise circulated in any form of binding or cover
other than that in which it is published and without a similar condition
including this condition being imposed on the subsequent purchaser.

A copy of the British Library Cataloguing in Publication
Data is available from the British Library

ISBN 978-1-78033-440-0

Printed and bound in the UK

1 3 5 7 9 10 8 6 4 2

MIX
Paper from
responsible sources
FSC® C018072

For Alex, Heidi, Luke and Betty,
four quarters of me, genetically.

Today, if Adèle Tapié de Céleyran and her first cousin Count Alphonse de Toulouse-Lautrec fell in love, they would very probably have genetic testing to make sure their children would not be at risk of deformities and other maladies provoked by marrying within the same gene pool. And when they learned that every child would have a twenty-five per cent chance of inheriting a rare form of dwarfism, they might choose not to have children together. They might even decide not to marry, which, given their basic incompatibility, would save them each a great deal of unhappiness.

Toulouse-Lautrec : A Life, Julia Frey

A million million spermatozoa
All of them alive
Out of their cataclysm but one poor Noah
Dare hope to survive.

And of that billion minus one
Might have chanced to be
Shakespeare, another Newton, a new Donne –
But the One was Me.

Shame to have ousted your betters thus.
Taking ark while the others remained outside!
Better for us all, froward Homunculus,
If you'd quietly died!

Aldous Huxley

Again the angel of the Lord called to Abraham from heaven and said: 'I swear by myself, declares the Lord, that because you acted as you did in not withholding from sacrifice your beloved son, your only son, I will bless you abundantly and make your descendants as countless as the stars of the sky and the sands of the seashore.'

Genesis

I

Everything Will Be All Right

1

Holman

IT'S BEEN AN HOUR since he told her about Jesus, and she has now sobbed herself to exhaustion. She looks old when she cries, which is usually only when someone close to her dies violently. Holman has only seen it a few times. The tears have dissolved into her make-up and drained it into the struggle-carved gutters of her face. He would like to paint her like this, maybe he will when he gets home. He tries to feel for her pain, he attempts to comfort her, but he can't help being fascinated by her. He can't stop himself thinking about how he could do something with oil or charcoal, to recreate what those streaked cheek creases say about her world. Even as he holds her heaving head and breathes in the longed-for, but rarely received, smells of woman, he feels detached. Like he is watching himself doing it. As if he is a tourist in the land of his own life.

The air in the studio apartment is stale, like the sheets of the drooping double bed on which they both sit. So he hauls himself by his cane and shuffles over to the stained-glass window, where the panes depict a grey-bearded saint. The arthritic creak as the window frame is forced open could have come from the stained-glass-saint's old bones.

Holman puts his head outside. It's no cooler out there and no fresher, with mopeds guffing out bacterial bio fumes into the already saturated air, but at this height there is a small breeze at least. They say it's the hottest June since records began, but such platitudes have long since lost all meaning: it always seems to be the hottest since records began. The sounds of the street – little burps from moped horns and the general tra-la-la – seem to have roused Dolly a little. She lifts her head and smiles a self-consciously brave smile at him. One of her false eyelashes is coming unstuck, hanging at the edge like a half-bitten thumbnail. A gash that shows the baseness of it all. A gap like an easily visible hole in a lie.

'Do you want a glass of synth?' he asks her. 'That might be the best thing for now.'

'I've got nothing left, and I can't be going out, not today.'

Holman winks a large dark eye at her. People seem to perceive something from his eyes: perhaps because the warm, permanently dilated pupils look pleasantly out of place on such a shrunken, uncomely homunculus as him. He limps back to the bed and sits down, thinking how he and Dolly make a comically chaste pair, side by side on this site of incalculable fornications.

Now that it isn't needed to support his weight, Holman is able to unscrew the top of his cane, and he pours from it a stream of frog-green liquid into the tea-tarnished china mug that sits on Dolly's bedside table. Though the sweet, strong smell of the synth instantly ignites his yearning, he leaves nothing in the cane's hidden flask for himself. But there's a decent dose for Dolly. Enough to medicate her troubles for a while.

She takes the mug to her face two-handed, looking childlike in her anxiousness not to spill a dear drop. He remembers her like that, and while she lies down to try and sleep away the pain, he starts to sketch her in the notepad that he always carries. Preparations.

Holman first moved to King's Cross – The Kross – in the hope of sanctuary. Some instinctive sense that he would blend in better. He had seen that the strange were more numerous there: the detritus from the closed-down communes, burdened with religion as well as imperfection; some elderly early failures; the dated, the cheap and the dull; the charity packs; and the ragged remnants of the city's Unimproved still lingered in the streets round that Elizabethan railway station. The Kross had become a beacon for the genetic underclass. Holman couldn't say that he grew to love it, but he grew to prefer it to anywhere else. And among the whores, the broodmares, the synth heads and the silk workers, there were artists, and many other bright splashes of colour on that drab urban palette.

His studio is not far from Dolly's. He hobbles out through the communal vestibule – her building is one of the many churches converted into council flats after The Dissolution of the Temples Act – and out on to the canicule street. He isn't dressed for weather like this, he never is, but his unusual uniform: the black suit and bowler hat acts as armour somehow, it helps push the world a little further from him. Already a grotesque oddity, to be odder feels safer than a pretence of normality would be. He passes a group of wall-leaning gavroches, most of whom wear their T-shirts tucked up under their armpits, in pretence that it cools them, but really to show off exercise-defined abs. Trying to look gene-improved, but exhibiting only self-loathing.

There is a languid menace in street youths like these, posturing that can flip instantly to violence. But Holman is left alone. He keeps his gaze ahead and down, so as not to meet the eye of one who might take that as offence. He hears a whisper of 'fucking cripple', but doesn't look up. To seem utterly defenceless is Holman's best defence.

Outside an unopened shop, stacked crates of dusty Coke bottles, filled and used so many times they are almost sheenless, still sparkle, so bright is the sunlight. So hot it feels like the glass should melt. Something about their neat segregated rows in the plastic slots reminds Holman of military ordnance: newspaper pictures, grenades that some tracksuited fanatic might have lobbed from the back of a moving truck, to make more martyrs to his insanity.

Vents from a few illegal air-conditioning units churn out ever more superheated air. Moisture drips from them on to the streets below. Dun sparrows try fruitlessly to bathe in the lens-thin puddles they produce.

Ahead of him – but making such slow progress that even-tually even Holman overtakes them – walks a boy, proudly holding the paw of one of those mini pandas that were popular a few years back. The panda looks mangy and malnourished: bare pink patches in its black and white fur – it's probably from a rescue centre, if it belongs to a Kross kid – but it gnaws eagerly on the bit of chorizo sausage it's holding.

Holman loves to watch children and at the same time hates them, and for the same reason, because children are a repository for all the joy left in the world. However they may have come – picked and modelled in computer simulation, or conceived in timeless two-backed tussle – at the points they arrive they are still just children. However those bluest eyes or that duskiest skin came about – with genes enhanced from ma and pa, bought entirely anew, or left to chance – they still arise like a gift of nature. They still laugh at life and discover old truths for themselves with fresh wonder. They still smile unblemished by guile. And they still remind Holman that he – perhaps not alone, but nearly so – was denied this joy even for those transient years when it should have been his right. In a world where physical perfection is ever more commonplace – and so of course becomes itself plain, in the striving for better – he has always fitted firmly in the lowest cadre of those who have been left behind entirely.

As he unlocks the front door to his building, Holman finds himself surprised, catching sight of the gnarled stubbishness of his own fingers around the smooth, slim, long-barrelled key. And simultaneously unsurprised by his surprise: because every time he awakes he is brought down anew by the realization that this is the real him, even though the other him, the him of his dreams, felt more real and more really who he was supposed to be. He never ceases to be disgusted by his own dwarfish fingers clutching the anchor-rope rim of his duvet.

When he paints, though, it is different. When Holman paints, his fingers become long and lithe like a pianist's or pick-pocket's. They float and fly about the canvas, deft strokes making the images of his mind more substantial than they ever were, either within his imagination or even in the original scenes that stirred them. He has a talent for capturing the inner vehemence of his subjects, for making the years of rage and despair and caved-in dreams explicit with a stoical stare or half-cocked leer. Holman has a rare skill for bringing to life the inhumanity of humankind. Somewhere within, he has always known this, from his snubbed art-school days, through the disdain of his family, and now, perhaps – he feels a smarting draught of hope – the world is starting to agree. Charlie Smith sold two of Holman's paintings last month, for enough money to keep him in supplies a good while, were it not for the fact that his rent was late and he drank most of the remainder in celebration. But people other than pimps and whores and the paupers he buys synth for are beginning to look Holman in the eye; even though they have to look down to do so.

He is not a dwarf, though, not a true dwarf – as such things are recorded and measured: he stands at four foot nine, with corns and blisters on the floor. If his fractal, valgus legs could be straightened, then he might have another two inches on that. If those foreshortened bandied limbs were in proportion to the rest of his frame, then he might be five foot eight, or more, which would have been respectable enough, though still strange in a world where only poor or religious males continue to linger below six feet.

But beyond even his height there is something dwarfish about his face. Dwarfish in the semblance of the minions who worked the mines and foundries of Vulcan perhaps, because Holman's skin is reddish, like it's fire-scorched from a forge. His lips are thick and would be lascivious, but they lack the look of intellect that word suggests and so they are merely brutish. Uncomfortably numb, drool will sometimes drip from his lower lip – with owner unaware – into his beast-thick beard. He has long since given up on shaving, an act that feels like an attempt to fight time or tide: since the hairs on his left cheek appear to have begun re-emergence even in the while it takes to shave the right. His eyes are dark, shadowed beneath thick brows and a tomb-front forehead. But they are, if not a window to his soul, at least not a mirror of his body.

Holman rifles through the meagre piles of mail in the lobby; then pulls out his pad and looks again at the sketches he made of Dolly, while he gathers his strength for the stairs. He made a show of strength for her – show or charade? – either way such displays take it out of him, leave little energy for himself. And inwardly, of course, he is still shaken from having found Jesus.

2

Gretchen Gerbi

THE SPIDER'S HISSED SHRIEKING startles Gretchen. The creature's ten-inch mandible fangs twitch and flare, though the noise doesn't come from the black gape they reveal. The screech emanates from its bulbous, wolf-haired thorax, or from the vibration of the flapping cage-door lungs that lie beneath it. There is no emotion in the four pairs of blank black eyes that stare at Gretchen, but the screech is horrible. Instinct erects the tiny time-whitened hairs on her elderly lady's frame, long past fight or flight. Seven of the spider's three-foot-long legs jerk manically, their triple claws clattering on the tiled kitchen floor. Its lame and trailing eighth leg is trapped under the door, again.

'You silly thing, Bojangles,' Gretchen scolds; but she looks on fondly as she frees the leg and the creature stalks across to its hardboard lair under the sagging but freshly scrubbed work surface.

Gretchen goes back to scanning her rescued copy of yesterday's newspaper, she'll use it to re-line Bojangles' lair when she's had a quick look. There isn't much of interest: another terrorist attack, but not a big one, bit of a botch job, it sounds like: blew himself up and the back wall of an empty library. Silly thing. There is editorial discussion about the morality of using a shark gene in people: it would allow for perfect pearly-white teeth that renewed continually through life. It would never get through parliament, though – they never cross the Rubicon of using non-human genes – the press just run these articles to shock. The newspaper ink leaves a smudged stain on Gretchen's fingers, which are looking greyer by the day anyway. Grey as her hair. Grey as her pinafore. But the day's not grey, she thinks, looking out the window. The sky's blue and you can bet it'll be a scorcher, but that's all right. That's not so bad.

'A bit of sunshine never hurt anyone, did it, Bojangles?'

Donald used to like the sun. Even at the end, weak as he was, he used to like to be wheeled out to sit on the parched little patch of earth in what passed for a front yard. No front yard now, in this new place, but she'd never grumble, plenty have it worse.

She hears the building's front door go and looks out of the spyhole next to her pantry that gives her a view of the entry. It's part of her job as the concierge, she always thinks, she's not being nosy, but she needs to know who's coming and going. It's poor Holman coming in. Hobbling across the hall resting on his walking cane. He really is a horrible-looking little man. 'But you can't blame him for that,' she says to Bojangles, with a sympathetic smile: the spider not being much of an Adonis itself. Bojangles doesn't move, just stares at her, not that it has too much choice, since its eight eyes don't blink or move. Actually, it would probably be quite a catch in spider world, Gretchen always thinks. It has lovely strong dark-furred legs, except for the gammy one, dances them ever so nimbly when something agitates him – hence his name – and makes her ever such a lot of silk. But Bojangles is a mule spider, of course, they don't mate, don't have the urge to. The breeders say it makes them calmer and stops them trying to run off, but everyone knows it's really just so you go back to buy another one when your spider dies after five or six years. Stops you ever really getting independent. Though people reckon it's hard to breed them anyway; it's difficult enough just to keep two at a time, without them eating each other. She knows enough folk who've tried. Sooner or later they'll find each other and struggle to the death. They've made them completely vegetarian – she's seen Bojangles sit spinning, ignoring a sparrow not a half-lunge in front of his fangs – but the gene-splice scientists still can't stop that urge to kill other arachnids.

It's like with people in a way: though, for the Improved, at least, sex is now completely separated from reproduction, the rape rate hasn't gone down and men still live in fear of being cuckolded; jilted lovers still murder one another. There's always something in the paper, when she fishes it out of the bin of Flat 10. There are some bits of nature you just can't get rid of. That's what she always used to say to Donald, when they were choosing their son.

'I don't care what the doctors claim,' she'd say, 'they don't know everything: you look at Mrs De Castillo's boy. They can have a go, but they don't know everything; nature will take its course too.'

Of course, the more you paid the less the chances were of unforeseen developments, but you can only afford so much, only do so much. They'd borrowed as much as they could, she'd said to Donald, so that was that; no point in worrying afterwards. Just let nature take its course. They were both the first generation of either of their families to gene-enrich at all. Prior to them, their relatives had all procreated in the same, slightly unseemly pot-luck fashion as their ancient ancestors.

And hadn't the investment turned out well? Their Paulo was a lovely boy, all their joy, and had grown into quite a man as well. Didn't come round so much as he might these days, but that was life. They gave him the best start they could. And anyway, if he was a bit too independent, well, that was probably old Donald's fault. Donald said he'd never been independent enough, wanted his boy to really make something of himself. Which he had, in a smallish way, but he never visited much.

The spyhole gives Gretchen quite a wide-angle view. She wonders if that's how Bojangles sees things, with his eight eyes. Holman's checking the mail now, sifting through all the piles to see if anything is for him, though he must know that Gretchen always separates it out. To think that his mother is that famous model what's-her-name. Donald had quite a thing for her, as much as he was interested in any celebrity types. She probably doesn't look as nice now, of course, close up anyway; though she still looks dandy when you see her in the papers, which you occasionally still do. You'd certainly never credit Holman as coming from her. All that money and those genes to work with, you'd have thought Holman would have been quite something. But no, they thought they knew best, didn't they? Silly things. She supposes he wouldn't have been Holman then though, if things had been different. He would have been *a* Holman, but not him. But he wouldn't have minded either, would he? He would never have known any different. That's what all the protesters and the religious folk didn't get: what you never knew never hurt you.

She and Donald could have chosen any number of other little Paulos, but the one that came along was theirs just the same. Their son. And he was the best they could afford anyway, so that was that. It would be nice if he called by a little more often, though. She wouldn't mind that.

Bojangles dances his funny little twitching-leg jig of anticipation when she gets his fly biscuits out. Who knows if there's real flies in them; Gretchen doubts it, but he certainly enjoys them. She uses the bowl of biscuits to tempt him out of his little den under the sink, the easier to change the newspaper in it.

Most people who keep silk spiders just do it for the money, for the bit of income the silk brings in. But Bojangles is her second now, and Gretchen finds them quite therapeutic. Well, maybe that's not the right word, but they ease the loneliness anyway. They help to fill the gap that was left when Donald died. It wasn't that she and Donald used to do much together, any more than she and Bojangles. But just having him sat there, even if he was in the other room, helped time pass. A day is a long time to spend on your own. Though not as long as a night: even in the heat of the summers there is a cold patch in her bed, where a funny little man used to sleep once. A man who shrank the longer she knew him. Whose eyebrows grew into great white clouds above his eyes as he aged. Once big eyes that eventually became little pinpricks, but were still the same kingfisher blue as the eyes she fell in love with and still belonged to the same man. And she can fully understand how people want to believe in life after death. Sometimes, in those first months, the thought that her Donald had just disappeared was almost more than she could physically bear. It used to hit her like a sickness, used to suck the air from her and leave her panicked. If there had been any religious groups to join, she might well have done so, back then; for the support, the solace. She supposes that's when they used to get people. But now she's mostly all right, she just keeps ticking on through the long days and longer nights. She knows she's not the first widow the world has ever known, and she'll not be the last. And she's not the worst off, not by a long shot. She did well to get this concierge job, with the free flat. And Bojangles gives her a little extra income as well. That was good luck, getting such a good spinner so cheap, just because of a duff leg. She's doing all right.

Gretchen smiles while she works; she likes making lasagne; she enjoys layering the meat and the dairy-ooze of béchamel, but most of all plating it with the pasta: overlapping the sheets, as if armouring a little creature. Like today, she often makes some extra that she can take up to Holman; pretends she can't get used to just making enough for one. Though of course she has, of course being one person in a world made for pairs sank in years ago. There's three of them now, really: her and Bojangles and Holman. They all might as well get used to never having that other half. But at least she's known it; and Bojangles was never made for love, he'd only eat or be eaten. It's poor Holman who really suffers. He likes to think he's independent; perhaps that's all he's got. But he'd never even eat a proper meal if it weren't for her.

It feels hot enough outside that she could just leave the dish of lasagne to cook on the windowsill. But someone would probably filch it, round here. She doesn't begrudge moving to The Kross. What choice did she have after Donald died and them still in debt from making Paulo all those years before? She had to sell up and move to The Kross, and it's not so bad. But there are a lot of folks with light fingers here; Gretchen doesn't see that there's ever a call to sink to dishonesty.

While the lasagne's cooking in the kitchen, she turns on the games station in her bed-sitting room. Bojangles seems to spin better when she's not looking anyway. She'll let him scrool out the silk from his little pincing second bottom for a while before she goes to gather and sort it.

Gretchen's game control pad is quite new, her last treat to herself, still a slight thrill to use. It's designed for the more elderly player, with bigger buttons and a kind of foam grip that is supposed to be more comfortable for arthritic hands. You'd have thought they could cure arthritis by now, but seemingly not. Perhaps there's no will to, now you can just choose a child that won't get it. Anyway, it's part of the price of getting old. Gretchen doesn't grumble; getting old is a privilege not everyone receives.

She's playing Civilization, quite old itself now, but still a popular game. The player is a kind of deity, directing a chosen people to different activities: hunting; building; farming; fighting wars. As play progresses, the bigger and more sophisticated they get, from a little clan to begin with to city states and whole countries. Apparently, anyway. Gretchen hasn't got that far yet. But she likes directing operations. Her tribe is still quite primitive and she has them spend a lot more time on agriculture and settling unoccupied land than on warfare. Which is probably no way to win. But, in any case, she's really just playing to make time pass. Mostly it's only old folks who play these games now anyway. They're all just passing time. Or maybe they're the only ones patient enough to put up with the brownouts. You can only save the game at certain points, and it's frustrating when the power dims, because the games station crashes and all progress is lost. After rebooting, it's like a plague has wiped out half your people; all the achievements and population growth you've made since your last save have been lost. There are actual plagues built into the game play too, and tsunamis and volcanoes and earthquakes. But it's the plagues that really devastate.

The oven pings, which has Bojangles all a-twitch again; she can hear his claws on the ceramic of the kitchen, over the calming music that plays in the background to Civilization when your people are converting forest into farmland.

Bojangles has made a lovely great wad of silk for her. She pats him on his mottled grey thorax, which bristles sharply to the touch, like new coconut mat. She wonders what it feels like to him, squeezing all that sticky silk out. Not unpleasant, she likes to think. He seems almost content, when he's discharging it.

Certainly nothing like giving birth was for Gretchen. Their Paulo had been difficult, though; they say it's easier than that for most mothers, the ones who still do it themselves instead of paying a broodmare. And he was a big baby, ten pounds. It's funny, almost quaint, how imperial measurements are only really used for human characteristics now. Gives them a certain mysticism, somehow. Their Paulo is six foot two, which is not quite as tall as the doctors said he might be, but plenty tall enough, and all in good proportion. She wishes he'd come round. She'd just like a hug. Like to hear him call her 'mam', like he does. After a while, you yearn for that contact. That little bit of touch with someone who was once an actual physical part of you, growing inside. You spend all of those years keeping them safe, keeping them healthy, keeping them fed. Until one day you realize that they don't need you any more; it's you that needs them. You watched the awkward adolescence, the bumblings and failings and frailties, and it felt like you would be needed for ever, and then you discover it's not true. Or not how you thought it would be. Or maybe that's just their Paulo. It was Donald who wanted to make him so independent. She'd love a hug from Donald even more.

The lasagne is baked to almost the same shade of brown as Paulo's skin. Holsten Mulatto, the doctor had called it, from Jon Holsten, the politician who had first popularized the colour. They were perhaps at the tail end of the fashion – not being the trendiest of people – which meant that Paulo would always look slightly older than he really was, but not much, not a lot, and it was a lovely look anyway.

Bojangles leaves his bed and tile-taps into the middle of the room, where he's left his toy. He picks up the cuddly monkey proudly and returns to his den with as much of a swagger as a seven-legged octoped is ever likely to pull off.

At least spiders killing each other like they do has kept it a cottage industry; given a generation of elderlies like Gretchen another little income stream, she thinks. The last cottage industry, if you don't count broodmaring, and you couldn't really call that an industry.

She leaves the lasagne to cool on the side. She'll put Holman's portion in a separate little dish for him. She goes back into the other room just to check how she looks, not that it really matters, but it's only proper that she's respectable before seeing any of the tenants. She wasn't given the job for being a sloven. Her hair is a bit bedraggled, bits hanging off all over the place, when she had scraped it back into a bun first thing this morning like always. She goes through the routine again, but there are big chunks left in the comb and it doesn't look much better. Old age seems to be coming at her faster with every day that passes.

Civilization has crashed again, too, while she's been in the kitchen, though Gretchen's not that bothered: it's pretty pointless really, and it always ends just when you're beginning to make some progress.

3

Holman

HOLMAN STARTS UP THE stairs, heaving on the banister. His apartment is on the fourth floor and there is no lift, but it is spacious and cheap and the light in there is incomparable to any of the others he viewed when he moved to The Kross.

Back in the security of his studio, still wheezing slightly from the effort of the climb, but surrounded by his canvases and crayons, his mattress on the floor, his little larder, his bar, he feels like a proper artist. He is a proper artist anyway, because surely that is defined by dedication, not success? But Holman also knows that so long as most of his meagre income comes from his allowance and not from work, he will never really persuade his mother and brother of that. Are they who he most needs to persuade?

One wall of the studio is covered by the huge canvas Holman has recently been labouring over. Its working title is *The Tribe*, and that's how he thinks of it, but so far he has only finished the dominating central figure, who is to be the leader of the clan. Holman calls him 'Adam', after that original patriarch. But the Adam in the painting is a barbarous savage of a man, stooped and staring at the viewer as if in confrontation. He is thick with muscle that he is tensing to make himself expand like a threatening animal.

Hands half closed to signal the ease with which he could snap bones. To look at him, one would be sure that he has done so in the past. He is naked and dirty, and Holman has positioned him so that the thing between his legs, hanging chubby and greasy, is in the precise centre of what will be an enormous anti-pastoral. It will hold the eye as if it is the focal point of this primitive tribe's world, to intimate that everything revolves around this tool of propagation. And the perspective is deliberately low down, as if the viewer is beneath even these cave beasts.

But Holman doesn't want to work on *The Tribe* today, he needs to catch Dolly while she is still fresh in his head and he still has the energy. He finds a painted-over canvas; some image he concluded the world should never see is hidden beneath a layer of white. He sets it on his easel, his back to the plastic-framed south-facing patio doors, which open on to the small balcony. The balcony is another reason why he picked this top-floor flat, stairs and all. It is protected from the world, not looked down on from any side. Only two metres by three, but big enough for him to eat out there, when he eats. Or to sit drinking synthetic sundowners in the battered deckchair he scavenged from a skip. Or to paint, when he wants something brightly lit. Now, though, he wants to create a sombre image. Such scenes are better painted inside. He pins the sketches he made of Dolly to a corkboard set on an older second easel that he often uses for this purpose and checks them occasionally while he works.

At good times, times like this, Holman approaches reverie, when the mood is there, when he is totally submerged in the painting. He works for hours, no thought of pause or even the nagging need for synth that preoccupies so much of his waking life. Perhaps he isn't awake, though, he is hypnotised by his own thoughts. If he could believe in muses, then the muse is with him – though today she takes the form of a broken, wet-eyed hooker – but he can't believe in such things, they are the fancy of romantics of a long-lost age. Holman sees life as it really is: the beautiful truth of an ugly world. When he has finished the painting of Dolly, he has an image that would provoke pity in the hardest heart, of a woman who probably wouldn't want it.

The paint on his fingers feels sticky and wrong, like boyhood masturbation. Scabs of it cling to his knuckles; street-fighters' hands would look like this, if they could only bleed in rainbow. This is the petit mort for Holman, the moment after his energy and exertion is over, the moment after his passion has suddenly emptied itself. This is the time when he turns to face his latest mistress to wonder whether she was worth it. And she is; this one is. He would like to stroke her, this newest oil work, but he would only undo her by doing so. He has just to marvel, for the moment, at the things his useless fingers and chattering brain can achieve when they gel, when they have their moments of synchronous clarity. Is this what it means to be an artist: to be without yourself at the moments of your greatest achievements? To be a rubbernecker. Holman could hardly even take the credit for his paintings if there were any to take.

But he's tired. He hasn't slept for who knows how long. He grabs the chunk of now stale bread that sits beside his easel and takes it with him into the world of his mattress on the floor. To the browned pillow, where unpaid-for love has never lain and where Holman's own head now lies uneasy.

Usually it is dog walkers who find bodies. From the newspapers it seems that if you have a dog, or one of the closely related chimeras, then you're almost likely to come across a corpse, sooner or later. But when Holman found Jesus, he was alone, making his way home from the Black Cat Bar in the heavy lead light of dawn's approach, his eyes and head misted with the green of another night of synth. Inadequacy gently rocked away by the emerald witch who never fails to come when he calls for her. Though a paid-for pleasure, like the whores, she is the dependable woman in Holman's life; the green fairy is always there for him, whatever whim his mother might be pursuing elsewhere.

Despite synth confidence, he had walked warily; he likes to be out in the oblivious gaiety of The Kross, but the night is not a time that belongs naturally to the likes of him.

Though Holman doesn't believe in God, he believes in Satan. That is to say, he believes in him as much as he likes to walk in the street lights not the shadows. At least as much as some chill piety makes him carry the wasp-knife when he ventures out in the dark. Satan, or the vague primeval list of fears that he personifies, has saved Holman from who knows what muggers and assailants and dark falls in his time. And he is quite certain that the fear of that old adversary must have protected many more people over the millennia than ever any God did.

So even as the relative safety of sunrise, and what is now today, approached, Holman studied every corner and shaded spot for evil eyes, listened close to the whines and creaks of the night. Well aware that to hear malicious intent in the yowls of a cat is not as foolish as to dismiss as the yowls of a cat something that might prove to have malicious intent. And like that – the senses heightened by Satan that the green witch had dulled – he glimpsed a foot poking from behind a stack of black sacks and fly-biscuit boxes down a side alley.

The foot was lying slump-ways; its possessor, if it was possessed at all, was clearly prone. And – though his mind felt synth-stretched, blurred at the edges – Holman deduced that this foot was too hard to see and too little alluring to be the bait for any kind of assassin's trap and so was more likely to belong to someone in need. Perhaps even in need of some assistance so basic that he himself might provide it. Fighting the instinct to flee and the more cancerous suspicion that he was incapable of really caring, that he was merely acting in a scene, he edged along the alley wall. Seeking to achieve an angle able to take in the rest of the foot's owner from behind the refuse, whilst still remaining as far from whoever they might be as possible.

The medics would later say that Jesus had not been dead for long. Even so, night flies had beaten Holman to the body. One, drinking from Jesus' eye, suggested a movement there, a wink from the void. More of them pranced and supped at the red welts where his dreadlocks must have been yanked from his head. Hair that still lay around it, in a strange pile, like a dark halo, or beams from a black sun in a child's painting. Holman wondered if this wrench-scalping had been done while Jesus was still alive. But knew the answer: they wouldn't have bothered if he was already dead. His face was swollen and bloated, turned piggish somehow by whatever blows of boots or blackjacks must have killed him.

Holman vomited then, the burn of synth and stomach acid caustic in his throat, spatters of bile in his beard and plashes on the street. Was that a sign of emotional capability, or merely a physical fear of death? Jesus hadn't been a friend exactly, but he had looked out for Holman a little, always acknowledged him on the street, even though that couldn't have aided his reputation. He had been a nice guy, for one in his line of work. He hadn't deserved this.

Holman called the police and the meds came along with them. He overheard one say that a post-mortem wouldn't be necessary: that being beaten to death was 'natural causes' for a pimp. But still, by the time an absurdly handsome detective had finished grilling Holman, it was well into morning. Weary with the duty as well as the lack of sleep, he went to tell Dolly.

Dolly said that Jesus was only in it for the girls. He loved picking them up from street-life despair and looking after them, grooming them perhaps, but caring for them too, and of course he loved the sex. Sure he liked the money, the respect and all the rest. But in his heart. In the beginning. It was just about his girls. And she had sobbed this, like it was the best thing you could say of anyone.

4

The Leveller

'TELL ME, PROFESSOR,' ILSE shouts, 'tell me why my children shouldn't have the same chances in life as yours?'

The professor carries on walking into the Prometheus Building, almost as aloof and detached as it is. A security guard opens the door for him and glares briefly at the assortment of outrage gathered outside, hand rested on a holstered pistol.

There is a marble statue of Prometheus himself near the entrance, white streaks through the stone like marzipan. Plastic spikes have been glued all over the top to stop parrots landing. And still the figure is covered in splats of dried bird crap. But that's about the worst the Generich have to suffer; Ilse's people get shat on daily.

Not all the protesters are Unimproved, though. There is at least one in the small crowd very evidently too handsome for that. Ilse keeps stealing glances at the guy, who is really too young for her, and in any case out of her league, but who is so beautiful that Ilse can't help looking – when her comrades wouldn't notice – just because the guy gladdens her. That's the problem with the Improved: so many of them simply are so nice to look at.

She read a quote on a religious protester's banner once: *Beauty is indeed a good gift of God; but that the good may not think it a great good, God dispenses it even to the wicked.* St Augustine or St Thomas Aquinas, Ilse forgets, but she thought it quite apt. Not that she believes in God, of course, and you shouldn't generalize about the gene-enriched; prejudice is wrong whichever way around it is. But what you can say is that when parents are selecting characteristics, they go first of course for what they can afford of health, looks, intelligence and athleticism; and then, if they're filthy rich, more complex bundles like energy, confidence, determination, nerve. Words like compassion, tolerance and empathy don't even appear in the brochures.

The number of Levellers outside the building has dwindled in recent months; inevitably probably. Some thought that the failure of the final high-court appeal would become a rallying cry, but really it has only served to demonstrate that the cause is lost, at least for now, maybe for another generation. There will be no equal access to artificial fertilization and gene-selection technology, not even the basic disease-immunity packs – the cheapest 'charity packs' – which the most moderate Levellers were calling for. The system can't afford it, the government says. Maybe there's some truth in that: the country remains broken from costly wars and all but devoid of export markets. But the Prometheus Building is still the most impressive modern tower in London, thirty years after it was built – they say there is a garden on the roof, a private Eden, that the trees there are the greenest in the city; there is still plenty of money in the genetics industry. How can there not be: for those who enrich, having a child is the most expensive thing they will ever do. Even the wealthy take crippling loans to buy the best for their unborn. Though probably not those wealthy enough to live in the

Prometheus Building: above the reception and conference rooms and the laboratories, the upper floors are residential, mostly occupied by senior scientists of Prometheus Industries.

The tower is protean, almost alive. It slowly spirals its ninety-six floors around a solid core. That number specifically chosen, to be double the forty-eight chromosomes of a gene-enhanced human: the chromosomes of a mother with child, perhaps; or a partnership of hopeful parents-to-be. The steel and glass shimmer in the sun as they imperceptibly shift the building's sinuous silhouette. Independent from the rest of the fuel-poor country, the gradual morphing is powered by wind turbines and the upper floors are covered with solar cells. Sometimes, when the sun catches the coiling flat ends, the tower itself looks like the double helix of DNA. With its movements speeded up, it resembles some kind of fearsome but beautiful insect, rearing into the sky. Ilse knows, because in the foyer they have a film on loop that shows precisely that, and once she made it in that far. The tower whorls skywards into a future that never came. Perhaps all building would have been like this, if war hadn't intervened. Now the tower is testament only to the power of Prometheus Industries – the biggest of the gene giants – and thus the focus of many of the equality protesters. But their complaints flow off it like the light.

The Levellers all wear green ribbons tied around their left arms, so that they can spot each other, so that they can feel a sense of shared purpose. Everyone seems so alone these days. Ilse can't believe it was always like that. Everyone alienated. Everyone out for number one.

It seems with the failure in the high court that the Levellers have reached the end of the road. There is no chance of political change. The ruling party has been in power for so long that people just call them *The Right* now, as if they have a born right to rule as well as to their beautiful lives. The only meaningful opposition comes from within their own ranks, from factions even more reactionary. A meritocracy of the genetically blessed means the masters of the universe are unassailable. An apartheid not just of opportunity, but of the very building blocks of life.

The Unimproved are barely represented at all. Aside from the Leveller movement, they are politically mute. And even a minor criminal conviction costs the right to vote; some estimate that almost half the male residents of The Kross are totally disenfranchised.

A workman, pushing a crate of something past on a sack-truck, pauses, looks for a moment like he wants to come over and join the diminutive demonstration. Ilse smiles at him, waves him across to talk. When he still doesn't come, she starts to approach him, but before she gets there, he shakes his head and wheels his crate away towards some basement entrance of the building; probably worried about keeping his job. The power is all in the hands of the enriched. They pay lip service to equal rights, but what use is having an equal right to apply for a job if you are less able? You still won't get it. The anti-genetic-prejudice laws were originally constructed to protect the rights of the Generich anyway; they were never intended to protect the Unimproved.

On paper everything is fair, but the reality is completely the opposite. Schools are streamed by the seven-plus SATs tests, so no further segregation is necessary: the smartest kids are the richest, and only the Unimproved go to the worst of the run-down remedials. Private schools have long since ceased to be, but the wealthy still rub shoulders almost exclusively with their fellows. Free university education, for those with sufficient aptitude, in practice only means that the taxes of the poor help fund the university and college places of the best of the Improved.

Social mobility is an historic term, *self-improvement* an extinct expression; all the improvement you are ever likely to achieve is acquired from people like those in Prometheus Industries. Privilege is bought before birth. Ability and life chance comes on a sliding scale according to how much your parents could pay. And for those whose parents conceived them in the lusty animality of nature's old ways – for the Unimproved – life rarely holds any great promise.

But every time Ilse comes here to demonstrate, every night she spends making banners, every feet-aching day of shouting is a little step along a road that Ilse has to keep believing will create change.

Ilse has a tattoo: a scroll underneath a heart, but the scroll is blank. Once it held a boy's name, a boy she expected to spend her life with. The name has been lasered away, but she keeps the tattoo as a reminder, a constant reminder, of how this division of society can cause the Unimproved even to hate themselves and each other. She means to fill it in again with the name of her child, when she has one; a distant unborn child who she fights for now, who will never have to worry about any of the unnecessary diseases that still afflict the Unimproved.

Sometimes she longs to give this up. Why not just do what the others do and forget about it? Blot it out with synth or drugs, dance each night away to salsco and rut till dawn. But that's what they want you to do. Ilse has her suspicions that the synth and drugs in The Kross are more than tolerated by the authorities, that they are secretly encouraged, even subsidized. They keep the urban underclass contented in their genetic and financial poverty. Now that religion is all but gone, opiates are the opiates of the masses.

5

Holman

HOLMAN'S STARVING WHEN HE wakes, a scrunch of blanket between his legs, a cushioning buffer to separate one from the other. They don't hurt too much today, thankfully, but it's a long-held habit. He's still wearing his suit trousers, which is by no means unusual. In a way, he would prefer even to bath in them, rather than have to look at his own crippled legs and the grotesque unemployed that floats between them. He doesn't bath now, though; heads to the Dead Rat for something to eat.

Holman orders a 'Cinderella Mary Poppins' – face-saving slang – while he looks at the menu. The bartender must be new; Holman doesn't know him. He has Holman's father's eyes, but then a lot of folk do.

Adolf, the absent usual barman, is an affable larrikin; Holman often has a chat with him. This new guy serves with a sneer from a charity-pack mouth that can't find much in life to be aloof about. *Cinderella* means to use the very cheapest synth, below even the A&B brand Holman normally has, but still legal, no moonshine. Not really something to be sneered at in this place. Holman's broke, his allowance spent; he's going to have to go and see his mother in Mayfair later to try and borrow some money. He's thirty-six and going to borrow money from his mother; that is far more humiliating than anything the barkeep could throw.

Holman orders fried rice and bean sprouts, the cheapest thing on the menu likely to fill him up, and takes the slatted spoon and metal pot of water that the barman puts down. Clumsily Holman clutches up a couple of paper-coated sugar cubes from the counter. A cockroach scuttles across the crusty carbon-fibre bar top as he does so, like it's using the movement as covering fire.

The heat makes Holman's joints ache; his knees throb as he walks to an empty booth. He wants to take the shortest route possible, but that would lead right past one of the Regans, who is playing patience or reading tarot or something, lots of cards spread out on the broken-skinned table in front of him anyway. They always seem to be alone, when they of all people surely have the least need to be. The Regan looks at Holman with narrowed eyes, as if trying to place him. Half beneath the card-cluttered table a giant dog-beast sleeps; so black it shines blue, where a beam of window-refracted sun highlights its fur; one big fang propping a drooping lip up.

Holman throws in an aching detour of a few yards. He has spent his life so far learning that a little pain can be an investment in avoiding much more. He wonders if it was the Regans who killed Jesus. Though it's said they kill with razors, lots of little cuts so even the brothers directly involved don't know for sure which of them dealt the death blow. The Regans are a tribe of reasonable doubt. A fraternity, in the truest sense of the word, who control The Kross as much as anyone does. The brother playing cards is probably in his early forties, around the middle age of the clan. He has a moustache, unusually, but he's definitely a Regan. Though Holman only risks a glance en route to his seat.

There must be those who don't know about the Regans, and Holman envies them their state of innocence. You can't unknow, that's the problem. Once you are aware that someone is capable of anything, and they know that you know, then it is over; you are in their thrall and your free will has gone. You're enslaved by your own comprehension.

The booth is wrinkled red leather, walled high enough to hide Holman from the Regan and the world. He puts down the jug and spoon and synth and sugars. Pleased to be free from another opportunity for his treacherous legs to make a fool of him. Pleased to have his cargo safe to port.

The spoon is white plastic, one that the synth wholesalers probably give for free; it's got a little riddle down the side, pocket wisdom Holman's too hot and tired to care about. He lays it across the top of the glass, the liquid lies like verdant turf in the bottom. Like the Irish eyes, for which there was a fashion some years back, until even the lower classes started choosing them and people started to call them 'synth-green' eyes.

He unwraps a lump of sugar and carefully places it on the slatted centre of the synth spoon. The jagged little edges of the spoon look like teeth; this could be the top view of a piranha in a murky pool, the last thing some creature ever sees. Only, piranhas don't get you like that, do they? You don't get one bite and it's over, piranhas get you with weight of numbers; they get you with tiny bites, but with teams and time. Like synth will most likely take Holman. But there still must be one, eventually, he thinks; there must be one that is the one that takes your life. Like whip lashes or heart murmurs. Or razor cuts from the Regan brothers.

Holman picks up the little steel jug of water. The hole in its handle is too small for his bratwurst finger to fit through, so he has to hold it in a neat pince, like a prim lady drinking tea. Which makes him think of his mother, strangely, since she is anything but prim.

Like many of the Unimproved, Holman comes from a single-parent family: 'it takes two parents to save for an enriched child, but only one to spawn' is a popular refrain from The Right. He really should phone his mother to see if she's home. Find out if he can see her tonight. No, not tonight. But soon. Tomorrow? Soon enough.

He tilts the jug so that just a drop of water falls on to the sugar cube, watches as the water discolours the sugar, trying to get through, but as easily absorbed as piss on scorched soil. He lets a little more fall, sees the sugar crumble slightly on the spoon, as the moisture percolates through. Yesterday he saw a tramp pissing; from the bus on a wasted trip to try another gallery owner. Holman had wondered why all the passengers were getting off at the front, looked out of the window to see a raggard old villain, spread-eagled at the bus stop, stubby wizened cock pointing skywards, from amidst string-fastened cast-off clothing, spraying into the air and all over himself, like an inexpensive municipal fountain. The real fountains have all been stopped, indefinitely, for the water shortage.

Holman lets a little more water drip down from the squat metal pot. With it, the sugar lump collapses like a sandcastle, and for the first time parts of it, soluble in water as they would not be in the high-strength synth beneath, drip down from the spoon as well. He watches them fall; not far to go, like with his own falls. How many times has he heard that? 'At least you didn't have far to go, mate.' Always *mate*, as if this makes it all all right. As if any insult is acceptable just so long as it is sweetened. Like with this drink: the cheapest synth, wormwood bitter, drunk as a Mary Poppins: a spoonful of sugar to help the medicine go down.

The Regan has gone when Holman emerges from his booth and hobbles out into the sharp sunlight. There are roadworks going on outside the Dead Rat. Mopeds and scooters are being forced to file through rat-run slots either side of a big hole in the ground. No workmen are in the hole and there is no evidence of its purpose, but concrete dust floats in the static air, coating Holman's black suit jacket in a powdery film.

On impulse, he hails a moped taxi to go to his mother's, without first checking to see if she's in. The guy he normally uses, Florian, isn't loitering in the usual spot. This driver tries to look casual, but discomfort is visible in his blond-framed face at his passenger's inept attempts to climb on. Holman sits as far back as he can, so as not to make the driver any more uneasy, and holds the pillion handle behind. As soon as they lurch away he regrets the decision. If Adele Nicole isn't home, he will barely have enough money to get back again. The worry stops him enjoying the journey as much as normal. Like on a bar stool, he is almost the same height as everyone else when on the back of a bike. And he goes at the same speed; not fast, in traffic like this, but enough to create a cooling wind against his rudded skin.

There is a feeling of liberation on a bike. But Holman's legs are not strong enough to support one when stationary, so he will never know what it is like to own one; to travel when and where he pleases. An almost god-like power of whim.

His mother is home, luckily. She's gin-breathed, beautiful. Wearing a kimono, like it's morning in fabled Manhattan in an old movie. She pays the taxi man with a big note delivered from a wrist drooped as if she expected him to kiss her hand; which he probably would have, willingly, given any more of a cue.

'Holman,' she says, 'I've missed you, darling, how are you?' She takes his arm to lead him inside and instantly fills Holman with the usual confusion of happiness and hideousness. The usual urge to curl back up inside her, into the place he never wanted to leave and seems destined never to return to, even in the Freudian surrogates most men get to discover.

She takes him through, into the room that is like a lounge that people with too many rooms have before you get to the real lounge: an ante-lounge. It has been redecorated again: everything is painted either coffee-tinted beige or a startlingly bright white. She has the air-con on full blast, never one to worry about legalities. Holman is staggered by the sheer cool-ness of it. He hasn't felt this refreshed in weeks. The sweat all over him absorbs it and bathes him in the lush sensation.

'Sit down, darling,' his mother says, pushing gently on his sweat-clumped curls. 'Let me get you a mojito.' She says this in a way that suggests that she is indeed getting it, though at the words Sebastian, her handsome houseboy, glides off to do the actual making and fetching.

For most people to drink real alcohol would be a sign of near-reckless hedonism. But for Adele Nicole it is merely a sign of wealth, since her liver, like Holman's, is not aligned to any of the synthetic brands. Rum and vodka are no worse for her than synth, though she nonetheless drinks them as if they were as harmless as the correctly prescribed synths are to the majority.

She tucks her feet up under her on the chaise-courte next to him, constantly pulling the hem of her kimono lower down her golden thighs. It is evident that she should have bought a longer one.

Sebastian brings a brace of mojitos. That his mistress would require one too is apparently intuited, though Holman suspects him to be none too bright. He has pestled the mint and crushed the ice to perfection as always, though. Droplets of water descend the glasses' sides, pure as tears from a baby. A single mint leaf swirls in the top of each, fresh and jagged and greener than any plant Holman has seen all summer. He plucks his out and sniffs it; it almost burns his nostrils it's so clean.

'Thank you, Sebastian. Adele Nicole would like to be alone with our guest now,' she says, and gifts both of them a smile that cost thousands and made so very much more.

Sebastian departs through another door; the house has many rooms. Holman likes Sebastian more than most of his mother's long line of houseboys. Perhaps only because she is now more coy about their extra duties than when he was growing up.

After the mojitos, Adele Nicole – who has never wanted to be called anything less formal, nor more maternal – leads Holman by the hand into her Jurassically green garden. Again he sits beside her, in her enveloping charisma, this time on a mahogany-slatted blacked-metal bench. He is, as ever, at her mercy. At the bidding of her hypothermia-blue eyes. But still he won't give in to what he knows she will ask:

'Won't you let me get you an exhibition, darling? Nobody would even know. I can be very discreet, just a few gentle whispers in a few ears.'

But Holman would know, that's the problem, and as if this paradise in his mother's walled retreat was a second chance at Eden, he resists the tempter and her lure. Well aware of the irony inherent in his arbitrary sense of what assistance he can accept from her and still call himself his own man; because, mere moments later, he will be asking her for some more money. Which will make him uncomfortable, but is also necessary: he could hardly get a job, after all. Art is his only chance. For that he needs his mother's support.

Holman wants to say that he never asked to be born, but he knows that's a petulant lie. Most modern children never asked to be born; they were selected, improved, created. But not him. Half of Holman out-swam and out-clamoured millions of others in the oldest race. Fused with the other half, which clung with all its might to a precipitous, slick wall, in the determined hope of becoming whole. He did ask to be born. He battled for it from the first.

'At least won't you go and see your brother, darling? He misses you. He wants to help too.'

He surely doesn't miss Holman, and Holman surely won't visit. So he accedes to the plea, because it is such a meaningless agreement.

***

Holman leaves after dinner, with the promise of more credit being poured into the guilty account linked to the chip inside his arm. And the press of Adele Nicole's flesh-ziggurat breasts into his neck as she crouches to kiss him goodbye. The same taxi-biker as before, suntanned and street-grimed, is loitering outside. He grins to see his gamble – of waiting for hours on the chance of a return fare, rather than burning fuel to try his luck elsewhere – paid off; he even tries a little shouted small talk on the drive. Florian, Holman's regular guy, would have given him a couple of swigs from a bottle of synth, but knows he doesn't like to talk much. Holman prefers just to sit, quiet and tall, on the bike; mouth shut against dusk flies; eyes full flared to take in the rushing world.

There's a billboard at the border: the unbuilt-upon, brick-and-shit-strewn wasteground between the opulence, which has dwindled all the way from his mother's, and its extinction at The Kross. Holman can't tell what the sign is supposed to be advertising, which means it's either not very good, or some kind of brilliant long-term campaign. It just reads: *Everything Will Be All Right*.

6

Detective Günther
Charles Bonnet

GUNT ARRIVES EARLY, AS soon as he gets the call, barely into another shirt-lacquering afternoon.

The weals left behind on the body where the hair has been pulled out look like bright organic spark-plug slots. The hair itself is not in evidence this time. A body-armoured officer who has been holding the perimeter – overtly muscular, busted knuckles like clumps of garlic – looks at Gunt with envy ill-concealed. Gunt has the best set of genes on the force, and everyone knows it.

'Second one this week. I hate The Kross,' the cop mutters under his breath. 'Why do we even bother?'

Gunt saw the corpse of the pimp, Jesus, the other day too. Gunt's got the case. Gunt always gets those cases: the Kross cases; the refuse; the scum. Gunt's fine with that.

Gunt's genes are so good he makes people tense. Why would someone like him join the police? It doesn't add up. Rumours about him abound. That he's a party mole. That he's not in the party at all. That he can smell lies. That he's a liar. That he's on the take; that he's bent as a left-handed corkscrew. That he's not on the take, that he grasses other cops. That he's a pervert. That he's a virgin. That he hates the Unimproved with unparalleled passion. That he fucks them. Gunt gives nothing away. Gunt does his job. Gunt doesn't get asked to the after-shift drinks. Gunt's fine with that.

Norris, the plump pathology lab guy, arrives not long after Gunt, wearing an anti-contamination jumpsuit. Looking like a chemical warfare trooper from the Third Caliphate War. As if they'd let someone like Norris in the army. Who knows how he got this job. He puts on spectacles, black plastic frames, blue lenses, stares at the corpse through them for a while. Gunt's seen the glasses countless times before of course: ultraviolet and infrared: show urine and semen and other secretions, as well as heat variations.

Norris gets out his DNA kit, puts the spectacles down on his metal case. Gunt picks them up and puts them on.

He doesn't see any traces of heat remaining, no lingering footprints on the baked-hard wasteland, but how would he, in this stinking summer? Only the corpse still glows a little redder than the dirt and bleached scrub it lies on. It will be hours yet before its core will cool in this sun. The body is criss-crossed with erratic rat piss, a visible pale blue, but no sign of human stains. Somehow the glasses make him focus his other senses too: Gunt starts to sniff, head winding side to side like a snake tasting the air. But he can't smell anything save the stench of dumped trash, which belongs here, and the scents of a body already starting the journey to decomposition: bacteria eating into putrid cells, rotting under the sun.

Norris starts swabbing the body under the fingernails, the most probable deposit points for the perpetrator's DNA. Gunt wonders if it's a waste of time. Two murders so similar in one week; maybe they were hits, and most hits are carried out in much the same suit and mask as the path. guy wears. Maybe not, though. It's a strange MO for a hit: the beating and the scalping: messy. And not the way the Regans do things either. Or this close to their turf, you might bet it was them. In which case, DNA would be just as useless.

Gunt slips the glasses into his pocket. If Norris notices, he doesn't say anything. Shortly afterwards he holds up the dead man's arm, so Gunt can scan it through his reader. The yellow writing says:

FLORIAN PETZINGER
29
SINGLE
NO CRIMINAL RECORD
NO MILITARY RECORD
NO EDUCATIONAL QUALIFICATIONS
LICENCE TO RIDE MOTORCYCLES INCL. PILLION
PASSENGERS
REGISTERED KEEPER OF VEHICLE K148 BRH
TAX BAND: D – VARIABLE
BLOOD: AB
EYES: BROWN
HAIR: BLOND
ALLERGIES: PENICILLIN
IMMUNITIES: NO IMMUNITIES

The anti-geneism laws mean that details of conception are never entered into official records, but 'no immunities' mean he's

Unimproved – scum – which could be guessed anyway by his sorry file. A picture appears on the reader that could well be the deceased, though the face is not broken and swollen, the eyes are open and the mouth isn't frozen in a rictus of sudden fear.

The reader is running low on battery power already. They don't last long any more. Gunt puts it back in his pocket; he'll go through the rest later, when he can charge it, back at the yard, where the homeless woman who found the body is waiting to be interviewed. Not far from the crime scene is her eyrie of corrugated plastic, sticks and sacks – planted, ironically, beneath a billboard that reads: *Everything Will Be All Right*. She claims not to have seen anything except for the deceased. She can wait. Gunt wants to look around.

The heat means more people on The Kross' streets. Overcrowding means more people on the streets. Rising unemployment means more people on the streets. Increasing alcoholism, prostitution and drug addiction means more people on the streets. They kill themselves and each other, like a self-cleaning oven. The police can't control this district any more; they victimize and brutalize, overreact when they catch, leave bruises and grudges. Some cops collude with the narc slingers, who keep people sedated and pay well. The forces of order who try at all are mostly arbitrary and violent, but ineffective. According to the stats from The Kross police station, less than fifty per cent of perps get arrested without 'resisting'. Gunt's own figures are nowhere near that good.

The deceased's moped is on the street, a decent walk away from the body, outside a betting shop. Tatty, gangster-parked mobility scooters next to it; slung side by side like crap greyhound traps.

Gunt throws the last bite of his McManna burger into the gutter. Instantly a ratty-pink snout protrudes from a dust-bowl drain to smell it. Gunt fingers his pistol. Wants to shoot the rat. Knows he'd hit it. Wants to shoot all the rats. He puts on the ultraviolet specs again to look. Finds he likes them. Finds them comfortable. Finds they help hide that shadow at the back of his mind, the thing that affects and infects everything he does.

There's more rat piss on the street. The darker blue of evaporated human piss pools beneath wall splashes and streaks where synthed scum have stopped to relieve themselves at night. The stains remain, like ghosts of the departed.

The ghosts all came from one place. He can see how they drifted. Blown by shitty genes along shitty streets. The ghosts all came from the end of the road. Where there must be a bar. There is ghost piss on one of the tyres of the dead man's moped. Which means it was parked there before the ghosts passed by. Maybe he was at the bar.

Gunt enters the bar ghostlike too: silent and unseen.

The floor is tiled and slightly sloped, so the slops and spillage drain away; so the whole lot can be hosed down, like a wet room or a torture chamber.

The waitress, who should presumably be opening up, sits staring evils at life across the top of the half-empty synth bottle next to her half-empty glass. She's a redhead. Pretty for a still-born, but mouth turned down at the corners by hangover or memories. She can't be more than twenty-five, but that disgruntled grimace makes her look older. And her eyes look older. Even her once white blouse looks older.

She forces a smile when she sees Gunt. Doesn't realize he's a cop. They never do. Gunt doesn't look like a cop. He's got the best set of genes on the force. She smooths back her hair, which is scrunched in a clumsy bun, except for the wisps that drift into her eyes. The wisps she tries to train with white wrists exposed. They say it's a signal: showing the wrists like that. Makes Gunt think she's probably attracted to him. Which probably goes without saying.

'Can I get you something?' she says, but doesn't get up, seems still torn between the handsome interruption and the edge of whatever sullen daydream she was wallowing in.

'Just a few answers,' says Gunt.

His voice is basso profundo, a guttural that makes what he says sound important. Which usually it is: Gunt is not one for pleasantries.

She raises one brassy eyebrow and pouts coquettishly. 'Ask away,' she says. Gunt's expression doesn't change though, and her face drops from its brief attempt at flirtation back to the same drooped churl.

Gunt says, 'Police,' but doesn't show his badge, and she doesn't ask to see it.

Instead he shows her the deceased's picture on the chip reader's screen; which beeps its pathetic semi-permanent low-battery warning. They can't get any decent kit any more. Sacrifices that had to be made for the war effort have never really been rolled back, at least not in The Kross. Except for guns. Since the end of the Third Caliphate War there are always guns.

'Have you seen this man before?'

She takes the reader from him, to look at the small scratched screen, and he can see by the way she handles it that this piece of shit-beat technology is impressive to her. Perhaps not surprising, for someone who works in this place. The walls of the bar are stained like an old mop, like it's soaked up all the filth that's passed through. Briefly he feels sorry for her, but it doesn't last: she wants mopping too.

'Well, have you seen him?'

'Yeah, I've seen him. He comes in here sometimes. I think he's a taxi biker.'

'Was he in last night?'

'I wasn't working last night. I was out.'

Gunt looks at the synth bottle and nods. 'Who was on?'

'Frank, he'll be in soon.'

'OK, I'll wait. Give me your ID.'

She stretches out her right arm. The skin is child-smooth, no needle marks. Gunt moves the reader in slow circles until it picks up her chip and digital stars tell her story on the screen. She's a typical Kross bitch: a religious cult runaway – not long before they were closed down – escaped into an underclass life that would doubtless appal the mother who has doubtless disowned her anyway.

She blushes, but juts her jaw a little defiantly, as it is clear he is looking into her past and present. Then she stares down at her glass, and takes a swig of the liquid that will probably shape her future.

The card reader gives out three rapid beeps and then the long sigh with which it habitually dies.

'I'll have a coffee then, while I wait,' Gunt says, 'and the paper.'

47

***

Frank arrives before the second coffee. Frank's a bulldog breed. Unimproved British beast. Hardy peasant stock, once noble yeoman, now scum. Frank's got something to hide. Frank starts to run, but he's stump-legged, barrel-chested, slow. Frank swings a punch from the doorway he stops to block. Gunt forearms the blow away. Gunt breaks Frank's nose. He isn't the first. None the less, Frank looses a strange, shrill noise: the swan shriek of the outclassed animal; the prayer of the prey. Frank tries to get away. Gunt kicks down Frank's departing calf. Frank's knee hits the pavement with a flat crack. Gunt stamps down on his broad back. Turns him over, delivers a slap. Frank wears a grubby tie, which Gunt tightens until flesh bulges over the sides. Bulldog Frank is dragged back in by the lead. Leashed to the counter. Beaten like he bit the baby.

The barmaid looks on. Rigid. Hand shaking as she pours out the last of her synth. The bottle and her glass rattle together. Her eyes dodge between the smashed pumpkin that used to be Frank and his interrogator.

Frank's talking while he bleeds now. Frank says that he found the man dead in the toilet. Doesn't know who did it. Says that he fronts this place for the Regans and they told him to dump the body. Says they will kill him for talking. But clearly finds this abstract future fear less pressing than his new-found fear of Gunt.

Gunt's fine with that.

7

Holman

BACK IN THE DAY, it was experimental for theatres to show plays with the house lights dimmed: to daringly suggest that the audience were not as important a spectacle, to themselves and to others and even to the players, as the play itself. Once upon a time, people came to the theatre to be seen. But it's dark in the cinema now, which is how Holman likes it. He comes here to watch, not be watched. Latterly he always arrives in the final anticipatory instant before the film starts, when the ceiling spots are all but extinguished. There is no joy in sitting lonely in a stretched desert row of seats, being effortlessly ignored by the people who come in afterwards; always in twos, like the rest of the world is born with another half in wait. Which is often what the films seem to be saying as well; but Holman can forgive it in films, because they are art and artifice.

The audience is sparse anyway today, quiet even for this last outpost of cinematography in The Kross. Hardly anyone goes to the pictures any more, so of course no one makes new pictures and ever fewer people go. The only recently made film Holman's seen had a nauseating agitprop plot, with a macabre Unimproved malefactor kidnapping a beautiful enriched child.

This film though, like most they show, was created long ago. People on horseback – centaurs – man joined to another beast. Bandannas up over their faces, like moped riders trying to keep the choke and dust of city heat from their lungs. Hard to decipher accents and features that are not quite right, which look antiquated, out of fashion. The bull they ride in one scene is spindly and weakling, by comparison to all the bulls that Holman's seen. The lighter-skinned heroes mock and detest the darker races, who are all either primitively armed enemies or slaves, strangely meek and pliant, though their masters don't look to be any stronger. And it seems bizarre that a society once focused on skin colour, this one random clutch of so many intricate genes, which told them nothing at all about ability or intelligence. Holman wonders whether prejudice today is less immoral for being better founded in fact. But these thoughts just depress him, and he comes here to be entertained.

And he is entertained, Holman loves the cinema. He is a bystander both more and less explicitly than in real life. Less, because here everyone is audience; all equally pointless oglers. More, because he doesn't even document this world of film, he doesn't translate it with paint, he serves no purpose at all. The film actors are already insured against passing time: long gone, but forever young, at least while people continue to watch them; eternal as the figures on a Grecian urn.

The US cavalry come in the end, but they come late, when most of the pilgrims have been killed and the survivors are huddled together, certain they will perish. Alike, Britain has been saved in two world wars and three Caliphate wars by the USA; each time grateful for the charge of their war machine, but always wishing it could have been sooner: before we were so broken, so diminished, so poor.

The ending of the film is happy, as always, though: everything is all right in the end. The natural order has been restored: superior technology has prevailed, men with telegraphs and rifles have exterminated men with smoke and spears; and, most importantly, the dominant male has secured the right to mate with the female of his choice. To celebrate, the victorious tribe unleashes a salvo at the skies. Holman's seen it before, this ejaculatory observance. It is clear that where men have guns, men fire guns in the air. At weddings; at funerals; to celebrate; to salute; just to remind others and themselves that they are men. They fire in staccato bursts or continued stream or by solitary shot, but until the chamber is empty. And it always makes him wonder what happens then, if anyone gets killed, because sooner or later, with inevitable certainty, all of those bullets must come down . . .

Holman asks Crick about this, later, in the Loup Hole Bar that he haunts. Scars twine like roots and vines about his face; weals pale instead of red, like their anger has abated, but he knows something of bullets and war. Near enough everyone in this bar does, except Holman. But these men don't resent him, because he would never have been drafted to fight for the supposed freedom he enjoys. They are, for the most part, Holman's comrades in deformity; though made not born. And although he can't share their solidarity – does that word come from *soldier*? – he can feel it, in this bar. Some drink to remember and some drink to forget. Holman drinks to them.

Crick has sat to be painted before – in his tactile mapped apartment – consenting, though he would never see the resulting portrait. He has no eyes. The scars flow over the place where they should sit and blink and wink. Eyes that might be dreamy – story-teller's eyes – to judge by the things he says. But perhaps it was the same fire that turned his skin liquid and the long months drenched in morphine that brought this need to paint a world with words.

The bar sells sunshine: synth laced with opiates. Maybe because it is an old soldiers' joint, this seems to be tolerated more than usual by the authorities. Though on the wall there is a poster that reads: 'If you are drinking Adulterated or Non Synthetic Alcohols, then you are slowly killing yourself.'

Underneath, someone has scrawled: 'We're not in a hurry.'

Holman takes a slug of Cinderella though – just the usual bottom-shelf shit – the first drink of the day, to kill the worm. Sufficiently wise not to envy a greater addiction. He's had his share of opiate dreams too, though only as a boy.

'I'll tell you about firing in the air,' Crick says, after Holman asks him. 'I'll tell you where the bullets go:

'Back in the Caliphate one time, we were patrolling larch forest, glairy sap slow dripping on your skin like water torture, while you walked. We came to this single scathed tree, ivory white, like it's been struck by lightning, all alone in a clearing. So white it was like clean sheets, we used to dream of clean sheets. But forget that, that sounds like comfort, and this was the most forlorn thing I've ever seen in my life. At the bottom of this leafless, lifeless tree was a guy – one of ours, but Regular Army, not a Para – hands nailed to it. Held up by nails through his wrists, face against the dead muscle of the tree, and they'd done the blood eagle on him. You heard rumours, but I'd never seen it; you didn't think they really did that, that anyone could really do that stuff. They'd macheted his ribs away from his spine, cut them right through and forced them outwards like a pair of bloody wings on his back, then they'd pulled his lungs out and thrown them over one shoulder, like the eagle's head and neck. You believe that? Believe me. I'm telling you a story. He suffocated to death. He was alive when they nailed him and ripped apart his back.

'It was no clash of civilizations out there, because they weren't civilized. It was a clash of reason against religion, and maybe that's enough. Maybe even after all the horror I'd go back and fight for that all over again, if I could. If there was anything left there to fight. You believe that?

'Of course the whole platoon went nuts; some of the guys start yelling stuff. You know: "Fucking show yourselves! Fight like men!" Things like that. But he'd been there for a while, the regular – stank like a stink you don't want to ever know about. The people who'd done it would be long gone, we knew that.

'De Castillo lost it, he was shouting: "I'm gonna plug your holes with salami, you fucks." He did used to do that sometimes, too, he was pretty messed up. Dried sausage, pig meat. They believe they won't get to heaven if they touch pork, so he figured he'd use their superstitions against them, used to push sausages in the wounds of the dead after a skirmish. Sometimes down their mouths or up their asses. It was pretty grim to see him doing it. Not to mention a waste of sausage. But no one was going to tell him not to, because, like I say, he was pretty messed up. And anyway, De Castillo was our lieutenant, he was in charge, after all. Someone told me he's a gangster now, but that's probably just a story.

'I don't remember who started, but pretty soon everyone was shooting in the air. M18s and combat shotguns and even the heavy guns, all blasting at the sky. Like we were trying to shoot down the god of a people who could do something like that to another human being.

'I've lost my sense of colours now. I can't remember if what I think is yellow is really yellow. Makes me wonder if we only ever agreed on an illusion to start with: we all agree that synth is green, but do we know we're really seeing the same colour? My green might have been your red. But now I don't even know if I remember even what colour I thought it was myself. Colours shift around in my head now.

'But the parrots were green, I know that; what we agreed was green back then. And as we were shooting up into the sky, these parrots started falling down on us. Some were like rags of birds: one wing spiralling down. Some were just bloody clumps of green feathers. And there were loose feathers floating all around, too; like the world had got its seasons mixed up and fresh spring-green leaves were falling like autumn. But lots of the birds fell whole, with no sign of damage at all. Big bright-green parrots, just like common London parrots, as if they just fell asleep mid-flight. Hundreds of them. I'm not telling you stories: there were parrots dropping out of the sky like some medieval plague of parrots.

'And we all started laughing our heads off. It was so weird, that was all you could do. We were still firing, clip after clip. Not wanting it to stop.

'Jaeger, he was my buddy, you kind of paired up out there. You don't fight for your country, or even for your family: you fight for the man next to you. I was looking at Jaeger, watching him shooting and laughing, and then the front of his forehead came right off. Just exploded in front of me. Covered me in a fine spray, like walking next to a waterfall. And I'm thinking, "What the fuck?" And that's what I thought: a bullet must have gone right up in the air and dropped down again. Taken out my buddy. He wasn't dead. We got a compress on him. Jacked some morph straight into his leg. He was screaming, but alive. Balls-deep in agony, in the middle of all these parrots, feathers still floating down on him.

'Jaeger made it home alive too, used to come in here, but they had to put him away. No frontal lobe left. He's got no control. He swears non-stop. Even by the standards of an old squaddie like me, he swears unacceptably. I've heard him swear in the middle of a swear-word: he'll be like "arsefuckinghole". But it's not just that, it's like he's lost all the rest of his language, he can only really say the words that you should hesitate to say. He just craps where he wants to, too, whenever he wants to, right on the floor or the street like an animal. But mostly it was because he tried to rape a girl that they had to lock him up. We're never too far from the beast, you realize that. You realize that when you see someone like Jaeger, and you realized that out there. The beast is always right behind you.

'But – your question, H – it wasn't a falling bullet that got Jaeger anyway. It was a sniper team. Guess the dead regular was a decoy to draw us in. They wounded our sergeant as well, before we realized, killed two others before we got them.

Obvious really: when you shoot bullets in the air, they go too far. Even if you used a spirit level, shooting straight up alongside that little bubble you'd be a tiny bit off and all that way it would never come down on you. Might kill someone, I guess, if it landed in a city, but not likely, and never you or anyone nearby.'

Crick puts down his glass with an exaggerated care, which says more about his need for synth than his lack of sight, and gets off his stool, walks with rigid certainty towards the stairs and down to the cellar toilet. There is an exit down there, a tunnel linked into the sewers, a place where deserters from the Second Caliphate War – before Holman's birth – once fled when the military police raided. Now the bar houses the human litter of the Third War. But these men don't detest deserters any more than they do Holman; there's a strange kind of peace in the Loup Hole.

Holman's still wondering about the bullets, though, as he limps home. The synth kills the pain in his legs, but it doesn't make him walk any faster. The street lamps always burn low in The Kross now; sometimes they even go out for a couple of seconds, when there's a brownout. But you can see the stars better, these days. And Holman knows there must be bullets up there too, far away. Though mostly in the amorphous ruins of the Caliphate, probably, where divided surviving tribes now fight each other and all half-expect a bullet. Where they wouldn't eat pig, they now eat people. Or so it's said.

***

He looks towards the concierge's door as he starts the haul upstairs. Yesterday he could smell lasagne cooking from there, which is normally a good sign. Normally that means she'll bring him a big slab up. He was looking forward to that, but it never arrived. He hopes he hasn't done anything to upset her.

8

Crick

C RICK TYPES:

There is no such thing as a just war, there is just war.

Then he runs his fingers back across what he has written, feels the reassuring bumps of Braille, knows that something has been produced there. Something ever so slight, but isn't that the nature of this endeavour: it is a battle of ant-slow attrition. These tiny Braille crumbs make up letters, which make words, which slowly, excruciatingly slowly sometimes, are forming something bigger. Even forcing himself to sit down at his table and work on the book is painful. But what else has he, what else is there? He is terrified that it won't be good enough, that a soldier's words aren't important enough. Horrific as his experiences are, does that make them more significant than someone else's? He has seen a lot of pain and destruction and now he can't see at all. Why would that be enough, why would the world care? This is the fear, the fear of failure more acute than death, but this is all he has. Only this old Braille typewriter and the Loup Hole and synth occupy Crick's days.

Once you're there anyway, that's all there is: just war. We were out on a plain, scabby grass wind-rasped, by the same injurious eastern wind that blasted it all. I couldn't say exactly where it was now, to tell you the truth – and that's what I'm trying to do – the places all became one a long time ago: Spain; Portugal; Northern Africa; much of France; most of Asia; of course Arabia; they all became one, all became the Caliphate, only the stories stay separate.

Subconsciously his fingers stroke his face, feeling the knots of scar tissue, which don't feel back. A sensation still strange, after these years: to feel a part of himself that might just as well be a mask. And he knows well from the gasps and gulps it evokes in others that it would be an ugly, evil mask.

Maybe that's not the right story to write, he thinks. Not yet. Or maybe that's not the right way to start it. He thinks of a different time.

The door was answered, when I tugged the bell-pull, by a brawny shaven-headed man with a flattened nose and a round Mongol warrior face, a bit like De Castillo's. He gestured me down a scarlet-carpeted hall, but himself remained by the door. The room that the hallway emptied into was vast, and lit by naked gas flames around the walls. Every fixture and surface within it was either a dark succulent red or else gold. The gold wasn't real gold, but it was gold in colour, it was as real as the senses required it to be, as real as the red. The air was heavy with perfume and potpourri, and something else: some kind of intense incense. It intoxicated, making you want to fill your lungs with its sweetness. Twin fires in grates on either side of the room kept it at a fiercely hot level, so that even my light uniform became immediately uncomfortable. But the great heat was necessary because, and here was the most glorious bit of all: in lounging chairs, settees, and chaises long and short; reclining, chattering, and sipping at sherbets and water, were seventy-two of the most beautiful girls I'd seen in my life, and they could hardly have produced a sack of washing between them.

None of the girls were actually naked, but what little they wore only seemed to enigmatize and empower what it covered. I didn't know where to look. I was mesmerized by the acres of skin, but feeling an ill-at-ease combination of politeness and bravado that made me want to pretend that I was always surrounded by sirens. Everywhere my eyes alighted they were met by rolling hills of smooth girl flesh. It was like being locked in a library of beauty, not knowing where to begin, not wishing to start on one book for fear of missing out on another. All the girls smiled and met my gaze; some giggled when I looked their way. I was stunned, as if by a grenade, and for a moment that thought threatened to ruin this paradise.

There was no one obviously in charge, just beautiful girls. I was as if under enchantment; unable to move from the spot and incapable either of sating my feasting eyes or of preventing their gluttony. It felt like I gazed for hours upon each girl in my innocent lewdness. I had no ability to decide which I liked the most and no idea what I should do if I could.

In the event, these tiny traumas of Shangri-La were taken from my clammy hands: with a flick of her legs, one of the ladies sprang up from her seat and walked over to me. Her arms swayed around her slightly as she walked, mimicking the movement that a flowing gown would have made. She wore a pale silk top, which stopped just below the breasts; breasts that poked through it like fruit beneath a fly cloth. Her legs were long, very long, and muscled like a dancer's. Her smile was cheeky, pale-painted lips pressed together, like the smile of a friend, a playmate, not a seductress. And even so it sucked the air out of my lungs as she moved towards me.

She said hello, and her eyes were as blue and bright as fresh ink.

I replied, likewise, through a mouth suddenly dry of the saliva that a moment before had been threatening to drown my tongue.

My lady took my hand, my right hand, and with it she traced a line down the side of her face. It felt natural, uncontrived; it was suddenly odd that all strangers didn't greet like that. She put me completely at my ease with that one movement, then stared deep into me with her beautiful eyes.

You're the loveliest girl I've ever met, I thought, and I think I may have said it too.

She smiled, just for me, and she asked me if I wanted to go upstairs with her. I think I said that there was nothing I could like more under a sky as blue as her eyes, though I only nodded my head. She led me up a stairway still holding my hand, through a door that I hadn't even noticed. I felt like a child

61

about to enter a magic kingdom, and I could feel myself hardening against my fatigues as I walked.

There were windows all about on the next floor, windows and doors, lots of doors too. She drew me gently through one of them into a little green room with a delicately made pristine green bed, and green curtains tied up to reveal the sky outside. Through the glass I could hear the clatter of the fools who went about their business apparently unaware of the nirvana above their heads.

'I like this chamber,' she said. 'Green's my favourite colour. But we can change if you like.'

I shook my head, and coughed to clear my throat. 'This is fine. Very nice. I like green too.'

She closed the door gently with her behind, not trying to be provocative, just as you would do if your hands were full. Then she slipped the bolt with practised ease, without even turning to it.

She came to me then, cupped my staring face in her hands and lifted it up to look at it. She kissed me softly, just once, a deliciously insolent tongue darting in like a robber. Then she eased me slowly backwards so that my calves hit the side of the bed and I was forced to sit on it. She bounced down next to me with a grin and took my hand again.

'You taste of synth,' she said, smoothing the downy hair of my knuckles with a forefinger.

'I had a drink over the road, I think.'

'Is this your first time?' she asked me.

And though it wasn't, though it wasn't even close, I told her it was, just because it felt like the right thing to say.

Tenderly she undressed me, taking my tunic off like a mother, a painful comfort: reaching right inside the sleeves to pull my arms out. She deliberately let her hair fall in my face while she struggled with the stiff uniform belt. Her locks were like straw and like gold all at once, mundane and yet magical. Her hand went down inside my trousers and she stroked it along me once, just once, just to remind me that she could. As if I was in danger of forgetting. Then she made me lift my arms up while she pulled my vest off over my head. I felt the static crackle in my ears, felt my hair rising. She held my arms up there, pinned them to the bed, though I could have thrown her off easily. And she looked into my eyes and laughed a guileless prankster's laugh.

'First the shoes,' she said.

Then she scampered off me to kneel where my feet hung off the bed. I inwardly cursed my high desert boots, as I felt her fiddle with the knots and then unlace them hole by aching hole. She pulled at them while they were still tight about my feet, so that they scraped along my stretched heels and came off with audible pops. I felt her tugging at my trousers, lifted up my bum with my back so they slid off, first snagging on my dick before it sprang up again uncovered. I swear I thought that it would burst. Then this loud wind started blowing, but blowing impossibly rhythmically, like a helicopter, and I remember thinking, Shit, is this a dream? Don't let this be a dream. But I suppose I must have said it out loud, because her head poked back into view and she said:

'Sorry, I'm afraid it is.'

And I remember feeling curiously flattered that she looked as glum about that fact as I felt. And then I awoke in terror and agony and unable to see.

Crick's fingers stroke back over his words. He isn't displeased with them; maybe they're all right, and they seem like an accurate rendition of that first morphine dream, but maybe they're not in the right place. The words. He is looking for the words to begin with. He has already written pages and pages, the main room of his flat is strewn with them, but he needs the right words to begin.

Once upon a time there was a young man; who, though he dreamed of being a writer, thought it better to face the risk of death in battle than to live with the surety of poverty. So he took the king's shilling, half in the hope of a life rich enough to write about, half in despair at the life he had. He only asked that it might go quick when his time came, if his time came. He only asked that, if he was to be shot as he ran, that he be running forwards at least. He didn't ask to be covered in glory, but he hoped he would be spared ignominy, he hoped he wouldn't let his friends down. And he hoped this wasn't too much to ask.

Once upon a time the young man believed in stories. He believed that to perish in a great endeavour would itself be a justification of his life, and he believed that his people were engaged upon just such a great endeavour. He believed that it was a clash of good and evil, of reason and ignorance, of knowledge versus religion, of enlightenment against the dark ages. Sometimes he still says that he believes that. Sometimes he still tries to believe that. Because if that was a lie, what has he left? If that was a lie, what have we done?

He pulls the page out and balls it in still-strong fists. Throws it somewhere, maybe at the wall. Maybe he will find it later and like it. But his own words hurt him for now. His chair screeches as he pushes it away from the scarred and sullied table and he feels his way the short distance to the sink. Pulls out from the cupboard a half-pint bottle of synth and takes a swig.

People say that your other senses compensate when you lose your sight. Crick has never found this to be the case. You rely on them more, that's all. You don't grow any extra nerve endings on your fingers nor any more taste buds on your tongue. You don't smell any better than the next man; the old joke: actually Crick often smells a good deal worse than the next man: his flat rarely has hot water, and washing is a chore he has little time for. Though time is all he has.

A Caliphate phosphorus grenade burned away his future along with his face. He has only a present now. But the present stretches before him dreary and pointless. Black and empty as the scorched towns. Fruitless as the charred orchards. Hollow as the craters. What have we done?

9

Detective Günther
Charles Bonnet

THE POLICE STATION IN The Kross is like a colonial trading post: a little island of civilization in the midst of savagery; sinking ever closer to the barbarism that surrounds. Neighbourhoods splattered with porn stores; peep shows; sex theatres, where people rut while the movies run; squalid beggar bars; calling-card hookers and straight streetwalkers; synth heads drinking out of mayo jars; street-corner narc slingers. Some Improved come down for the frisson of slumming it, to buy drugs, to fuck, to play at impecuniosity. A few own businesses. But mostly The Kross is peopled with scum. Scum like an algae or an oil slick, pointless pollution on the surface of the gene pool.

There are any number of slang words for the Unimproved, many of which began as terms of self-defensive humour, when the Generich were few. But most have become expressions of genuine abuse, now that the Unimproved are so much lesser in number and stature. The strengths of the words vary like brands of synth: some could be used lightly, possibly, between very good friends, though such intra-group friendships themselves are rare; some have become hyper real, to mean more even than an insult, to mean 'blasphemer'; to mean 'auslander'; to mean 'your way of doing things is wrong: to have sex to procreate is sordid and selfish and even sinful'.

Of course the anti-genism laws – though initially enacted to protect the Improved – outlaw such abusive speech in officialdom. As a police officer, a detective, Gunt would never use such terms. Not if a superior was listening anyway. Because even those superiors he knows to hold such views themselves – which is most if not all of them – might well use it against him at a later date. Gunt's superiors don't like him any more than the men do. They just know he gets the job done, and anyone can see he's got the best set of genes on the force. Gunt keeps his head down. Gunt gets results. Gunt doesn't contribute to retirement whip-rounds, because no one would do it for Gunt. Gunt's fine with that.

Frank retracts, of course. As soon as he's got a lawyer. As soon as there's a recorder. As soon as it's not just him and Gunt. The Regans disappear from his statement quick as acid dew from the scorched streets. The rest remains, though: Frank found the body in the toilet. Forensics back that up: though Frank gave the toilet cubicle the best clean of its fetid career, traces of hair and skin remained. But Frank was behind the bar all night. Probable time of death is well before closing. The witnesses say he was never gone for long enough to beat a man to death. From seating plans and cross-referencing, Gunt reckons they've got hold of everyone who was in that night. No motives. No connections. No one giving nothing up.

And the cubicle was apparently locked from the inside. That's what Frank says and the forensics say: at least so far as the door has been kicked in recently and splinters from the busted wood match fragments on the deceased's clothes.

So who could have done it? A midget who crawled underneath the door? The gap's only thirty-four centimetres; the deceased doesn't look the type to be beaten to death by a midget. A midget who eased slowly into view while his victim was on the throne. There is no gap at the top, so if not a midget then a magician who walked through it. Or else someone who went in with him: for drugs or sex, maybe, but no traces of either. And the lock mechanism is a circular dial, perhaps not impossible to close with a length of wire or something, but difficult and probably time-consuming. It had no external screwdriver override of the type common in bar stalls, hence the busted door.

The fact remains that no one the lab's produced so far, apart from Frank, left significant telltales on the body. The man was a taxi biker; he got hands around his waist for a living. He had cloth and skin samples from probably fifty different sources on his clothes. But all were slight, Frank aside, not what you'd find from such a violent attack. Unless the assailant walked through a fairly busy bar wearing a path. suit and mask, then it doesn't make sense.

Plus, Frank has a rock-solid alibi for the other one, the night the pimp died. Gunt is beginning to suspect that they're unrelated, when the call comes in. A third death with the same MO is beginning to look like a serial killer.

In the heart of The Kross again. In the midst of the cess. People so fat they use crutches. People so fat they have fat backs. Backs that look like fronts. Fat fucking fronts at that. And white-faced Goths, painted ugly to hide the fact they're ugly. Fooling no one. Not fooling Gunt. Gunt's the best-looking guy on the force.

Gunt's got shoulders like a section of sky. Gunt puts on the pathology spectacles he picked up somewhere. Wonders whether they soften his look. They don't; he looks like what he is: a beautiful thug, in glasses.

Ancestral eyes lost the ability to see ultraviolet the better to see colour. To see pattern. To see camouflage. To see snakes and snow leopards. Because of this advanced colour recognition, we can see art. But with the glasses on Gunt sees art better than anyone. Gunt sees art everywhere. He sees things no one else can. He sees art in places others can't. He sees the magic of the street. The irroration left on shadowed walls where girls leaned. The scurried pale cornflower strokes of rodent trails. The Rorschach butterfly beauty of sweat stains on a burly Turk's shirt, emanating white-hot heat.

The crime scene's a sangria tenement block. The victim's a hooker. Gunt makes a note to check out possible connections of the taxi biker with the sex trade. Pimp, hooker, biker. Maybe they saw something. Maybe they knew something. Maybe they were just born unlucky. They were all born unlucky: they were all born scum.

This girl's last luck ran out a long time back. The flat's painted tobacco brown and you can still see the dirt on the walls. She's sprawled on a heat-dappled sepia rug in the middle. A few pikey possessions knocked about, like maybe there was a struggle. You'd think so, by the bruises that cover her. Her face is kind of manly, square-jawed. Blue eyes still staring, china-glazed. If you could get an image from those eyes, the last thing they saw, would there be a face? Would it be grim, or would it be taking pleasure?

'Ecchymosis caused by trauma extravasations of blood,' Norris, the path. guy, says. Norris is as close to a friend as Gunt has on the force, which isn't very close, the chubby fuck.

'You mean she was beaten to death?' Gunt says.

'Probably.'

Most of her hair's been pulled out. The main link to the other two: the pimp Jesus and the taxi biker. Finding a hooker beaten to death is not an everyday occurrence, even in The Kross, but neither is it unknown. Three similar deaths in just over a week, though, that's certainly unusual.

'I hate The Kross,' says the cop on the door.

10

Holman

HOLMAN WAS TEN YEARS old and his legs were almost smooth. Almost entirely devoid of the hairs that would one day grow from them dark and dense as brush heads. Back then there were just a few faint blond wisps. They could have been the legs of almost any ten-year-old, except that they were shorter than they should have been for a boy of that age. Except that they were shorter and they had scars in them; two big, round, recent scars on each side of each leg. Holes where bolts once protruded, not so long ago. Bolts that supported metal mechanics for stretching; for growing; for Holman's own good, not for torture; though for that purpose they would have served just as well. These could have been the legs of almost any ten-year-old boy, except that they were shorter and they were scarred and they were both bent outwards in places that legs should not be bent. Not just the bandied kinks at the knees, which were a normal aspect of the boy who was Holman. These legs – which, even dazed as he was from the fall down stairs, he was still forced to conclude were his – were splayed in ways that no legs habitually splay. The left leg was bent, slightly but noticeably, at a point mid calf where there is no joint and therefore of course should be no bend. The right leg jutted grotesquely sideways almost from the place the thigh exited Holman's grey shorts. And because his life so far had not been so very long; because time is experienced subjectively and this was a larger proportion than it would have been for an older person and the very worst portion of his life; because he was alone and in agony well beyond anything he could previously conceive of: the minutes while Holman screamed for his mother felt like hours. And even after she came to hold him – against her exertion-sweated hair and hastily tied gown – the hours before the ambulance arrived felt like days.

Perhaps it's the similarities that make Holman think of that time now. Though the differences are more apparent: now he is well versed in falls. The blood flows from his nose, more rivulet than a drip, both from a gash that his fingers feel running across the top and from a bleed inside, which may be severe, as he suspects his nose is broken. Now Holman knows something of breaks. This fall was not even a clumsy stumble, it was just that his legs dropped away beneath him, sending his nose into the far concrete lip of the hole in which he now sits.

The world went black as Holman left the Dead Rat, street lights out. But he edged on across the road; even synthed to the lids he knows the way home. *Especially* synthed to the lids he knows it. But malevolent pranksters or scavengers must have removed the wooden barriers he now remembers were around the hole he now remembers was in the road. He's never known it as dark as this. It's like being in a cellar or cave. Or an oubliette: the pits of medieval lords where the unfavoured were both imprisoned and buried.

He shouts for help. For ten minutes he shouts for help continuously. Opening his mouth hurts his nose and makes it difficult to hold the bridge, which Holman knows he must do to stem the flow. This time his mother does not come. No one comes. And the lights don't go back on. He could almost think it's him who has lost his sight and the world itself continues to be lit by street lights; but now that his always large pupils have dilated to their limits, Holman can faintly see his pale hands, caked with blood as well as the oil paints that linger in finger cracks.

For another hour he shouts sporadically. His nose has not yet stopped bleeding, and slimy blood drips down his throat like choked-back cough-snot. It is a warm night. Were it not for the gradually encroaching fear that he might bleed to death down here, forgotten in his oubliette, it would not be an unpleasant place to be. Holman's slept in worse places. The soil at the bottom of the hole is dry and sandy, not uncomfortable. But every time he removes his fingers from his nose's bridge, the slow drip speeds again. Not a gush, but enough to make him think about how quickly a trickling tap can fill a washing-up bowl. And about how many washing-up bowls of blood might be inside a short person like him. And about how many of those one would need as a minimum.

The next hour Holman doesn't shout at all. He tries to keep as still as a statue. As still as the statue of his father at his brother's. He only swaps the hand he holds his nose with when cramp sets in. But the drip continues; into his throat or down his shirt front, depending on the angle of his head. A constant edging closer to death, which he supposes every second is in any case, but not so evidently as this.

Holman vomits then, stomach unable to take all the blood he's swallowed. He spews it in congealed balls and clotted chunks that barely fit back up. Tasting a second time what he would have preferred not to have tasted at all.

His panicked heart pumps faster, sending more blood to his nose. More blood to flow from him. More blood that he needs. This would be a dumb way to die. Holman doesn't want to die dumbly. So he tries to calm himself and slow his heart, and sits holding his nose's bridge once more. Cross-legged – so far as they do cross – like a bleeding Buddha, he meditates, he wills himself serene.

By this time he would not be heard anyway. By this time there are shouts from the street. There are crashes of metal on metal and splintering wood. There are smashes of glass being broken and light pops of lobbed bottles exploding. By this time the darkness is no longer complete. There are flickering glows in the sky and sometimes sparks blow across the window on the world above Holman's head. By this time the bleeding has stopped – he will not die, not now, not from that – and he has edged himself back into a small cave at the end of the hole. A space covered on four sides where a mammal such as Holman can curl in some comfort and some protection. By this time he has realized that the world outside the pit may have become a far more dangerous place than within it.

11

IN THE GLIMLESS MURK of the blackout, division was illuminated. Though the power failure was city-wide, the havoc was largely confined to The Kross; and those places ill fated to border it.

Elsewhere, people dined by candlelight. People danced to string quartets and to salsco beats played by battery or by bongo.

Elsewhere, people fucked. First-timers gradually tripped further forward along the oldest path. Long-comfortable couples, who knew the other's body almost as well as their own, found freshness in the unhackneyed black. Emboldened co-workers, who had long harboured the urge. Strangers trapped in lifts, passing the time, or fearing it might be the last time. Orgies speeded up, as people ceased to care utterly about their performance; some even ended up with their own partners, so confusing was the dark. Under spider-silk sheets. Under the suddenly visible stars. Sweat stuck shirts to backs. Panties were ripped. Butts were gripped. No children were conceived.

In The Kross, a primal freeze instinct first set in. No one moved from their immediate surroundings, except those few who were certain they were unlikely to meet anyone more to be feared than themselves. And that such people as these would be abroad was precisely the worry of those who stayed put.

But swiftly afterwards followed greed. And greed created movement in many more. When the light failed to return, the professional criminals realized that this might be their moment and quickly began to capitalize. They were, however, proved wrong: this was not their moment; this was amateurs' night.

From out of the darkness sprang an enlightenment urge, and while others bunkered down, the residents of The Kross sought self-betterment.

The Cash Converters were the first to go. Where people's own property had long mocked them from behind grilled windows, for want of buy-back money. On Lockerbie Lane a team of four descended within ten minutes of the lights going out, to sledgehammer down the door. Battering rams appeared elsewhere in the shape of scaffolding poles and disused railway track.

Those burglar alarms with battery back-up clanged out – at least until they were smashed from the walls – the message that a one-night amnesty had been announced: an opportunity to enter the world of adverts.

It wasn't long before haphazard-stacked shopping trolleys were clattering down The Kross' tired tarmac streets. Streets soon strewn with goods too heavy to be carried far, abandoned for lighter spoils, or upon sight of a newer busted-open door. A second-hand sofa sat widthways across Smeaton Street, sprawled like some beached water-beast. And a near-mummified matriarch, toothless as a turtle, had been helped out of a despondent tenement, either to save the beige paisley seat, or else just to sit on it and enjoy the night. A fine night it was, to watch the sky and the prancing passing people and to revel in the festival. Fridges and washing machines, like boxy cartoon characters, staggered along with legs beneath them. Mannequins were dragged through smashed windows, stripped bare by thirsty lovers. Angle grinders treated steel shutters like wrapping paper. Happy birthday to you. Happy birthday to you all. Welcome to the world of whim. Welcome to the world of wealth.

Police lunged into the crowds but the revellers danced around them to re-form on the other side, like the fractal ballooning of fish schools about clumsy predators. In The Kross it was a carnival; a Mardi Gras to which the sirens and flashing lights only added.

When the lights first went out, those off-duty police who could be contacted were told to report to their nearest station. Their nearest station was never near The Kross. Cops didn't live near The Kross. Extra police patrolled safe streets, while those in The Kross got swamped.

Some looters stood their ground, which left outnumbered cops even more confused. Many backed away again. Perps that got arrested meant cops who had to go back to a station, taking them out of the action. Some cops made arrests for just that reason. And every arrested looter was replaced by ten more eager hydra's heads, as the clamour and the glamour and the word spread. Some of the cops couldn't care less: let The Kross eat itself; let them smash their own shops; pile the trolleys high, see what you eat next week! The serious cops removed their shields and nameplates: the one glinted in the dark; the other showed they were playing rough.

Gunt was in the thick of it. Gunt was dealing out turbans – bandaged heads – with his retractable steel club. Soon that was snapped, broken on scum-skull. Instead he took a baseball bat from the hand of some fat gene-lack. Smashed it into the man's own kneecap. Gunt didn't arrest anyone. Gunt didn't want slowing down. It was like truncheoning the sea. But Gunt was wading anyway. Gunt was bloody. Gunt was happy.

Good bar owners plied free drinks on their regulars, who stayed and protected their local. Bad bar owners gave away their synth anyway, and their stools and tables and mirrors and fridges.

Sackers passed bottles between them, swigs shared with the smiles, as they waited their turn to climb through broken windows. People who couldn't normally queue for a bus politely waved strangers on ahead.

As the night went on, more business owners arrived. But most didn't live in The Kross; most were too late. Most were under-prepared and underarmed.

Some premises paid protection to the Regan brothers, and generally these stood safe. Jacob and Kieran Regan – called away to protect a threatened bar – nailed a failed looter's hands to the door of a store, so he could explain its status to others.

The Regans controlled the situation better than the police. Not just places that paid protection, but their own properties and the shops either side. The Regans had plans in place. The Regans had cameras. The Regans took photos when crowds too big to beat back started encroaching. The cameras held them off like water cannons. Only a few people got so drunk with tonight that they forgot there would be a tomorrow.

Some shopkeepers were more concerned about their tally books, their credit lines, than the stock. Some tally books were the first things taken.

Soon smoke laddered into the hot black skies and flames snaked up graffitied walls. Landlords burned buildings for the insurance, sick of struggling to collect tenement rents from flats already subdivided like ice-cube trays. Looters set fire to shops to destroy the evidence. Arsonists set ablaze everything they could, because that's what arsonists do.

Sparrows shot from burning lofts, like startled bats fleeing daytime caves, or sluggish winter bees: out of place, bewildered and out of time. Their feathers singed, or even aflame, they spiralled earthwards.

As the night grew bright with fire, some looters stopped the pillage to form gangs around their own blocks. Human moats to block flames and invaders. Because, as goods grew scarcer, amity dissolved. Looter preyed upon looter; size prevailed. The strong took from the weak, only to be robbed in turn by the numerous.

***

Watching the distant flames through locked windows, hearing the lament of the sirens, those outside The Kross had their long-held suspicions confirmed: the Unimproved are to be feared; they are not a part of what British society has become; they belong to a different age or a different place; they lack guilt, therefore they aren't fully human; they are animals. They are other.

II

Everything Will Be All Right,
In The End

11.
Everything Will Be All Right in the End

12

THERE IS A MAN in the darkness; gently rocking; softly praying. The man, a jihadi, had to stop putting the bomb together when his light went out. Bomb-making is black work at the best of times; though this man finds it relaxing. It soothes away his troubles, just as his finished works smooth away the creases: leave the world a little neater, a little closer to how the Lord intended it; a little freer of the soulless ones who now overrun it. His praying body bobs like a lake reed in an evening zephyr, a movement natural and timeless. Though the blackout has stopped his work temporarily, the man doesn't take this as a sign that he should stop it entirely. The man does not subscribe to signs. The man talks with his God directly. He whispers to Him now, in the night, words inaudible except to them. Words laid down in ancient scripts, in a book now difficult to find, but the man knows much of it by heart. He has a good heart, this man, a courageous heart. A heart open to his Lord and His word. In the beginning was the word.

A Leveller sleeps, her blanket unknowingly clasped to her womb. She needs this rest, from her world of protest, but even asleep her mind is unquiet. By day she dreams of a better world. By night she dreams of this one.

The electricity supply to the police morgue has been cut, like all the rest. And in a labelled drawer in a wall of identical drawers, like an ingredient for a giant apothecary, a pimp is putrefying. Two rows down and four along, a taxi biker renews the rotting process as well. For now, many of the other drawers are empty, though there's a hooker in there somewhere too. Soon there will be body bags stacked up on the floor, piled like rubbish would be if the refuse collectors were on strike. And the refuse collectors *are* on strike. In a room down the hall, blood samples are going off. Whatever little messages they had to convey are being lost. But then it is a night of loss.

The blue spark of a stun gun is seen in The Kross, a jagged flash visible for an instant before it is buried in someone's neck. They drop to the floor and twitch among the sharp confetti, tinsel crystals of broken glass. It is a crystal night. Might yet be harbinger to such things as crystal nights have signalled before. The assailant is just protecting his property. Defending what is his. Though being one among so many brothers, there has been little in his life that was really his, and this shop he now guards, with stun gun in one hand and the choke chain of a babottweiler in the other, is no different.

A prostitute, on her own in the world, warms a tin of baked beans over a candle in her small apartment. The clothes iron that she normally uses to heat her canned dinners won't work in the power cut. She is not given to self-pity, but she is scared. She knows she needs protection, and even more she needs protecting from those who would protect. With Jesus dead, it's only a matter of time until some new pimp comes round. Bringing punches and kisses. Jesus brought love, but she can't see that she will ever find another like him. But for the candle, she can't see at all.

In the darkness, a writer is working. Though it is no darker to him than any other evening, since he has no eyes. Only direct sunshine ever shows itself: a burning sensation on his already burnt skin. His typewriter pings at the end of the line, like an empty rifle clip. The hubbub outside doesn't frighten him. Not even when it is outside the door. Not even when the noise is gunshots. But he is terrified that no one will ever read his words.

Seven sets of triple claws clatter on Sacred Heart Street. Patter on a scullery floor. Four unblinking pairs of eyes, incapable of pining, stare at an old lady. Maybe the creature is trying to understand what her stillness means, but probably not.

An artist is caked in his own blood, curled up in a hole in the ground outside a hole of a bar. He's sleeping now, unlikely as that seems. And ash from burning shops floats down dreamily, like snowflakes, on to the black suit jacket that blankets him. He has never seen snow.

A houseboy walks quietly on bare feet, not wanting to stir his sated mistress on the divan where she sleeps. Even by oil lamp she is beautiful. And even though he knows he is just the hired help, he cannot help loving her.

A narc dealer is making his deliveries by torchlight. Some of his regulars are probably too scared to go out, so he's dropping by like the milkman. Though real milkmen don't deliver in The Kross. He's got a gap between his two front teeth, a wide space that he sticks his tongue through and sometimes, like now, whistles through. He wouldn't normally operate like this: everything bagged up and on him, walking round with the collected cash as well. But he figures cops and robbers both have other things to be getting on with tonight.

Skilled, precise fingers pick a fleck of lint from the trouser leg of a beige flannel suit. It is strange to be wearing such attire at this time of night, and to be able to see such a small thing in a power cut. But this man's room is well lit. And he not only has power, he has a computer. The monitor's light caresses a classically proportioned face. He looks at the screen, upon which are a series of numbers. A vast, jumbled, senseless clutch of numbers. But when the man looks at the numbers, he can read them, like reading a journal. He looks at the numbers and he sees helixes, double helixes. He looks at the numbers and he sees lips and eyes; charming smiles and entrancing irises. He looks at the numbers and he sees sinewy shoulders dropping triangle-neat to slim waists. He looks at the numbers and he sees perfect ratios of buttock to breast. He looks at the numbers and he sees proud parents laughing and cooing. He looks at the numbers and he sees money and prestige. To him, these numbers are pictures; they are art, and he is an artist.

A detective, bloody but handsome, is grinning through the gumshield he is wearing to protect his tiger-white teeth. He has a half-time victor's orange-slice smile: sweet and smug. He is wearing special spectacles, perhaps to see in the dark; or because the colours they create are beautiful; but maybe just because he likes the brightness of Unimproved people's dignity flowing out before him, luminous rivulets in trousers, puddles on the pavements. He wields a nightstick, commandeered from a uniformed cop who was running away. He doesn't draw his gun, he doesn't want to scare them off. He lures the pond scum in or chases them down. He breaks their Unimproved hands, their kneecaps, their ribs, their heads. He smacks it out of them, away from him. He shows that he is not like them. Though anyone can see that. He's got the best set of genes on the force. Anyone can see that.

There is change on the breeze and gunfire in the sky. And somewhere, sometime, all of those bullets are going to come down.

13

Holman

HOLMAN WAKES WITH THE dawn, curled in a hole; which carries a curious sense of correctness, as if this is precisely how he evolved to awake. Daylight shows an exit to this tomb. No rolled-aside rock, but a scaffolding pole, field-promoted perhaps to battering ram, but now discarded into the pit in which Holman lies. One end is wedged in a corner and the other still pokes clear above the lip. Usable, Holman thinks, to clamber out with. In any case the walls are not so sheer, now that he can see them clearly, there are small rock protuberances and softer soil where he could kick in a toe. A man taller and more able than him could scramble out without the pole at all. A man taller and more able than him would already have done so.

Suit covered in dust and blood and dirt and spats of ash, Holman emerges, on to a street that looks like a war zone, like somewhere Crick might have described to him. A hellish city not much like London. Only twenty metres away an arm is lying in the gutter. Dirty pink and chokingly sick. Only when Holman sees the rest of it further on does he realize it is a dismembered manikin. A small relief, but nausea remains and The Kross remains a land laid waste.

Greasy water burps from a lately busted pipe, unable even to make a puddle because the heat-cracked concrete thirstily sucks it down. And all around are discards and broken glass. Streets rarely cleaned now look like landfill.

The Dead Rat is still intact, but most of the other shop fronts have been smashed in. A mangled wheelchair hangs half out of one, like a partially swallowed lump of refuse being gulped by a gull.

Holman tries to calculate what effect this altered world will have on him. He has the money for synth; perhaps such emotionally spastic self-interest thoughts would go better accompanied by a glass or two? But grey smoke furls up in the near distance, like the tabby tails of a tribe of cats. The safety of his flat and paintings must first be ascertained.

At what pace he can muster he makes his way home: through broken crates and shredded paper; round upturned trolleys and wrecked display cabinets. He hobbles past martyred goldfish, scattered like carrot peelings, drying amidst the shards of their former home. Everywhere is broken glass. Everywhere are the marooned objects too cheap or too damaged to be prized. A building side is pocked with melted choc ices, pelted as if valueless; alone it would be vaguely comical, vaguely comforting: a humanizing prank. Amidst this ruin it seems a gutless, senseless waste.

Look on our works and despair! has been spray-painted on to the axe-gashed front of a discount shoe store. And Holman does.

The Kross wasn't always this ghetto, filled with the other, the excluded, the feared. Once it was an area similar to the rest of London. But between the first two Caliphate Wars, when the refugee trains started pouring through the now long-blocked Channel Tunnel to St Pancras and the surrounding streets became near permanently filled with anxious hungry families awaiting assistance, the better-off Londoners moved further out.

Blockbusters moved in. Blockbusters paraded the Unimproved immigrants around to scare residents into selling cheap and quick. They subdivided flats with plywood walls to cram twice or thrice as many tenants in. And as the area's demographic started to shift, all the remaining original residents were panicked into selling. Only the blockbusters and the slum lords were buying. They made fortunes buying cheap and letting dear. Ironically, the Unimproved and the refugees, those with the least money, had to accept high rents, having nowhere else to go. The Generich could live where they wanted. The Unimproved were largely intimidated into staying with their own.

Construction funds got skimmed over many decades. Councillors and builders got fat. There is very little sky now in The Kross; the buildings are high and the streets narrow. Already crowded conditions were swelled more when the religious communes in Britain were closed down. And as the Unimproved from all areas found themselves unwelcome in, or priced out of, places their families had lived for generations.

The Kross was re-zoned, to permit twenty-four-hour synth bars, gambling, and soft-peddled prostitution. It became an alternative economic system, which has little contact with the outside save for slum tourism and broodmaring.

Though right in London's centre, like a rotten yolk, The Kross is now *extra muros*, outside the walls; like the anarchic Montmartre once was to Paris – home to deserters, robbers and hookers – back when Paris was the city of lights; like the ghetto banlieues were to a later Paris – before the Caliphate was declared – from where the darkness spread, the Taliban within.

There is pattern, if not method, in the destruction; which leads Holman to divert his route. His flat isn't far from the Rat, but he now needs to check something else. Holman feels like he's always walking somewhere, when walking is probably the thing he does worst, of all the things he does. And now every step is upon streets slick with liquids and scattered with obstacles. But he must go to the gallery. The gallery that has his paintings, the only gallery that has his paintings.

Charlie Smith, the gallery owner, sits outside, his skinny legs making coat-hanger triangles in his wet jeans. His face is in his sooty hands. Ash, some of which Holman fears may be his works, drifts in dirty water towards the drains. He sits down beside Charlie on the fire-scorched step and puts an arm around him, momentarily pleased at himself for thinking of the act. Charlie looks up; there are no tears around his sunken eyes, just tiredness.

'I came as they were taking the last of it,' he says, 'before they burnt the shop. I said to them, *I'm Unimproved too*. You know what they said?' Holman shakes his head. Charlie continues. '*We're not prejudiced, man.*'

Holman thinks of his lost works. The hours that will never return. The things he will never have the passion to capture again. Some of his early religious-inspired art: the Aztec tower with thousands of hopeless, helpless people lined up on each of its four giant stone stairways; waiting on piss-soaked collapsing legs for their turn to have their hearts ripped from their chests by the priests. His painting of Abraham, in those dark creeper-slung woods, a sleepy and trusting child Isaac gripped in one large hand, a honed stone knife in the other. All the paintings from the 'Immolation Opus', painted in ironic take on eight-eenth-century style, with breasts tumbling carelessly from Biblical robes; everyone in a permanent state of semi-undress and semi-arousal; all pale skin and golden hair and adoring gazes, even the elderly improbably well muscled; even those being martyred seemingly having a good time. They are gone now, gone with the 'Green Series'. Holman can only hope they will end on a looter's wall and not in ashes or the rubbish. If he could let himself dream: maybe they will be found in an attic – when he is highly acclaimed dust – and be sold for a fortune by the progeny of larceny. But today is not a day of dreams.

As Holman walks home, he sees a Down's syndrome boy. Disability has all but disappeared now; only in The Kross does it linger; like olives left in late-night glasses, an acquired taste. But he is beautiful, the kid. He has a round, unfrowned face, crowned by a bungle of hair that demands a tousle. Eyes wide by nature as well as in wonder. He must be the first stranger in weeks not to tear their gaze away from Holman, usually only to glance back as if unfazed, or to affect that prejudiceless, middle-distance, over-epaulette stare. The kid waves, which Holman prefers and returns. A salute to a fellow traveller, as different and yet as familiar as a desert might seem to an ocean.

The front door to Holman's building has been kicked in, but inside it seems unscathed. *The Tribe*, his work in progress, and his recent smaller pictures must be safe.

A message is pinned to his door. It says that his brother needs to see him urgently. Utmost haste. Utmost importance. Holman lets it drop from his fingers and it wafts like a feather down the stairwell towards Mrs Gerbi's door.

14

Detective Günther Charles Bonnet

'KING'S CROSS' SOUNDS ANTIQUATED and strange, since of course there is no king. Once the royal family began genetically enhancing, the utter absurdity of a bloodline head of state became obvious. But if they hadn't Improved, they would by now seem as ugly and irrelevant as some of the scum in The Kross, would have forfeited the last vestiges of respect in any case.

The power is back on in The Kross, but the balance of power may never be quite the same. Gunt notices that people look him in the eye more readily, even those who know he's a cop; but not those who know his reputation, and not those who try to stare him down. Gunt walks down the middle of the street. Other cops have been hit with chunks of debris flung from damaged buildings. Most refuse to patrol on foot now, and there aren't many cars available. The Kross is becoming like enemy territory. It was always enemy territory to Gunt. Gunt's fine with that.

The murder case book is bulging since the blackout, papers spew from its sides like meat from a kebab. Pathology samples have been lost, bodies are rotting. But Gunt has to clear the previous cases anyway. That's the way it works: you clear it or you declare it, before you can move on. 'Declaring' means you are leaving it open or calling it unsolvable. That's what most cops do in The Kross. Blame it on the Regans and declare. Who cares? Gunt cares. Gunt doesn't declare. Gunt kicks down doors. Gunt breaks fingers. Gunt gets answers.

She's in, when he calls, one of the dead pimp's whores: Dorothéa Oveja, *aka* Dolly. Who would pay to screw her? Gunt thinks. She's a skank: rank red head; black bin bags beneath her eyes; cheeks swollen like an orang-utan's with age and fake tan. But men would and do. Men who pay for it anyway. Men who aren't fussed. Though men are quite choosy by the standards of animal males, they are still animal males.

Disease is rife among the Unimproved. Those who are immune to common illnesses do not prioritize their treatment, and the political classes are all immune to the highest levels. But despite the risks, the unimmunized slammerkin scum of The Kross continue to ply and buy sex. The primeval urge to procreate is stronger than self-preservation.

She lets him in without saying anything. Either she knows he's a cop, or she thinks he's a john, or she lets everyone in. She gestures to the lonely reglued chair, by a dressing table draped with dirty dishes. Herself sits down on a denuded mattress; a greying sheet is drying over the wardrobe, making it look like a feeble ghost. The stained-glass window throws strange lights on the hooker's face. Which intrigues Gunt. He puts the glasses on; the infrared plays with the palate of the stained-glass glow, makes her look attractive, in an eerie, other-worldly way. He can't help a half-smile, but kills it quickly, and doesn't sit down.

'I'm investigating the murder of Jesus Jackson,' he says. 'You knew him.' It's not a question.

She nods.

'ID.'

Gunt runs his chip reader, freshly charged, over her thin arm. The yellow words on the black screen spell out a decent sheet: soliciting raps; drug raps; affray; assault on another's unborn – from drug use while broodmaring – no immunities, of course; most of her education in juvenile rehab clink; most of her known associates broken, empty flat-backers like her.

There are no whores with hearts of gold, their hearts are full of synth, street-cut sunshine and self-pity. If there's any gold in The Kross at all, then it's stolen property.

'You knew he was murdered?'

She nods again. 'H told me, right after it happened.'

'H?'

'Holman, his real name is, can't blame him for not using it: 'specially when he's more of a *half man*.'

'The freak who found Jesus; you know him how?'

'He's a john, but a good one. Not a friend exactly, but he treats me well. He's an artist.'

'And Jackson was your pimp?'

A nod.

'You know why anyone would murder him?'

'No more than any other pimp. Less, I guess. People liked him. He made you feel special. He probably had enemies – he was a pimp – but no one I knew about.'

'Anyone tried to take you over since, make you work for them?'

She hesitates.

Gunt comes in: 'Look, I'm murder squad, I don't care if you're a hooker – like anyone does round here – I only want Jesus' killer. Or killers.'

He pushes his hand into a box of her stuff that is sitting beside her on the bed, like she's been looking through the silt of her wasted life; trinkets and tat ooze over Gunt's fingers: rumpled photos; plastic mementos; chipped seashells.

She seems barely to notice, long inured to the invasive.

'No, no one has come round. No one's tried to take me over yet, but they will . . . ' She drops her shoulders noticeably.

'So you're safe, for now.'

He plucks from the lucky dip of shit a little matchbox with a handle. It has a faint blue hue through the glasses, because of the cold metal inside. He turns the handle slowly and it plays a quiet, tinny Happy Birthday.

'You know why anyone would torture him first?'

'Jesus saved,' she says, without irony. 'He had a lot of money put away. Everyone knew that. He wasn't flash, never spent much, but he did all right so he must have. Maybe they were trying to find that out: where it was, to make him tell them.'

'And the hooker, the murdered girl, you knew her?'

'I heard. I've seen her around, I can picture her, that's all. Everyone's scared.'

Through the spectacles her bare legs are a warm terracotta, heat up to venetian red at the approach to their conjoin: a scarlet shadow that keeps her secret place, which isn't a secret, because they both know it's there.

Gunt opens his wallet, takes out his card, places it carefully and meaningfully on her bedside table. 'You can call me if you think of anything else, or need help, if anyone leans on you, tries to take you over, if you're scared.'

She looks up with realization, grateful but weary, mouths 'thank you'.

The air is heavy. The sweat on her breasts leaves visible trails. It's been a while since Gunt's had sex.

Already wet with her saliva, he slides into her. Way too easy for how big he is. Whore. Unimproved flat-backing scum. But maybe that's just how wet he's made her. He's probably the best thing that's ever happened to her. Though she must know it's just release for him. Sure she knows, course she knows, that's her job, but right now that contact's enough. That and the protection he's just offered: a strong hand reaching from a lifeboat. Soon she's murmuring 'you're the best'. So many millions have said those words so many times before, and she has probably said them herself innumerably. Even so, it's probably true. He probably is.

'Pull my hair,' she says, once he's flipped her over, showing the dirty soles of her feet in parallel to her white, plump arse cheeks.

She means it to show trust, or complete surrender. Maybe that's what her pimp used to do. Gunt pulls it all right. Yanks her ponytail out of its tie. Some comes away in his hand, he pulls so hard. But she likes it. Pushes back on to him. Her arse cheeks crease as she does so, fold like old apples.

He hates her as he comes. Silently snarls 'scum bitch' with a curled lip. Wants to punch the pea-round back of her Unimproved head. But he doesn't. He just wipes the curds of sperm from himself on her dress and dresses. He almost takes his business card with him too. Scrapes it from her bedside table in deliberate antithesis of the norm. But thinks better of it, throws it back down to where she lies, balled foetal on the bare bed.

'You hear anything, you come to me. Then I can protect you. No info: you're on your own.'

Well what did she expect, a fairy tale? Being handsome doesn't make you a prince. There are no princes now. There's no queens and no kings. Just The Kross.

15

Valentine

VALENTINE WHISTLES THROUGH THE gap in his two front teeth. It's not a sign of happiness, though he's not unhappy; it's just what he does. Once they thought such gaps were a sign of a lascivious nature. Valentine's not particularly lascivious. He probably doesn't get any more sex than any other twenty-three-year-old narc dealer on the salsco scene. But that is hand over fist. Hand over fist, mate.

Some kids – girls – are skipping in turns over a long thin rope that two of them keep spinning. It drags trails of slime from the ground when it hits, flicking them up into the air. The cord is wet and oiled from the puddle caused by a leaky hydrant. It twirls so fast that sometimes it tricks Valentine's eyes into believing that it doesn't move at all, that it hangs like a rainbow above the kids who dance in the middle. It's been forever since rain, never mind a rainbow. They sing as they skip. Valentine thinks it sounds like the refrain from that track you keep hearing at the moment: 'Strange Fruit'. But it's not really, it's just some nonsense child rhyme.

The bus is taking ages. Valentine ought to get a moped really. He's doing all right again now, and the bus is no way for an upwardly moving man like him to be travelling.

Valentine's got a mane like a lion, blond Samson locks that loll around his shoulders. No one has hair like him these days. Most guys on the salsco scene wear it brilled back and short. But his hair's become kind of a trademark for Valentine and it helps them identify him in the clubs, which is handy for a businessman. One day it may help some cop identify him too, but that's the way it goes. Few retire from this game, you get bumped or you get busted. He used to be part of a street team, but Pedro and Alex both got busted. Not him, though, Valentine's quick. He's got a double-arched foot, runs like he's nuclear, has to wear a balled second sock under it for comfort it's so high, but man is he fast. Not from improvements; Valentine didn't come from a line with the means to speculate like that; just one of those things nature throws up: a little experiment that seems to work. In the world of the street dealer, a double-arched foot is a fitter model.

There's a brace of even younger kids playing by the hydrant, butt-bare under the spray it's sending into the air. Valentine wouldn't mind being naked under it himself, in this brutal heat, but you can never know that innocence again. Not like those kids have it, two dumpy cupids splashing each other. Water soaking little bodies, dripping off of tiny loins that are just cold bits now – sideways smile and pointy stub – but will soon become something else; something singularly significant.

The bus eventually turns up, bringing with it the distinctive stench of bacterial chlorophyll fuel. Valentine secures a seat, its plastic perforated like a tea bag from years of minor injuries, scrawled upon like a long-term con. He wonders how Pedro and Alex are getting on.

Valentine climbed in the world, when they went down. He had to leave the street corners and move his game up a gear – you can't work on your own on the street – so he got into the salsco scene, and are those jivers mad for their kick biscuits? Hand over fist they neck them, hand over fist, mate. And there's none of the shit you get on the corners: no one's trying to rip you or roll you. No one brings a gun to a buy, just a grin.

Valentine always gives people a swig of synth to knock his pills back with, when they want to drop right away, which they generally do. Doesn't cost you much – just a few extra bottles a night – and people appreciate little touches like that. That's become part of his trademark in the salsco clubs, that and the hair and his styles: 'Valentine the boneless' they call him, because of the dance moves he's perfected. The jivers like them, he's seen his moves spreading; that's what happens when you get in on the scene. And it's a good scene: people don't judge you in the salsco clubs, everyone's together, wilfully obliterating their circumstances. All reckless revellers together, all part of the new transmute. Classless but classy, that's salsco.

Through the dusty bus window there's a man selling clearly looted goods outside some flats. People are selling all sorts of curios on the streets of The Kross since the blackout. Valentine had a guy try to swap a set of saucepans for a couple of sleepeasies yesterday. Would have taken him up on it, except it was a bit far to carry them. In this line of work you can't afford to have a conversation with the cops about where you bought something. It's a weird business, though, all the looted stuff; kind of like going back to some ancient barter system. But then it's always operated a bit like that in the narc world anyway.

Valentine's started doing some deliveries now in the early evenings. Thought of it during the blackout, when some of his big-buying regulars were afraid to come out, and found it steals a march on the competition: delivery. You got to innovate in this game.

Stocks are running low, though; he needs to buy first, so he's got to go to the Regans. They shift their meets about, just give you a bus number and a stop and one of them takes it from there. Kind of handy: them all looking the same, more or less. Means they can send anyone and you'll recognize them. Course it tends to be the younger ones who do meet-and-greets like this. The old boys have got bigger fireworks to light; one of them's a bloody MP now.

The bus's automated voiceover calls out, 'Stop forty-two – Charles Martellus Street – we hope you enjoy your business here.' The Regan at the stop is really young, must be only sixteen, the youngest Valentine's seen. His face hasn't yet got the podge around the jaw they get when they're older. You can still tell he's one of them, though, if you've seen enough of them. He tells Valentine to go to number 151, along the street.

Number 151 is under repair. Scaffolding bars manacled together in clumps of bolts lattice the frontage; a skeletal barricade bristling with ladders and planks that have paint and mortar from a hundred building sites splattered over their weather-greyed beams.

Another Regan opens the door. The one with the moustache like a pair of slugs flirting. Valentine's never seen another one with a soup-strainer, which is understandable, because it looks really dumb. He's got the most massive babottweiler with him too. All black but for its ridiculous purple arse and panting pink tongue. Its face could be handsome, but the eyes don't look right: too closely set for a canine face. Valentine can't remember whether you're supposed to look them in the eye or not look them in the eye. But when it yawns to show off a set of teeth like white latchkeys, he looks away anyway. Thankfully the Regan knocks a code and another door is unbolted from the inside.

It's Paris. Valentine recognizes Paris right away, because he has a cobweb of scars over his face; every line running into the others like smashed safety glass. That's probably why the Regans keep him inside, away from witnesses, and why he often does the drug wholesale stuff. Their names are alphabetical, Paris is probably in his early forties, though the scars make that hard to judge.

'Valentine,' Paris says, 'good to see you.' Extends a handshake that is just hearty, not painful, but with a very explicit sense that it could easily have been painful.

'Back so soon? You're clearly keeping busy?'

'Hand over fist, mate,' Valentine says.

Paris looks a bit thoughtful and says, 'You know, if you ever fancy working for us properly, come and see me. We can always use good soldiers like you.'

This irks Valentine a bit: 'soldiers', like he's a bloody general. There's no war, just people trying to get by. But he nods a polite uncommitted 'thanks'. Valentine's a groover not a gangster. He's quite happy making his own moves. Being loosely hooked up with the Regans offers a bit of protection, and opens some doors

– particularly those tricky club doors where the brawny bouncers hang – but he's not about to get into bed with them. Valentine's pretty pan-sexual – he'll go to bed with anyone if they're attractive – but the Regans aren't, not even the younger ones.

They're pros, though. You have to give them that. The buy is as straightforward as ever. Paris does a quick cash count, not distrusting, just to keep everything clear; flicks briskly through the money with the manner of one accustomed to flicking through a lot of money. Valentine's totally confident anyway, the Regans are businessmen, they don't try and rob you, they make plenty. Though the rumors say most of them are miserly enough to suck a shilling from a shit and never spend nada.

The kick biscuits are unusual, flecks of dark yellow in their white, like tea-stained sugar goes in the bowls of greasy spoon cafés. But Paris says they're new and super good, and you have to trust the Regans, they're pros.

This is the time of maximum exposure: leaving the buy. This is the time when, if he was busted, he'd be looking at some real time: possession with intent to supply carries a sliding scale for what you're caught with. But the Regans don't want to fuck about with peanut sellers, so you've got to buy in bulk. Valentine is relieved when the second bus of his day comes quickly.

Paranoia keeps you alive, but it can also give you away. Valentine stays in his seat when a cop gets on the bus, fights the fear that makes him want to bolt. And also resists the urge to whistle through the gap in his teeth, which he suspects might look like deliberate – and thus suspicious – nonchalance.

The cop just has a look around, though, and gets off again, no ID scans.

Alex used to have the logo of The Right tattooed on his arm, so it would be the first thing cops would see when they asked to scan his chip. So before they became privy to his every imbedded sin and secret they would have a slant on what they were reading. He hoped that would help. He still went down for a nine stretch, though. Caught cock in hand, should have saved his money.

You don't have to have an ID chip, of course. Britain is a free country; this isn't the Caliphate, as they keep saying. You only need a chip if you have a criminal record, or have ever worked for the state. Only if you have a bike or driving licence. Only if you have any qualifications worth recording. Only if you have immunities or other medical records that a hospital or emergency team might need. Only if you want to vote. Only if you want a bank account, a mortgage, a loan; or you claim any benefits. Only if you don't want every interaction with officialdom and authority to be a punishing pain in the ass. It's completely up to the individual to choose. But it's considered suspicious if you don't. It marks you as a probable lefty or illegal refugee. A chip's absence in itself can be sufficient provocation for arrest until DNA tests can be processed.

It's six o'clock by the time Valentine's home and got his stash separated and hidden. He keeps it in the loft crawl hole, technically part of the common area rather than his flat, which he hopes might help his case if he got busted. Though of course the stuff would be smothered with his DNA, and such technicalities might ultimately make bugger-all difference.

It's not a big salsco night, but there are a few things going on. There's always something going on: now is the summer of our discotheque. So he slips into some mid-range duds, nothing too flash, but slick enough to look good with his special belt. Had the belt hand-made: little stash pockets that lie pretty flat on the back; it's sturdy, but comes off with one hard pull if you know the right spot, so it can be dumped instantly. He puts in a few from his full range – neo doves; pips; purples; sleepeasies – but mostly kick biscuits, they're what they crave on the salsco scene.

Figures he's got plenty of time for a delivery first, though. And for the delivery he has in mind, it's best to leave plenty of time. He always delivered to her, even before the blackouts. She's not the kind of lady who buys on the streets. She used to send her boy Sebastian out to pick up. Until they got some trust going on and figured it would be easier just for him to drop it off. Home service she calls it. And she likes a service at home all right. She used to be a model, still stunning; fit as any of the teens Valentine routines. She was the last Miss Natural; they stopped after that. Maybe it was to do with the anti-geneism laws. Or maybe natural beauty was falling too far behind where the standards for improved beauty lay. But there was no doubting how hot she was, still is. Valentine knocked a couple off over thoughts and pictures of her in his youth. And now he gets the real thing. Hand over fist. Because she's a hungry one. Hand over fist, mate.

16

Holman

ONCE UPON A TIME Holman knew this second-storey hallway intimately, though now he rarely comes up here when he visits his mother. He used to crawl on hands and knees along a carpet that he thinks was drinking-cocoa brown back then, though currently it is ice white and it has been at least two other colours in between. It was beige, glazed-eye beige, the year Holman spent the most time aware of it, the year he spent staring at it for what seemed like day upon unaltered day. By the end of that year the wheels of his chair had carved little troughs along its surface: tram tracks of the world's most cloistered, pointless tram. When they eventually removed the treacherous stretching steel leg braces, which had been promised as friends but turned so quick vindictive; when he slowly began to walk once more and could finally escape this second-floor prison, his legs a precious three inches longer, his muscles wasted; when he ran along this hall in startled fear and fell down the stairs to shatter his unprotected femurs, by then the carpet was green, parakeet green.

Holman hasn't been on this floor for a while, but Adele Nicole wants to dine in the redecorated room that was once his bedroom, and Sebastian leads him there. Though muscular,

Sebastian glides like a toreador; makes Holman feel more than usually ungainly, while he follows with his uneven clump, walking stick pressing navels into the pile. A small mahogany dining table now sits where his click-cogged, tilt-topped child's art desk once was: in front of the window that was his whole world for so many months before and after the fractures. The view to the street below is not so different now from then. *Am I?* Holman asks himself.

His mother is not; she is as beautiful as ever. She seems barely to age. Surely soon he will overtake her. Her hair is piled up on top of her head, buoyant and tangerine. Holman isn't sure what colour it really is; it changes to suit her whim. She has just a hint of a double chin: a little curve small as the top of an egg floating in water. That aside, her skin is still French-polish smooth.

She invited him to come over and help her eat some of the food that threatened to spoil when her freezer was off in the power cut. That is the only sign that there was a problem here: the street outside, framed by leopard-print spider-silk curtains, isn't troubled with wreckage and waste the way The Kross still is. A policeman in black body armour with a stumpy pump shotgun saunters past as Holman looks. The table is spread with cold cuts – porpoise and wilderbuck; peacock and hedgehog – and pickles to accompany them, lightly toasted loaf lumps.

He kisses Adele Nicole hello, looking over her shoulder as he does so at a framed photo of his father. The man Holman never knew, whose final act on earth was to curse him. He reminds Holman of his brother, they have the same eyes, but then a lot of people do.

***

Adele Nicole turns to the subject of his brother while they eat:

'You need to see him, darling, he said it was urgent and he couldn't get hold of you. Why won't you let me get you a phone?'

'Because it would be expensive and pointless: no one but you would call me. It would just be a stone in my pocket reminding me that no one cares for me and I care for no one; and that fact weighs enough already.'

And then, because he realizes that this sounds self-pitying and petulant, Holman gives her a smile, which he hopes converts what he said to a bit of self-deprecating humour. To his mother, who grew accustomed to decoding the awkward expressions of his partially immobile mouth, it may even have done so. Subconsciously he wipes his lip on the back of his hand, in case there is drool there.

'Well you need to see your brother. He cares for you, Holman; we all do.'

She fails to elaborate on precisely who the others involved in 'all' are; but she is so ripe with life that he's almost ready to believe it anyway. He's not going to go and see his brother, though. The last time was a disaster. And Holman will never completely clear from his head the image of that other time he saw his brother . . . He looks rapidly around the room, as if to shake loose that thought. In here he was taught by his kindly but – he now sees – incompetent teacher, Mr Routledge. Learning by rote important dates in the simultaneous but incompatible rising of Islam and genetics and the wars where their realms met.

Was it this lonely home-schooling that separated Holman from the world? he wonders. Denied him what he thinks of as normal human emotions? He sometimes feels like he is a machine that goes through the motions of humanity with no understanding of it. As if tutored to pass a test: he knows the correct responses, but not why they are correct. Does this realization that he may be autistic mean that he is not?

After luncheon he sits and reads his mother's paper in her forget-me-not-splashed garden. Most of the stories are still about the riots: *ANIMALS*, reads the front-page headline.

London feared the worst and The Kross didn't let it down. These 'people' weren't hungry, writes a columnist inside, they didn't loot to eat. They looted because they think they merit ever more. By supporting the dregs of our society, by not requiring enough of them, we have created a strata of people who do nothing, who achieve nothing, who do not even seek to invest in their children so that they might one day amount to something. There is a sector within our city, it is becoming clear, who think that they are owed a living and who, even when given that, will not hesitate to steal more for themselves. The streets of The Kross need to be cleaned, not just of the detritus from the carnage its inhabitants have wreaked, but of their attitudes, their very mind sets and (dare I say it?) their very make-up. Can we continue to live with these relics of another time in our midst? Britain spearheaded the second enlightenment, the genetic enlightenment, we fought and won wars costly in our children and our treasure to secure this future free from insidious religious superstitions. Can we now continue to live with peoples of the dark ages, those who outbreed us by breeding like beasts? Or lower perhaps than that, when even the cows in the fields and the pigs in sties have all been selected for their qualities, have been enhanced and inseminated with care and cost, unlike some bottom feeders in our inner cities.

We took in the incomers who fled to us from Europe; our fathers and grandfathers welcomed them, in the long and noble tradition of our land. But we can't expand, we are just one small island, and while most of us sensibly have but one child and save and borrow all we can to make that child all we could wish for, a section of society thinks nothing of having three, four, five, six offspring spawned from them, which they cannot even support. Our country cannot cope with the numbers. We cannot feed everyone. We cannot feed those who would have as many children as they whim. There must be a limit. It hardly needs saying that it is thanks to this that we continue to live in fear of terrorism from within, even as we protect our borders. Let us not neglect the lessons of history: the Caliphate first erupted in countries where native peoples were outbred by interlopers, with all the catastrophe that wrought on the world.

Something now needs to change in Albion; the beautiful British people cannot thrive while we fight a second front within our isle. Our green and pleasant land has been sullied with a primeval ooze, the slime of riot and disorder, which should have been long left behind.

The words make Holman sick, not least because his mother's paper is supposedly part of the dwindling liberal press. What then might the right wing be saying? Suddenly he doesn't feel like staying in this house. He never really belonged here. Despite a beautiful mother and wealthy father, Holman is undoubtedly a part of that primeval ooze. Why? Why did they make him like this, when he could have been anything? But Holman knows the answer: hubris.

17

The Professor

'TELL ME, PROFESSOR, TELL me it.'

'I love you.'

'But you don't believe in love.'

'I believe in a measurable physiological condition called *love*.'

'And you love me?'

'I love you.'

'Why do you love me?'

'Because I made you.'

'Why did you make me?'

'Because that's what I do, I make people.'

'And do you love everyone you make?'

'No, just you.'

'Why do you love me then?'

'Because you are perfection. You are art,' he says.

And she is.

This is their game, this is their ritual, this is their daily grace: the prayer offered between a god and his creation. The confirmation of devotion.

They lie together on their shared bed in his fortune-filled apartment and he gazes at her with undiminished awe. She is his greatest ever design, he still hasn't bettered her: English rose, without the propensity to sunburn; just a hint of a Romano-Jewish bump on the nose to break up the flawless Asiatic cheek-bones; heavy lids, an effect borrowed from the heroine-chic years, which always suggests a desire to go to bed, but not quite yet to sleep; her smile looks Javan, though the top lip is actually Spanish, arched in the perfect cupid's bow when closed, and the buoyant lower lip comes, of course, from sub-Saharan Africa – where all lips first emerged, those genes still produce the finest. An impossibly difficult task, and yet there she is: a masterpiece of science and sculpture. Perfection. And a laugh like a pre-fall Eve. The laugh is her own.

Tabby rolls the solid silver love balls around in her hand; her fingernails always look French polished, so glossy are they, the cuticles and tips so perfectly pale. She would merit the name Tabby either for her quartz-grey eyes, or because she slinks her hips like a slow-stalking cat, but she is called Tabitha in any case.

She's young enough to be his daughter, of course. In some ways she *is* his daughter, but not really – she has two loving parents already. Indeed, she's young enough to be the professor's great-great-great-great-granddaughter. Not because the professor is so very old – he's only fifty, looks forty – but because he knows so very much. Of course, all baby girls – save the very poorest and the deeply religious – now routinely have their eggs stored. A tiny ovarian aspirator, which takes no more time and is barely more invasive than the once traditional slap, extracts all the eggs from the newborn child, already replete with every ovum she will ever produce. But the professor could go far further than that if he wished: using embryonic stem cells he could produce children from parents who have never been born themselves. He could run through generations in weeks, the parents in Petri dishes; only the final offspring need ever know a womb. He could produce twins, in gestational terms, one of whom is the other's mother or grandmother or even female father. These things are more than theory, of course: because they are possible, they have been done.

Tabby's hips are slim, not skinny, but slight enough so two little curves of bone, just visible, poke into her hot-pink hot pants. The professor swallows as he notes that the seam of them has her flesh gently parted. She is a wonder, she is wonderful; what a wonderful brave world that has such a girl in it.

Tabby has told him that her parents are torn by the relationship: they would like to disapprove; but they are so grateful to the professor for her that they find it hard not to like him. And anyone can see that he cherishes her. He is like an ancient Japanese poet: a man who has worked and walked through cherry blossom all of his life, who knows those pink petals so intimately that he knew instantly when he had found the perfect bloom.

Of course, her parents can rest assured that their soon-to-be-born grandson will be beautiful and happy and healthy. In normal 'natural' reproduction – the word 'natural' is of course absurd, since it has no measurable qualities and therefore properly belongs in the 'supernatural' world, with witchcraft and Wicca and Yahweh – but in 'natural' reproduction, three quarters of all fertilized eggs will die before gestation is complete. If one were to believe those laughable old falsehoods, then heaven would be largely peopled by floating motes of soul-endowed cells and angelic peanut foetuses. Tabby and he and their soon-to-come sturdy son will have no such fears, nor worries about birth defects or harm risks to the mother. Birth has become so safe that the leading cause of death in pregnant women is now murder. But, of course, many broodmares come from the classes where murder is more common anyway.

Putting down the love balls, which make gentle jingles as they nestle into the silk bed sheets, Tabby starts to unbutton his shirt. His skin grows younger to her touch; she makes him remember what it was like way back when: before he was so jaded, so experienced, so world-wise. She makes him remember what it was like to feel strange fingers on him: not in the way that all fingers on us not our own are strange; or even the fingers of strangers; but a time when for fingers to be there at all was a strange thing. She makes him remember when he believed in life and though he was a cynic it was just a stance. That is why she is so precious. That is why children are so precious: innocence alone is of value, but innocence and beauty combined? What glory; what worth. Truth is beauty and beauty is truth.

'Tell me, Professor, tell me the story of how we met.'

'We met at your birthday party.'

'Why were you there?'

'Your parents had invited me.'

'How old was I?'

'You were sixteen. You were sweet sixteen.'

She calls him professor, but, of course, he is more specialized than that. He is a genetic ordinance doctor, a pleasing acronym, no doubt chosen deliberately by the early pioneers of such techniques.

Her fingers sharply pinch his nipples, forcing a soft moan from him that makes her smile. She bites his lower lip with her smile still wide.

'Were there other girls there?'

'I don't remember.'

'But you remembered me.'

'I couldn't forget you.'

'Did I do anything unforgettable then?'

'You watched me all night.'

'Is that all?'

'No, that's not all.'

Even in his high penthouse apartment it's hot. In the corner is a standing fan, with a gyroscope design; as it spins, it looks as if it's sucking you inwards, like she does. A pearl of sweat runs down her face and he licks it away, relishing the salt. Humans loved salt long before they had any notion of loving other humans.

Evolution is not a goal in itself, but a means of solving a problem, and the problem is extinction. Genetic and fossil records show that ninety-eight point eight per cent of all the species that have ever existed are now extinct; among them the dozen other lines of Genus *Homo*. Those doubtless louse- and disease-riddled early experiments, which failed, or were outcompeted, or – in the case of the Neanderthals at least – were probably slaughtered by mighty *Homo sapiens*.

Every human alive today – a population, it must be said, significantly smaller than before the Caliphate Wars – came from a single common ancestor who existed something around 150,000 years ago. As is true in all evolution, none of those descendants can have looked remarkably different from their parents or children, but jump back a few hundred generations at any stage of those seven or eight thousand generations and the ancestor would likely appear to its descendants to be a creature abhorrent: a misshapen, ill-begotten bog thing; more distant even than Tabby would be from the Unimproved today. The professor wonders whether primitive man would appreciate the beauty of Tabby; probably not.

She is undoing his cord belt loop now, eyes gleaming with tease.

'Did I do this at the party?' she says, as she frees him from his linen trousers.

'Yes, I believe you did.'

'And you let me?'

'Yes, I believe I did.'

'But wasn't I just a child?'

'No, you were never *a child*, you were *the child*, you were the most beautiful girl in the world.'

Is it fair, this new world order, that he should live this life of luxury, that he should be able to have Tabby? Hardly, but then life never was fair. Intelligence, athleticism, health and attractiveness were never distributed equitably, not even in the eras of communist regimes, which probably failed for that very reason. And because 'natural' genetic inheritance was not under an individual's volition, meritocratic capitalism was never a fairer system, in the strictest sense, than feudalism; it only randomly selected different winners and allowed more people to win. Now that the castes are genetic – with the hopeless breeders lingering far beneath – life's winners are generally predetermined and genuinely superior, it's no fairer, but is it really any less fair? The best prosper and leave ever-fitter offspring, it was always thus, only the speed has improved.

Lovingly she rubs the underside of his glans with her thumb, as if she is trying to smooth the crease from it. His penis strains upwards to meet her ministrations.

'Did I do this?' she says.

'Not so well as you do now. You learned fast, but never so well as now.'

He wonders how their life will change once their son is born. Will there still be time for lazy, sexy mornings like this? They will have a nanny, of course, but Tabby will want to do so much herself, that's her way. She's insisted she wants to breastfeed. The hormones she's taken have swollen her already large globes. She frees them now, pulling her Lycra vest over her laptop-black hair. They jut from her above her slim flat stomach. Breasts full and full of promise, like some fantastical fruit: the fruit of the tree of knowledge. It was only a sin to eat that fruit because God wanted to keep people ignorant and hungry. The first genetic revolution fed the hungry, the second promoted people to the rank of angels. No wonder the religious objected so vehemently. But since religious credulity itself is substantially genetically determined, such people have long since disappeared from positions of power in Britain.

He cups her breasts from beneath, as if he is weighing them, though they need no support, moves his thumbs to push against her nipples. Nipples that he knows are precisely five centimetres in diameter normally, but which have grown with the lactation hormones. She works his shaft with slow, accomplished strokes.

Her other hand teases his perineum, palm upon his testicles. She could patent the technique, but then it is probably something her mother taught her in any case. Mothers like to pass on their little tricks ...

The facts of life long ceased to be the facts of life. There can be no disguise about birds and bees because people, most people, the decent sort of people, do not procreate in such ways. So sex has evolved into its most explicit ever incarnation. It is only about the performance, the entertainment, the pleasure.

And what pleasure. She sucks him down. Gathering as much as she can into her mouth and pulling from behind his clenched buttocks as if she needs more. She murmurs and moans into him, as if the sensations run through her body, not his, though all his fingers do is clutch her fine-spun hair.

She is his everything, his houri, his princess, his partner, his perfect artwork. It was almost inevitable that she should worship him; he was her creator after all. He was her God. But he is in equal thrall to her, her silken skin. He could spend hours stroking her, days in her sweet coney. She makes him feel like the lord of all he surveys. Which, he supposes, he rather is.

Unlike in evolution, stability in a social system requires the greatest number possible to win. But in order for them to know they're winners, there must be a curve to grade upon: some – like the professor – must win big and others must lose. It's not fair, but it's fairer than nature's all-or-nothing way. The Unimproved would by now be extinct, if London were a jungle. But no one starves to death in merry England; or at least, not many. There is social support, and their women can find work being paid for pregnancy, if nothing else. Tabby's surrogate was carefully selected from the upper echelons of the profession, of course. A girl fully qualified in womb massage and mood music. They wouldn't leave such a thing to chance, nor let a 'natural' carry their son. But not everyone can afford such luxuries, there is plenty of broodmare work. Some of the Unimproved even get off prison sentences because they're carrying another family's child, which might suffer in incarceration.

Tabby kneels above him, her coney lips like slices of carpaccio, which he would indeed like to eat, but she has other plans. She is natural, thick-lipped. In common with most modern girls, she is 'afflicted' with the previously obscure genetic condition of neck-down alopecia. But he's glad her parents chose to keep her whole. The professor dislikes the practice of labial diminution; though the customer is always right, of course.

'Tell me, Professor, did I do this?' She holds him as she eases down, taking just enough of him to cause them each a slight, exquisite pain.

'Yes, yes you did.'

'And did you like it?'

'I loved it.'

'Did you like me?'

'I loved you.'

'Do you like me?'

'I love you.'

He made this girl, who rides him, bucking her hips like a gaucho. He constructed the artificial chromosome pair to be added to the twenty-three pairs from her parents. Their genes are in her, she is their daughter, but much of them has been silenced by anti-genes. Alongside the most up-to-date immunities and synth sync packs are all the things he added. Those are the things that really made her; he designed her, he created her. And yet she owns him as much, if not more, than any claim he has on her.

She makes him child again. You can never appreciate orgasm like you do the first few times. After that, you know what it feels like: it feels like orgasm. But that first time, it felt like nothing you'd ever dreamt of. It was cold through your dick and hot through all the rest of your being. It's still like that with her.

She rolls her hips, so that it feels like he is being twisted inside of her. Like she is milking him.

To keep himself from coming too soon, he does what he always does, something intellectual, some little memory game. Let's remember the names of all the extinct human species, then: *Neanderthalensis*, of course, our erstwhile companion. Then who? *Homo habilis*; *Homo erectus*; *Homo rudolfensis*. The last ones: *Homo floresiensis* and *Homo denisora*. *Homo georgicus*; *Homo ergaster*; *Homo cepranensis*. Who else? *Idaltu*, our older brother. *Sediba*, or was that one still an ape? *Homo heidelbergensis*; *Homo rhodesiensis*. Is that all of them?

It's not enough, anyway, it's barely slowed the quickening she creates. She makes him feel like a teenager. He thinks of work, he tries to think of the projects he has to do. The appointments with the super-wealthy parents-to-be he has coming up. Still no help; there is pleasure in his work. He enjoys his work. Something odd, something strange. That thing they made him help with. But that's too strange. That's sick. They'd never do it, though. *Homo sapiens*. He comes, and yet it is an empty orgasm, a mere squirting of fluid.

18

Detective Günther
Charles Bonnet

THE SUPER'S HAIR IS smog-grizzle, cinder-grey. He suits this place. Grey as pavements, grey as old gum, grey as his grey blazer and grey desk plate, grey as smoke and freight. He'd probably even look grey through the specs, but Gunt wouldn't waste them on him, and anyway, wearing them would smack of insubordination.

'There's been another one,' the Super says. 'Prostitute again. Dorothéa Oveja, ring any bells? I only ask because, interestingly, your card was found at the scene. Which says to me that either you're getting close to the killer, or you've fucked up, or you're fucking whores . . .'

The Super stares into Gunt's eyes. Gunt meets the gaze. Doesn't try to stare him out, but doesn't flinch or blink.

'No,' the Super says, 'I don't think she'd be up to your standards would she? If you're not too sodding perfect to fuck at all. Anyway, pathology tells me all the substantial DNA traces they found on her showed 'no immunities' – they were all Unimproved – so I think we can assume you're in the clear. But get this thing solved! I don't need to tell you that word about these murders is starting to get around. The last thing we need is The Kross more on edge than it already bloody is.'

***

Gunt's desk. The Super's gold pen flops like a rigid gymnast, somersaulting along Gunt's fingers. Dextrous fingers, strong fingers, nails bitten down as if their owner were nervous.

Dolly's flat. Same as Gunt remembers it, save for the kids' chalk drawing outline of a person on the floor. With the glasses on, Gunt thinks he can see Dolly, sure he can see the shadow of her, on all fours on the bed. Then balled up, begging for his retracted help.

Norris from pathology, chubby brown berry, sends through a long list of established DNA matches from the corpses. One name at least Gunt knows to be innocent, so the list is immediately redacted, investigating officer deleted. No single person's traces were found on all four victims. No overly strong criminal or psychological correlations either. But a couple of people's deposits were found on a couple of bodies, worth checking out for a start.

A little matchbox with a handle. It has a faint blue hue through the glasses, because of the cold metal inside. Gunt turns the handle slowly and it plays a quiet, tinny Happy Birthday.

Big dangerous animals don't move much and don't make much noise. Little scampering bleating prey animals do. Humans register: it's always the quiet ones you have to watch for. Gunt is silent, walking through The Kross.

It's too hot for much noise anyway. Builders repairing the riot damage, taking a mandatory break from the midday sun, hardly have the strength to leer. One manages a half-hearted 'want something else to suck on, darling?' at a young woman with an ice pop, but his spirit is not with it and she doesn't even look up.

There is a man selling what his sign claims are genuine fragments from the Statue of Liberty, but they could be anything, probably came from a busted building a block away. America, O America, our ally against the Caliphate, who sobs for what we did together. We used to be special friends. But oceans are wide when fuel is scarce, and over there Christ is still king. So like former partners – in murder or marriage – we don't mix much now. People are buying the Liberty fragments, though, like they want to believe it's true. Let them. Gunt's fine with that. Gunt's got his own problems.

The Super was right: The Kross is on the edge, you can feel it. Humans get violent when they are overcrowded and undernourished, much like all other animals. The Kross has turned man-eater, you can't help it now. You can only alleviate its pain.

A parrot flies within range and Gunt punches it out of the sky, instantly and without thought. A passer-by looks as though they are about to say something but meets Gunt's eye and shuts the fuck up. The bird, broken-winged, flaps weakly on the dusty pavement. He can't leave it like that, so Gunt stamps on it, feels a series of splinterings under his foot.

Once, pursuing a suspect, Gunt went to Hastings, down by the sea. Saw the fences and the ploughed and poisoned ground beyond, denuded of vegetation, flattened to reveal footprints. The hairbrush clumps of razor wire piled down the gullies that would have been easiest to climb up. And he supposed that was right, supposed that was our right: to hold on to what we ourselves had built, to keep out the refugees who had no part in building or protecting this fair isle. There isn't enough space for everyone. But weren't they the very ones we needed? Because the cowardly never leave; and the stupid can't find a way; and the weak don't make it; so those who try must be genetically superior, in their way. Only that's not good enough now, not any more. But Gunt couldn't help wondering what became of those who made it that far. They can't have turned back at that point. They must have continued. They had no choice.

Gunt could have gone anywhere at the beginning. Gunt could have been anything. But now there is only this. Possibility has been squeezed through the bottleneck of previous choices, until this is all that is left. So he goes on too. So he goes on making the choices even narrower.

Three names come up linked to more than one body. There's one that Gunt's already spoken to: the limping, lisping dwarf freak who found Jesus Jackson – his swab was taken there to eliminate him from that body – but he comes up again as a trace on the other hooker. And he knew Dolly, she said so. Should be prime suspect then. But the guy's a bloody cripple. No way could he beat Jackson to death, or the taxi biker. Probably not even the whores, certainly not without more of a struggle than showed. But he needs re-interviewing, might be something he knows.

He's not home anyway. Gunt doesn't leave a note. Better not to warn them off.

Suspect two wears a T-shirt that reads: *Go Ugly Early, Beat the Midnight Rush*. This shows significant self-knowledge: he is an ugly fuck. Typical unenriched Kross scum. He's sitting out the front of his building when Gunt approaches and recognizes him from the reader picture. He's got a snake on a lead. The snake is one of those that have been given legs. Overcoming a curse to slither on its belly. It's still unmistakably snake, though; barely uses the legs as it follows its master inside to talk to Gunt. It slips the feet flat to its sides as it writhes along the floor, shows how its ancestors must have come to find them surplus to requirement. The man talks easily, doesn't really need the slaps Gunt gives him, but it's better safe than sorry. Who gives a shit if you beat the odd still-born? He's just a john, Gunt doesn't make him for the killer. Anyway, he was working during at least two of the deaths, pretty solid alibi, if it checks out.

Name three has the slightly dreamy delayed response that sunshine heads often have, even when they're straight. He has *LOVE* tattooed on his left hand and *HAT* tattooed on the right, which seems to suggest that it once had more fingers than the three it has now, against the prevailing fashion of humankind. Gunt breaks two of the remaining trio before he's satisfied the man is being truthful. Gunt tells him it's a small price to pay to be in the clear. Much better than spending weeks on remand, alone in a cell; alone in a cell if you're lucky . . . The man agrees, moaning and rocking. Every society gets the police it deserves.

People think that police work is glamorous. It's not. There's nothing glamorous about The Kross. Or they think it's drudgery. It's not. Not the way Gunt does it. It's just about being the apex predator. And Gunt's fine with that. It's just about scaring some fuck more than some other fuck scares them. It's just about who's got the thick neck and the brick wrist and the swinging dick. And it's pretty bloody obvious: that's Gunt. Gunt's got the best set of genes on the force. Gunt's made for this work. Gunt's never happier than when breaking bones and taking names. Someone's got to keep the scum down. Someone's got to strim the stingers. Albion has no need for nature now. The womb rats have to be kept in check.

So why is it that – when he gets home to his apartment; when he pulls out his pistol, his truncheon, his brass knuckles and his butterfly knife; when he drops his blood-flecked suit jacket over the back of the chair; when he puts his chip reader on charge and pulls his size twelve steel-toed shoes from his feet – why is it that Gunt slumps down at the table and cries?

19

Holman

THE CROWDS HUSTLE PAST him on the way to the stadium. Bustling towards the blood. Holman would be a fast walker, by inclination; he sees the gaps that he would like to be in, spaces through the throng. But he is frustrated by the legs that will not allow him to be where he'd like and the sluggard pace his life must therefore take: leaning on his stick; swaying like a wave-rocked life raft; marooned in this body that seems not to belong to him.

There is a protester on the broad parched pavement outside the stadium. He isn't against the entertainment; just making himself heard where he knows there will be a multitude. This isn't the Caliphate; Britain still enjoys freedom of religion, of a form: the freedom to assemble only in groups smaller than twelve; the freedom to be ignored or mocked.

Man in God's image. Not God in Man's! reads this poor pongo's sandwich board. And he shouts phrases from the Bible, which supposedly support his objections to technology its desert-dwelling authors could never have dreamed of. While Holman watches, a youth throws a plastic cup of liquid over the preacher, who is brought to a spluttering stop. It might be synth; it's probably piss.

In the beginning, most God-fearing folk used to believe that gene selection was inherently wrong. But it became so mundane, so mainstream and everyday, that eventually even some of the religious couldn't help but suppose it to be one of God's mysterious ways. And with it there were no more abortions, no more birth defects, no more menstruation even – Eve's curse had been lifted – so most of them came to suppose that the world had become better. Indeed, some became the most passionate advocates of genetic improvement: fervour, it seems, is substantially genetically determined, but not which faith.

Actually, Holman pines for the days when the existence of God was truly in doubt. When one could have argued about that. There is no doubt but that God's death has left Britain a poorer place. If only because it means another grand topic is finished. The final limpets on the rock of religion rarely argue or reason now; they just blow things up, kidnap and murder. That's all that's left them, but perhaps they're right anyway: from what Holman knows of the major holy books, it seems likely that's what God would have wanted.

Holman buys a bottle of synth from a trestle counter outside the stadium, even though his liver feels scuffed, like a leather football used too long on a concrete playground. Childhood games were a visual experience for a home-schooled cripple; Holman always served as a watcher, not a doer. This arena, where all are onlookers, is the perfect place for him.

The synth seller tries to short-change Holman, doesn't even have the decency of a blush or an averted gaze when he spots it and politely challenges. Instead she stares at him with contempt and resentment, for having the audacity to secure his own money. Who gives a shit if you swindle the odd still-born? She drops the change into Holman's out-held palm, as if she doesn't want to touch his skin. His hands are, as usual, stained with the greasy oils of his art, but he knows it isn't for this that she avoids his touch. Holman knows the look well: she inwardly fears that his handicaps may be contagious, however much she knows they cannot be.

There is no such fear of contagion once inside, not in the cheap seats: Holman shares his synth with the strangers either side of him and they gladly take slugs. More bottles and flasks do the rounds. This is a part of the ritual of watching. Waiting for the game to begin. Holman tries to keep the grog glugs well back in his throat, though, away from his lips, where he is aware that synth's delicious anaesthesia can increase his tendency to drool. It is best not to try the good nature of the bottle-sharing strangers who surround him.

The man next to Holman sucks greedily on a long clay pipe. He wears the knitted black cap of an aficionado, but it's battered, and, sitting where he is – high up on the sunny side – he must be too poor for a season ticket. He has even brought his own cushion with him, a sure sign of a hollow pocket. Most people, like Holman, sit on the inexpensive rented cushions, to make the red-brick tiers of the amphitheatre more comfortable.

The dirt on the arena floor is dry ochre like some exotic spice; still tinged with a mysticism that familiarity cannot overcome. Holman takes out his sketchbook. This circus is one of his favourite haunts, because life and death are so very explicit here; the energy always demands documentation, and now he has much work to replace.

Drums announce that the pageant is to begin. The fighters troop in, sinewy, poised, bred for this sport every bit as much as the aurochs they will meet. Most of these men are from families with a lineage in the arena, and with each fresh generation their characteristics are chosen to improve upon even that stock. They wear the recortes style, of course: not the brash gold threads of the originators of the sport, but the more dour street wear; but they still have the cropped boxy drummer-boy jackets, the black neckties, and the knitted caps – which have also become the uniform of the aficionados; and they still wear white stockings and uber-tight breeches, which make the jumbled assortments of male adornments squashed down tight trouser legs look like quart offal bags from the butcher.

Holman starts to sketch, as the fighters circle the twenty-thousand-seat stadium, waving and blowing kisses to the crowds. The figure he crafts is a composite – all and none of the fighters – alone in the amphitheatre. His pictures often produce this alienation, this separation of the subject from the rest of the world, and with pencil this seems to be even more pronounced: dark, solid strokes lend themselves to pictures of isolation and violence.

The aurochs don't parade; they won't be seen until they fight. They will have been driven from dusty Cornish estates today. The aficionados have a saying: 'the bull has only one bad day in his life'. Which is true, but it's a very bad day: torn from the herd and the endless, fenceless fields it roamed; corralled by horsemen; loaded on to a livestock lorry; driven for hours through the sweltering heat, on legs that find it hard to stretch or stand comfortably in the confines of the truck. When it arrives at the theatre, it is swollen with rage. And at that point, for the first time in its life, it encounters a man on foot. It isn't scared; it is angry, it is incandescent. Adrenalin and fury bowl through its veins faster than it charges around the arena. It doesn't occur to it until the final instant that it is not going to destroy this puny, hornless beast one tenth its weight. It only knows – and although Holman realizes it's foolish to imbue a bull with human emotion, he is sure of this – that someone is going to pay for today.

The fighters troop out, except for the torero who will take the first bout, and his team. They remain, a tight circle, a hub in the centre of the huge wheel of the plaza. The drums start again, beating to signal the opening combat. The torero's name comes up on the LCD scoreboard. He's not a complete unknown, but hardly a star; the better fighters will come later.

The crowds cheer as the auroch is released through the sliding gate. Its heavy hooves puff up mini mushroom clouds in the dust, then trot it to a baffled stop, as it looks about its new surroundings. It's a magnificent beast, velvet black, long, pale horns sweeping directly forwards. It weighs probably a mite closer to two thousand kilos than to a thousand and is six foot plus at the bulbous shoulder, which is humped like a diving whale. The same beast found in Stone Age cave paintings and Cretan art, hunted to extinction in the Middle Ages. Recreated by backtracking genes from modern cattle, which descended from it, to the DNA of a mummified beast found in bog land. Extinction overruled. One of the easier marvels of the modern age.

In a carefully choreographed volley, the torero's team fly from him to the protected palisade sections of the stadium edge.

Leaving their leader alone and suddenly the object of the auroch's ire.

The toreador spins his cape about his waist like a cancan girl showing her wares, but with the aloof precision of a flamenco dancer. The bull stares at him a moment, and then begins the lumbering bolt that always begins a charge.

The crowd claps, started as always by the aficionados in the season-ticket seats, but the man next to Holman senses it and claps along. It is the sign of a good bull to charge at once. It will be a good fight.

Holman sketches, trying to capture the muscles of the beast: it is hard to show their fullness without their looking inflated. But then it is all exaggerated already. The fighters are much taller than is common, even among the Improved; they are selected for this as much as the bulls. 'Normal' people couldn't reach to place the darts and swords in an auroch's neck. The gigantism of both participants gives the sport a hyper-real feel. As if this is some kind of epic struggle. The toreadors are lean as well as long, elegant, designed to fit their clothes more than the clothes have been designed for them; with the celerity of house flies, the agility of cats. The reanimated bulls are like living history. Perhaps that explains the popularity of these spectacles: they remind of a time when men fought nature and not just each other. The grand battles of both wars are finished now: the Caliphate has been finally broken, all but obliterated, and nature has been banished utterly, to intrude only as a cockroach in the kitchen.

The auroch snorts as it makes its first pass, horns lunging futilely at the cape, which floats just out of their reach, like a butterfly on a breeze. Of course Holman can't hear the noise of the bull's snort from where he sits, especially amongst the cheers and chatter, but he saw the spray that ejected from its fierce nostrils. When Holman squints, it is as if he has taken a photograph. He can pause the image even as time continues. It is this that allows his studies of action to be so precise. He can picture the instant that blood or sputum flies.

For now there is no blood. The toreador lets the bull make several passes. He plays it close to his body. More dangerous, but danger is the only way to progress up the rankings of public perception, to begin to command the top fees and the top billings. Holman suspects this fighter will never make it all the way, though. Holman's no aficionado, but you don't have to be to spot the true maestro. There is something about their grace and fluidity that separates them even from the graceful and fluid.

One of the toreador's team holds the two banderillas aloft now, flower-garlanded spears. And forces them with deft fingers into the distracted beast's back. They are to weaken the neck muscles of the bull, to make its charges easier to control. Already its head is lowered slightly, closer to where the toreador wants it. Two more banderillas are added. Bright barbed kebab skewers flapping lazily, bouncing as the auroch runs; held in by jagged hooks that must be excruciating, however much adrenalin and testosterone course through it.

But Holman cannot pity the bull. Most male cattle are castrated at nine weeks and slaughtered within the year. Led on trembling legs to smell the abattoir's death and fear; watching the animals in front get a bolt through the brain. The fighting auroch lives to five or six or more, roaming vast sun-drenched estates. It doesn't occur to it until the final instant that it is not going to prevail in the sudden strange world of the arena. Who would not rather go like that?

But that is the question: not 'to be or not to be', but how to go. Some days Holman longs to open a vein and slumber in a crimson bath. To escape this prison of a body and this lonely, paid-for, perishable life. To disappear into the same void as before he was born. But he would sooner go like the auroch. He would sooner have its strength for a day, even if it had to be that one bad day, than to die with his own frail limbs.

Because of paediatric sicknesses and frequent fractures, Holman has never enjoyed the unconscious sturdiness of childhood. He has always been aware that he is dying by degrees. And he knows the others are too, all the others, even the beautiful and the lucky, perhaps especially them. But they at least have the years of ignorance and then the joy of some fleeting years when they think they can fight it. Holman feels like he has only ever been watching the short stubby hands of his own personal clock ticking away.

The torero is better than Holman thought; he puts on a good display with the charging auroch. A bullfight is like ballet: a spectacle entirely pointless save that someone has made it their life's work to perfect the meaningless exhibition, and that in itself produces meaning. Holman's neighbour murmurs the moves as they occur, whether for the benefit of others or his own satisfaction: 'revolver', a swirling finishing flourish; 'lager cambiada', a kneeling cape pass; 'public mirando', a devilish daring pass performed while looking at the crowd, not the bull;

'abanico', or Spanish fan. Of course all of the moves were Spanish originally, in the way back when; brought to this country by the waves of refugees from the first Caliphate incursions.

A saddle of blood now coats the animal's shoulders, running down towards its forelimbs. It is for this reason that the fighter's cape is red: so as not to show the bloodstains on it, not because the bulls somehow hate the hue. Aurochs, like all cattle, are colour-blind. They attack the movement of the cape, its impertinence in the air. They can't see its red side, nor the Union Jack flag upon its other face.

The fighter cocks one knee and raises his hand to summon applause. Somehow his gestures seem deliberately feminine; is that all grace is? The bull is panting, bleeding, dirt up to the knees of its widow-black fur. Muscled flanks, still burly and ferocious, but caked now in shit.

To watch the bullfight is to see the lie in what is nonetheless true. The spectacle is beautiful, it is as close as we get to the primitive essence of our existence, and yet that essence is hideous savagery. But these two facets coexist. Holman is able to appreciate the skill and daring of the fighter, even as he feels disgust for what is done to the fought.

The fight is not entirely unequal, though. On the next pass the auroch catches the torero on the leg. He is not gored, but is knocked to the ground by the force of the blow. The animal slews round at the end of its run, spraying up the arena's dirt. And paws, begins to charge again. The fighter tries to regain his feet, but cannot get there. The beast is diverted from its charge by one of the torero's team, who runs across its path, daring it to follow. It does, head crashing into the wooden shield at the arena's edge, which the man darts behind. The shambles is given whistles of derision throughout the theatre, not just from the aficionados.

The torero limps off. He would be stepping aside anyway around now, though preferably without this ignominy. The three other members of the team come on, each armed only with a cloak. They are here to tire the creature. To let it waste the best of its anger, before the toreador must lean between its horns to deliver the death blow.

The bull gapes, and with its mouth open, it is more visibly herbivore. There is something placid about it with its tongue dangling that detracts from the size and the muscle and the horns. Blood doesn't pour from the open wounds, but it splurts periodically, when the beast breathes, and it is becoming clear that such breathing is getting harder.

It still charges, though. And for some minutes the men attempt to best each other in bravado. Trying to win back the crowd's approval. 'Too long,' Holman's aficionado friend mutters, shaking his grizzled chin, pipe moving like a finger ticking off a child.

Sure enough, the auroch's head is now lowered, not to charge, but because it is at the end of its strength. Stationary, the beast stumbles to its knees, too weakened to fight on. In the wild, the wolves would have it at this moment. Perhaps they would have pursued it for far longer and with more savagery than that committed by the fighters. But then this isn't the wild. The jeering, whistling crowds show that. This is civilization. And it is not humanization to say that the bull is now aware of its own death. However much before it was cloaked in fury and adrenalin, it sees that fact with open eyes now. It's the first time that Holman notices that its eyes have white within them. They are not pure brown, so they must be wider, or the pupils narrower. This is fear, as real or realer than anything Holman could experience. The bull lacks imagination, but now it doesn't need it. Its back is a two-litre pot of red paint. Its tongue lolls from its mouth, coated in the same bloody mucus as drips from its lips.

The torero runs back on. Leg pain gone in his anxiousness to salvage something from this disaster. He's too late to square the bull's feet for the kill, which should be his task. Instead he goes straight for the death blow: the sword stabs toward its spine. But at the last moment the creatures denies him even the consolation of the clean kill. It rolls on to its side, hooves curled up as if in supplication. Pulled into its body for protection or from exhaustion or just because it knows not what else to do. It is at the end of its experience as well as its life. The toreador's stab goes into its side and the crowd boos him. It is messy. His team tired the bull too much and the crowd has had to face what it didn't want to see: not art, but slaughter.

The tumescent internal tissue bulging from the skewered bull's side reminds Holman of his own swollen, bursting lips. The dribbling slash across his face. Self-consciously he wipes his lips before taking a swig from the bottle that is handed down, seemingly for its previous holder to better take to his feet and yell abuse. Chants start, spread and join, throughout the amphitheatre, like ripples on a lake. The torero storms off. Blood bursts from the auroch's nose, it tries to raise its head, but this time it's too much. Eyes wide in terror, it dies.

Man has triumphed over the beast. Dancing and bragging at the top of the food chain. Perhaps a little prematurely, for a creature barely a hundred thousand years old: when sharks have been around for 350 million years, evolving a hundred million years before the dinosaurs. The article that told Holman this, in the newspaper the other day, was saying that some scientists now think it was disease that killed off the dinosaurs. Their only surviving members, the crocodilians, have the most amazing and powerful immune system on earth. Though whether this was gifted to them and allowed them to prosper or was won at that time of upheaval and mass extinction by the few able to survive is now a matter for conjecture.

A chain is wrapped around the auroch's horns and the carcass is dragged from the arena by a tractor. A man sits backwards behind the driver, waving a Union Jack above the body. From the sidelines, sawdust is flung over the blood and the arena dirt is raked smooth behind the hoof prints and tyre tracks.

To the obvious disgust of the man he begins to pass it on to, a strand of drool, like a dewy spider's silk, still joins Holman's lip to the bottle. Holman wipes it hurriedly and clumsily with his kerchief and motions that he is going to get another anyway, starts up the amphitheatre steps.

The man holds up the stub of pencil that Holman's been drawing with from where he left it on the stone seat.

'Wait, mate, you've forgotten your walking stick!' the man says, to laughter from his friends.

Always the 'mate' . . .

20

Crick

CRICK'S NAILS ARE BITTEN down, half-moons of hurt. Sometimes he tastes blood, but he can't help biting them every time he pauses. Writing is the only way to stop and to halt the head monkeys that jibber through his thoughts.

Crick types:

It was in the dying days of the Third Caliphate War. Of course we didn't know it was the dying days until afterwards. Dying days are only apparent once there has been a death. But a country won't take war for ever; nations do not endure limitless conflicts that sap their economy and steal their sons. Eventually they have to end. If you have the means, it has to finish. Whatever the cost. Whatever the morality. Such things cannot be tolerated in perpetuity. That's what they said afterwards anyway.

We were deep in the Caliphate – around Avignon, I think – far from the front. Often you felt safer like that. Most of the people we encountered had no love for the Caliph and no desire to get shot. Everywhere we went they became docile as our platoon passed by; cowed like slapped children, there was little open hostility.

Their villages weren't like our villages. They were more like villages drawn from memory – but maybe that's just how I remember them – turnip-headed scarecrows smiled at us, and kids with catapults waved from the golden depths of wheat fields rippling like sun ponds. I'm sure of that.

My mother once told me of a fabled woman who runs among the corn. Barefoot, scarlet-haired, pupils dark and free and cool as minnows in a stream. She's the poppy planter, the crimson interloper among blond sheaves. The one that scatters sand-fine seeds amidst the crops, who spreads a little joy, a little difference, who paints a little colour in the corners. Of course she's not real, but I always looked out for her, out there. She's as real as you let her be.

We rarely saw any women, though, they were either hidden inside at our approach or they were just nervy eyes in a wrap of black cloth.

Most of the roads in the Caliphate were really just tracks, once paved but long since cracked and covered in dirt, as if by determined effort to travel backwards in time. Scorched vegetation by their sides concealed occasional skeletons of animals, like discarded preliminary sketches. Sometimes the walls of bombed or crumbled buildings survived high enough to form a fence, and mangy goats would hide from the painful velocity of the sun in the corners of what might once have been a bank or a school.

Derelict villages were common as crows, abandoned utterly or home only to cellar dwellers. But that last month we came across something different: a place that felt like it had been deserted in moments and only hours before; a dry-docked Mary Celeste. *Washing still hung on lines, limp in the breezeless air, not wet but not taken in. Plates and cups stood on tables, food dried into scabs but not old, nothing rancid, no mould; only the first expeditionary scout ants in evidence, yet to call for reinforcements.*

Our platoon cleared house by house, fanned on to two sides of the street, sheltered beneath buildings. We moved as sticklebacks will, to meet a threat: taking turns to dart forwards and then hold. All the doors were already open. Some kicked down. We weren't the first search team in town. There were no signs of a fire fight, though, no bullet-hole spiders, no cordite flowers. No bodies either, but in places there were tracks, like you get when a corpse has been dragged.

Those first searchers found us before we found them: Special Ops, or Interfectors – military intelligence agents – or both. No insignia, grey silk fatigues, matt-black body armour. They had us in a three-zone crossfire before we even knew they were there. We would have been exterminated like sprayed flies if they weren't ours. De Castillo was more pissed off about being caught out like that than he was relieved to be alive. They must have been heli-dropped: they had too much gear to have come far. A dozen of them walked us to the main square, where their command group was. We weren't disarmed, but we were covered.

What was probably the whole village was gathered there, a few hundred people. All lying in long rows on the ground, as if quietly queuing for something going on in the sky. All

bald like convicts or concentration camp prisoners. All still as
slaughter. Arms reaching out above their heads, as if in
belated surrender, but most likely from being lifted from
stretchers into this orderly indifferent horror.

Three Interfectors knelt beside the train of bodies at
various places, taking samples or something. There were no
bullet wounds, but many of the corpses looked as though
they had been beaten to death, raw-faced, bruised. A pitiful
collection of the villagers' abstinent armaments was piled
against a wall: a few shotguns and bolt-action hunting
rifles.

The leader of the group that took us discussed something
with an Interfector who must have been in overall command.
They looked our way, then came over. The Interfector's eyes
looked dead already. All the stone-cold killers I'd known
before, I realized they were scamps next to that spook. He
didn't care enough even to kill you for kicks. We were just
something he had to make a decision on.

'Any of you Unimproved?' the Interfector said. They
weren't allowed to ask that and we weren't allowed to answer;
that was the army rules. But there weren't any still-borns in
our platoon and De Castillo told them so.

'All right, pull out then. Depart and forget, men, depart
and forget.'

But Crick can't forget the child's hands, palms upwards,
fragile knuckles in the dirt. Hands are specifically human,
more so even than faces. There was something about that
child's hands, so very clean, like they'd just been washed

before whatever happened happened. A mother must have washed them, or supervised the washing, for them to be so clean. The sight of those hands remains, even after sight itself has gone.

Crick gnaws at a raw nail.

21

Holman

HOLMAN IS QUITE CERTAIN that the men are real. Though yesterday he saw a four-foot millipede that wasn't. He knows that now; it seemed real enough then. It had black reticulated plates that clicked as its flock of translucent legs drove it steadily and unstoppably over the floor's obstacles towards him. He was shaking from fear as well as morning withdrawal as it reared up and its glassy mandibles tasted the air before him. But then it vanished.

Holman needs to tone his drinking down. Probably he needs to stop drinking altogether, if he is to survive, if this is not soft suicide. But first he needs to survive right now, and he is sure these men are no creatures of delirium tremens. But if real – and it seems safest to proceed as if they are – what are they doing lurking outside his door at seven in the morning?

The men are Improved, he would say, though it's hard to be certain when peering through a slit in the door of the fourth-floor cleaning cupboard; and while ink-wash shadows of the ill-lit hall mask their features. They are both looming and sharp-dressed, and seem out of place for The Kross and in particular for the age-mottled section of hallway outside his studio.

Holman fingers the wasp-knife in his pocket. His brother gave him the knife, after he learned that Holman had moved to The Kross – maybe he does some work for the military. He said to call it 'Sting' and laughed a croaky little laugh that said this was an allusion to something Holman wouldn't get. Though he did; he's read Tolkien; he got the joke: little short weapon for the funny short man. But it's still a good blade, a proper wasp.

Perhaps it is paranoid to assume the men mean him ill will. But Jesus and Dolly have both been murdered of late, beaten to death with objects unknown. Paranoia can keep you alive. While he watches, one of the figures tries the door handle, which is not something casual callers do. And casual callers don't call on Holman anyway.

He doesn't owe money at the moment, so they are not bailiffs, but they have something of that look – hired muscle – twitchy, when they should be men of confidence; as if they have no moral right to be here. One looks directly at Holman, staring into the black slash of cupboard crack from which he looks out. Can the man see light reflecting on Holman's eyes? No, the body language says no. But Holman trembles nonetheless.

If he hadn't lost his house key last night, he would be inside his studio. Would presumably have opened the door. Might be in even more trouble. Though maybe he wouldn't. Maybe he would be curled on his mattress on the floor, ignoring the raps of the world on his door. Blanket pulled high over his synth-sweating form.

Here he feels more exposed, tucked against a mop and a broom; the malconformed twin peaks of his knees, near as they will, towards his chin, in a childlike security hug. Is he sure they can't see him? Momentarily it reminds Holman of another time, peering though a door, but the present is too perilous to dwell upon that.

The men leave. They don't leave a note. They leave looking back. They leave with a look of men who will be back.

Holman waits a watch-ticking, nervous hour before exiting the cupboard. It's not the first time he's slept in there, curled among the cleaning things. They felt unused somehow, this time. It occurs to him that he hasn't seen Mrs Gerbi in a while. Anyway, he'll see her now: she has a spare key to his flat, and 8.08 seems an almost reasonable time to disturb her.

She will not rouse, though. Holman pounds her door, with fearful glances towards the front entrance – still unfixed since the riots – for as long as he can bear. Then decides he needs to get out of there.

Feeling vulnerable and visible on the almost empty, workless early-morning streets, he backtracks to the Loup Hole Bar of last night, to see if they have his keys.

En route he keeps seeing the same poster; a new one from The Right. There isn't an election due for years and there is nothing resembling an opposition, but they like to keep the rallying cries running. The poster features a strapping sorrel youth, muscled like he was carved from hardwood, almost at the landing point of a barely conceivable jump between two precipitous rocks. *Taking Britain Further into the Future* reads the banner. Beneath the mythic leap, at the poster's base, are a jumble of small shadow figures; in silhouette except for unaligned white eyes and highlights upon humpen misshapes and part-lit crucifixes, turbans and petrol bombs. The intimation is clear: *Taking Britain further away from these creatures of the dark and the past*, it might as well say.

The Loup Hole never closes, it only changes watch. Already there is a detachment of veterans in there: the heroes and the haunted, and Holman, the hunted.

A demi-man – shorter even than Holman – legless before he takes a drink, pushes himself along in what looks like a child's cart. Holman had one himself once upon a dream, with colourful lettered building blocks in it. A was for Apple, B was for Boy, C was for . . . what? Cursed?

A painting of Crick hangs behind the bar. He's a well-liked regular. And Holman swapped the oil against his account one time. Streaks, in shades of autumn leaves, descend Crick's eye-vacated face; it isn't what he looks like exactly, but it's him.

Holman takes his early-morning leak, leaning against the plywood wall of the Loup's solitary cubicle. Even without the fact that all too often his leg has given way, leaving him splashing down his own trousers at the sudden movement, he despises the conversationless forward stare of urinal troughs. Marked for the silent ridicule of the firing squad. Sometimes not silent: 'hey, auroch cock'; 'hey, blunderbuss'; 'hey, mate' – always the *mate* – 'that thing's bigger than you are'. In final irony, the one part of Holman's frame he visibly inherited from his father was grotesquely magnified. The sturdy pant trunk that fitted that Attic patriarch on the billboards of old was distended in the genetic lottery to hang on Holman like a third leg. What should have been a source of consolation and pride is instead a last insult. So large the whores call him tripod and coffee pot. So large the whores charge him extra or turn him away.

There is paper in the bowl from the last visitor: white toilet paper inlaid with strips of blue, run through it as a pattern. And as the stream of his piss disintegrates it, the blue strips remain, writhing and dancing in the dehydration-amber water like ecstatic sea snakes.

The barmaid says she hasn't seen his keys, but has a token search through the places they put things handed in. She's wearing the green ribbon of a Leveller and in apparently unknowing irony a Prometheus Industries T-shirt, which bristles over her breasts. Some promotional giveaway thing that is unlikely to recruit a following in here: it's for a brand of synth pack that allows you to drink during pregnancy: 'Mum's drinking for two!' says the strap line, above the smiling, suave, synthetic-cocktail-sipping pregnant lady, who couldn't look less like the harried homely barmaid, face faintly green lit by the bottles.

But who is Holman to think 'homely'? He is Frankenstein's monster: except that it was deformed and unnatural. Holman is deformed and natural, stranded in a world where that is the most unnatural state: where those created by scientists are the normal and beautiful beings. The barmaid wouldn't give Holman hand relief for hard cash. Even some hookers won't have him.

Art is his only chance, because art is still open to all. The last dream of those who had failure mapped out from birth. A few of the Unimproved still break their circumstances as artists. Maybe more do than those supposedly gifted the latest, greatest brains. Perhaps because there is a hint of mental illness required to be a true master. But genius sits rocking in the dark, uncertain night air with more madmen than poets, so what prospective parents choose the intensity of the schizotypal, the drive of the obsessive, the peculiar clarity of the autist, or the reflective vigour of the manic-depressive mind for their offspring, risking greater perils than potential? None. Parents who enrich stay well within the bell-curve of comfort. And Britain becomes ever blander, even though more beautiful.

Holman chokes the first parrot before breakfast, draining the glass of every clinging dreg. Bacon and greasy tatties soak into his bloodstream shortly after, to ease the wooden skull of last night. He refills his cane's small flask with his second glass, to keep in reserve.

'Always one in the chamber, eh,' an old soldier winks.

He has one arm of flesh and one of metal, with just three digits: two fingers to salute with and a kind of steel stalk of an opposable thumb. But he handles his glass as well as Holman, and beats him for pace.

The third glass Holman takes leisurely anyway, the louche method: a dose of synth in a shot glass placed at the bottom of a larger vessel. He pours cold water in on top and the synth curls out into it, sticking to itself at first, like sperm in the bath, then turning a cloudy green as the oils free up.

And so the morning runs; Holman's pad and pencil in his pocket aren't intruded upon. Soon his head, still suffering from a night of sleep shared with buckets and brooms, is resting on the bar top.

The tortured whine of a mosquito wakes him. He instinctively, but vainly, slaps at his own ear. The clap into his eardrum's airlock shaking him further from stupor. That he couldn't hurt a fly is more a mark of inagility than any compassion, but the mosquito lives to bite another day.

In the mirror of the bar, a far more disturbing sight: the two men – Holman's sure it's them – seated, sipping, next to the door. They don't look at him. But their not looking feels purposeful. And they belong in this cannon-fodder dive like wasps in a beehive; their being here is not coincidence.

Dread in his chest. A fear to which all his previously known fears feel like awkward fumblings. Holman is ill designed for flight, even were they not within blocking space of the door. There are no other exits.

Except of course there is. Except that is what this bar is famous for: the deserter's escape hole into the sewers.

Holman clunks clumsily and noisily from his stool – there is no way they won't have noticed – and descends the stairs and down the passage towards the toilets, but through the door to the storeroom that holds the manhole. Once it was a wine cellar down here, but real wine is long gone, gone with the double-dry regions that grew it, now both abstinent and barren. The walls are flaky; red brick crumbles beneath Holman's fingertips, like the corridor is bleeding.

The manhole cover is a dirty moon. The handle pokes out above its iron face, but Holman can't pull it from the floor. He gets a long metal rod from a corner of the cluttered room – a part of something that is broken, which most things are – and pushes it through the handle for more leverage. It works; with grunts from Holman and ogre groans from the metal, he lifts the lid free from its dust-crumbling casement and slides it aside.

A rusted ladder leads down into a bottomless trench of darkness and filth. But the men must know the reputation of this place too. They will be coming down after Holman, when he doesn't reappear. They will be faster and stronger than him. They may have torches even. Holman is a documenter not a doer. He wasn't designed for tasks like these. He wasn't designed at all.

The men appear only five minutes later. They both have too much jaw and too much muscle; they look like henchmen, or even Interfectors. They move straight to the chasm in the floor, and with little discussion one drops down it. His partner produces a slim steel torch from his jacket pocket and shines it down. There are protests about the stench from below, but he too climbs down the ladder.

Holman waits a minute before exiting the self-created nest of empty crates from which he's watched. He slides and drops the manhole back in place and pushes what he can find of weight on top. Leaning on his cane, teeth a little gritted against the pain of speed, he mounts the stairs and leaves the Loup Hole.

Somewhere on the streets of London the men will emerge. Figures made more repugnant by slime and night soil. They will gratefully breathe the hot air. They will find somewhere to clean up. But Holman will not be forgotten. Men who need something sufficiently strongly to wade through sewers do not forget. And they clearly already know the places he goes. So Holman must go somewhere new.

III

Everything Will Be All Right
In The End.
If Everything Isn't All Right,
Then It's Not Yet The End

22

Adele Nicole

'AND FORGIVE US OUR debts, as we forgive our debtors, and lead us not into temptation; but deliver us from error. Amen.'

In middle age, Adele Nicole had returned to the religion of her childhood almost organically, as if it were not something she'd ever relinquished, but only put to the back of her mind for a while. Today, such observances are of course a private pleasure, unlike the shared prayers she was raised with, but they are a pleasure and a comfort nonetheless. She enjoys having someone to thank for all that she enjoys. And life, on the whole, has been kind to Adele Nicole.

Growing up, it was not considered proper to exult in good looks, but it was noted by all in the commune that Adele Nicole was uncommonly handsome. She was courted, in the solemn, regulated, chaste way that such courting was done, by boys years older than her, before she had but wisps of hair on her inscrutable parts. Though as she blossomed, she grew too wilful for most of those suitors and it became apparent, no doubt, to some of the elders that she would one day leave the commune. Such girls always did. 'Butterflies', the girls who stayed behind called them; a polite term, but with derogatory undertones and often a hint of ill-concealed envy.

Adele Nicole rises from her supplication; her knees ache a little, even though she kneels on a cushion. She wonders if this slight inconvenience, which has only come latterly, is the half-seed of the condition that has stricken her son all of his life: a recessive yin which found its yang in her husband. Poor Holman seemed to get dealt all the bad cards.

Sebastian, her houseboy, comes into her room and tuts in mock frustration when he sees the cushion, not because he has to pick it up, though he does anyway, but because he doesn't approve of religion.

Adele Nicole does not, as so many still do, make the mistake of believing sex to be some evidence of affection, but she is well aware that Sebastian loves her. And maybe she loves him too, a little. She has kept him on longer than any of her previous houseboys, and she has recently started to entertain the idea of growing old with him. Letting their relationship gently drift, like leaves in the brooks of her youth. It would not take so very much to flow from mistress and servant to calm, contented couple. So that, when she is very old, she can sit out in the sun and hold his warm hand. So that when he fetches her drinks, he will do it because he wants to make her a drink, not because that's his job. So that when she dies, she will not die alone. She hopes her God will be there too. But if He isn't, it would be nice to have someone. And she can't help fearing that Holman will be gone before then. In a way, it is selfish to wish him anything but that: he seems so tortured by this world, it feels almost mean-spirited to keep him against his will. Sebastian will be enough. He is kind and devoted and quite devilishly attractive, and he makes sweet whimpery noises, like a sleeping dog, when he makes love to her.

Adele Nicole goes downstairs to water her plants. Silk trailing as she walks, her kimono day-coat is about all she can bear to wear. Her garden is bijou but high-walled, so she doesn't need to worry about the neighbours seeing her or the hosepipe. The walls are washed white and the garden looks greener for the contrast. The spatter of the hose on the dry earth creates little foxholes. Water droplets tumble down from the frothy acid-lemon petals of her lady's mantle and nestle on the leaves like pearls. She has a thicket of dark mint in an antique iron-legged bath: she loves mojitos, but mint will sprawl like a shanty town if allowed the freedom of the soil. Everything wants to spread and breed, she thinks, that's what we all have in common.

Adele Nicole was fifteen when she was first led into temptation. Lazarus, he was called. She smiles slightly at the thought of him. Not wistful for Lazarus the boy, but for that time, for the discovery of such things. She and Lazarus had talked about running away, in their pilfered, illicit afternoons; grass stuck to their skin; basking in the aftermath of fledgling sensations. She wonders if Lazarus would still be at the commune now, if it still existed. In her commune, those who left could not return; the rule was rigidly and vigorously adhered to, because that was their greatest coercion against butterflies: if you left, you lost everything you had ever known.

Adele Nicole lost Lazarus too, left on her own. She was offered a room and a job by the creaking old matron of a dining house on a rare trip into town, and that felt like it might be her only chance. She loved her mother, but dull drudgery seemed to have stripped everything from her: her looks; her laughter. She was as worn out all over as her day-to-day dress was at the elbows, and Adele Nicole knew that she did not want that life. She was not going to marry some boy from the scant selection the commune presented and look forward to nothing more from then on but the harvest festival feast and a conveyor belt of birthing. Her mother said, 'You do what you have to do,' and then submitted to her tears as meekly as she suffered all else the world sent her, but she didn't ask Adele Nicole to stay. 'We'll meet again in heaven,' her mother said. 'I'll pray hard enough for two. You just worry about you.' And for a long time that was exactly what Adele Nicole did.

Sebastian makes a four-egg omelette for lunch, yellow as the sunshine, with feathery mushrooms and *in vitro* crab. On her suggestion, they eat it together, under the tessellated shade of the pergola draped with purple bougainvillea vines. Sebastian glances up at her constantly while they eat. She supposes that she ought really to cease sleeping with other people. It probably upsets Sebastian, even though he never shows it.

Her husband had no such qualms. He used to love her to perform with other lovers for him; boys and girls. Of course, he was too old to get up to much himself too often. That was his way of enjoying her. That was what no one ever got at the time – and of course it wasn't the sort of thing it was proper to make public – but they had a beautiful relationship. It was just different.

Adele Nicole still has scars from the things that were said of her back then. The innuendo made in the press and the just-in-earshot snipes of the social scene: 'What was her chat-up line? Can I pre-chew that for you?'; 'She worships the ground he wheels upon'; 'Worships the ground his laboratories are on, more like'; 'She has to dress slutty enough that even his poor eyes can make it out'; 'Engaged for two months; that's probably half the time he's got left now they're married and twice as long as she'll mourn'.

She went from being a cherished star to a despised gold-digger. But no one but them knew their relationship and how much they really meant to each other. Love is more complicated than anyone is willing to accept.

The first night they spent together they stayed in a cheap hotel, to go unnoticed. His physician had equipped him with a controlled confection of auroch hormones and powdered horn, sildenafil citrate and cocaine. Not something to be used often – his heart couldn't have sustained it – but all right for an occasional treat. The medication cocktail made his eyes shine bright but black, like photographic negatives of the stars they watched from the balcony. The hotel wall was the screen for an outdoor movie theatre. Lights danced over the windows, while Ennio Morricone music played and shots rang out. And the bed rattled like a feverish fool was in it. When in fact there were two.

Adele Nicole leaves a couple of mouthfuls, as always. Never to entirely finish a meal is one of the surest ways not to get fat, and she spent much of her younger days worrying about that. Now of course she has pills for it, as for much else. She supposes she'll have to give up thanking Valentine for his troubles quite so fully as well, if she is to allow herself to love Sebastian – but that's all right: Valentine is fun, but life moves on.

'Thank you, Sebastian, that was lovely. Adele Nicole is going to retire to the withdrawing room now. Would you bring a cup of tea, please?'

She retained the habit of referring to herself in the third person, which was perfectly normal in the commune, but considered quaint in London, even affected. Not that it seemed to have harmed her career; if anything it reinforced the naturalness and wholesomeness of her looks. How fast things change, she thinks, no one sees anything wholesome about the Unimproved now, not even the beautiful.

Adele Nicole was the last 'Miss Natural' before the competition was dissolved. They used the second war effort as the excuse, and Adele Nicole's engagement to Prometheus may have been what stuck in the mind of the public, but neither was the real reason. Partly that period marked a turning point in the perception of 'natural'; after that, it began to seem like a very unnatural state of being. And by then the anti-geneism laws made a farce of the show anyway. Tests for the extra chromosome pair were no longer allowed. Tests for immunities could discriminate against people who had them naturally, or worse, encourage parents to recklessly choose not to immunize their daughters in the hope of winning. But being the last made Adele Nicole the forever queen, and her subsequent marriage ensured that she would remain in the public gaze.

She took her husband's name: Adele Nicole Prometheus. His father had chosen it way back when he founded Prometheus Industries. A company that went on to become the largest of the genetic enrichment laboratories. Inventors and refiners of the extra chromosome pair. Her Prometheus used himself as the scaffold for chromosomes 47 and 48. Though often silenced, his own genes went into every baby that used the company; in effect, impregnating more women than any man in history. Next to him, Genghis Khan's thousands of successful breeds looked positively chaste. Of course Prometheus didn't really have sex with those women, it was all clean and clinical. But he had sex with a lot of women; he became the pin-up of progress. Billboards sported his image and he sported with the stars. He dined with party officials and partied with diamond heiresses. It is almost certain that Prometheus, having gained such fame and wealth, eventually slept with many of those carrying his own genes, his own daughters. But then who could judge him for that? Why, even in the Bible, Lot slept with his own daughters.

Adele Nicole has never felt any incongruence between sex and her religion; she has always considered sex to be one of God's greatest gifts. Had there not been so many silly hypocritical prohibitions on it in the commune, she may never have left at all. But her commune, like all the others, was expunged anyway in the event. 'Terrorist training camps' the government called them; 'breeding the enemy within'. None of her family made any attempt to contact her after the communes were demolished, and she could find no trace of them. They must have felt the butterfly rules applied even outside. At least, she hoped that was what it was.

***

That evening, Sebastian catches her praying again. He takes her arm at the elbow and turns her to him gently – so gently. There is something to be said for finishing up with a man as gentle as him.

'You know it's not true, don't you?' he says. 'You know deep down that there isn't a God?'

'Why does it matter?' she says. 'Why does everything have to be true all the time? What's this obsession with truth? Isn't it enough for things to be beautiful? Can't we just keep believing, or at least trying to? Who does it hurt?'

'You know who it hurts: it hurts everyone: the honour killings, the ignorance; the bombs, the terror, the wars; the Caliphate's rise and razing; half of Europe laid to waste; all those people dead.'

'But their God isn't my God, and anyway, it isn't just horror, is it? Look at the garden; how can the world be filled with so much beauty if there is no God?' Tears await behind the wall of her eyes now. But if they are to progress, if they are to become a couple, they must pass this place.

'The most beautiful plants, like the most beautiful people, are made by men, by gene selection and improvements, not by some omniscient deity.' He pauses, like he knows he is going too far but cannot help being carried by momentum. 'I know you love your son, but you have to admit, he's not exactly beautiful.'

'But he is,' she says, 'that's just it, he is.'

23

Detective Günther
Charles Bonnet

T HE DWARF'S STILL NOT home. This time Gunt lets himself in.
He has his own set of skeletons; the department-issue ones
aren't worth their weight. The dwarf's apartment doesn't look
like it's been used for a few days. Cups on the counter have syrupy
evaporation gunk at the bottom. Dust lies on the higher rumples
of a furled black sheet on the mattress.

One wall is dominated by a vast painting: foregrounded
figures bigger than life, so that those at the back are still man-
sized. There's a subhuman human in the centre, naked and
angry, staring at Gunt the way Gunt stares at the mirror: instinct
tensing his muscles, wanting to strike this other him that he
hates.

Gunt looks away first. The painting man still glares out
surrounded by the spoils of his primitive success: half-clad,
half-grown girls and cave catamites gnaw at strips of stick-
grilled deer. Unlooked-for babes, filthy slammerkin cherubim
toddle the cavern's fire-shaded recesses. And at the right side
front sits a hagfish harridan, big-bellied with child. Impregnated
with designless bestial gushings, as such creatures did things in
this primordial past and some scum still do today. And Gunt
sees that it is Dolly. The dwarf has made this figure into the

likeness of the murdered whore who Gunt screwed, who holds traces of his DNA, whose corpse might yet undo it all. The dwarf is laughing at him. The dwarf is laughing at Gunt.

Gunt smashes the solitary chair across the bar, sends glasses shattering. Kicks the chair into pieces, rakes them across the painting on the wall. Slashes the Dolly matriarch with the sharded wood of a chair leg until she hangs in rags from the corner, face hidden, belly open. Stabs the eyes from the staring other him in the centre. Finds paint. Prises off lids with his butterfly knife, throws the pots at the wall. Finds more paint, squeezes oil tubes so they burst and splatter, jet across. Spreads it all around the painting with bits of chair, pushes it to the top with the dwarf's stepladder. Nothing is left to see. Gunt is not like these primitive cave pigs. Anyone can see that.

Exertion spent, Gunt wipes the worst of the paint from his hands; dabs the splatters from his shoes. His suit is marked too, but Gunt knows a cleaner adept at stain removal, perhaps the paint is no harder to erase than blood. Nothing is harder to erase than blood.

Gunt leaves. He doesn't bother to relock the door. It will be apparent to the dwarf that someone has entered now.

Downstairs, there is a familiar smell, though Gunt hadn't noticed it on the way in. Maybe the rage opened up his senses. Gunt locates the smell's source: another door, but locked from the inside, the key is still in the lock, so skeletons won't work. Gunt doesn't have time for trying to push the key through, and the stink empowers right of entry. He kicks at the door and the wood around the lock splinters, gives entirely on the second try.

A silk spider shrieks and rushes at him. It's emaciated; thorax shrunk like an empty scrotum. Gunt boots it across the room. It hits the wall. Clambers to its multiple legs again. Scuttles back at him. Gunt stamps down on its back. It thrashes wildly. Sending judders up Gunt's leg and clattering its claws on the tile floor. Gunt keeps pushing down with his foot till the spider bursts like a grapefruit. Yellow flesh squeezes from its mouth and arses.

A baking dish covered in mould sits on the table. It looks like it might once have been lasagne. Whatever it was, it still smells better than the old lady who's dead on the floor.

She smiles up at Gunt, the rhesus sardonicus of the dead, lips drawn back from her teeth in their shrivel. Borehole eyes gaze at the ceiling, like she's thinking of England. Her hair is half peeled back from her head, creating a cloud of grey on the floor.

There's a noise from the other room, but upon investigation it's just a computer game. It must have been playing endlessly and pointlessly since her death. Monotonous music drums. *Your people have been wiped out by plague,* the screen reads. *Would you like to restart?*

Gunt goes outside to call a path. team. The glucose-sweet stink of uncollected piles of hot trash bags smells good compared to the stench in the old lady's flat.

There are salsco dancers across the street. Busting their moves on a sheet of taped-down plastic to help their feet slide. They have a hat out, but they're mostly doing it for kicks. They must be: people who like salsco mostly aren't up yet and mostly have no money anyhow. The dancers are just kids really anyway. One of them reminds Gunt of a younger him; but they're still-born scum, can't be. One of them reminds him of her: what could have been: what wasn't: the hate.

Gunt tries to block it out. The same way they fence off the crime scenes. Tries to unfurl rolls of wasp-striped tape in the mind. But it doesn't work, the senses override it. Even without the glasses, Gunt's started to see things. It's safer with them on; with them on, the world is confused and beautiful. Without them it is a world he no longer knows. Strangers trying to look into him. Strangers laughing. Everyone on the force knows. Gunt's got the best set of genes on the force. Anyone can see that. Can't they? What can they see?

Gunt pulls out his pistol, puts it to his head. That's how you stop the voices. Pulls it away again. Fires in the air. The salsco kids get up and run.

Gunt's together by the time the path. team arrives. Locked down. A strict mind is a tidy mind, a tight mind. Safely compartmentalized. A place for everything and everything back in its place.

Each fresh shame ousts and yet rests upon the previous one, like layers of London streets, infamy lasagned over what came before. Easier to blot the memories and build on top than to delve down into that first foundation.

24

Holman

THEY'VE CHANGED THE BILLBOARD on the wasteland: *If Everything Isn't All Right, Then It's Not Yet The End*, it now reads. *Stop here, breeder scum!* someone has sprayed underneath.

Gulls shriek, cutting the sky like Regan razors, as Holman stumbles over the refuse and the rubble. This is the dividing line between the way to his mother's and The Kross, but he is self-exiled from both. There is still no sign of what the hoarding is supposed to be advertising; maybe he just doesn't get it.

Gulls and parrots, rats and roaches, all he has seen in days. Save for once a lone bee, far from home, struggling to fly up but making it only a few paces further along. A creature of soothing sun and gentle breezes blown in to a scorched city. She tried a final heave but fell on her back onto the frazzling pavement, from which it seemed impossible she would ever arise. So Holman crushed her with the tip of his cane, easier to move and defter than his foot.

His fragile bones ache from time spent evading unknown foes – haunting alleys and urban fallows – femurs in atrophy at those points where they should once have experienced the glorious growth spurts of adolescence.

The call of Adele Nicole is strong here, but to go there might be to condemn his mother too. If the men know he frequents the Loup, then what chance that they don't know of his childhood home? Home is where, when you have to go there, you cannot risk their lives.

And crowning the horizon the Prometheus Tower shines, like an emblem of all that Holman is not.

At dusk he has a drink by the side of the road from a street vendor. Grateful for the brittle road-grimed plastic chair slid his way. Stunted by cheapness, it is a perfect height for Holman. A feed-sack windbreak separates him from the two-stroke thud of scooters and hides him from their passing and any other eyes. He relaxes into an ill-washed mug of sweet synthetic beer and rests his legs.

The proprietor of the shanty establishment cooks his dinner on a pot-bellied stove, fuelled by something that the stench declares should not be burnt. He side-eyes a boy child who wins solo games of marbles in the mustard dust. And they both, as well as the snaggle-toothed cat that stalks flies in the stall's shadows, are beautiful.

Holman knows much of beauty, who stands so far from it. Like a river fish watching the bank-stranded land of men, everything is mediated and altered by the prism through which we stare. There is beauty everywhere, if it is regarded with sufficient detachment. The only requirement is that you are not a true part of the world. And in this Holman has succeeded. He has finally abandoned himself fully to being other.

But to have nothing is only to be free for as long as the money holds out, and without the bank cards still locked in

Holman's flat, that time is not far away. He licked windows all day, in this strange part of town, eyeing things he could not buy. Trying not to look behind, where only guilty people look. To beg means to risk exposure, and so, when this last drink is supped with the last of his funds, he doesn't know what he'll do, or where he'll go. Perhaps tomorrow he can pawn his watch and the wasp-knife, maybe even his cane. But first he needs somewhere for tonight.

Even outside The Kross, there are places for the likes of Holman. There are dank bridges and plank benches. There are corrugated-iron roofs so rusted as to look like cardboard, and cardboard ones that envy them.

Holman passes a pierced-dustbin brazier, where an old man sits and gives a gentle, old man's nod. The jowls of his face droop loose, like he once lost weight quick as sickness. Holman turns in half-question and the man produces a pipe from somewhere within a faded denim shawl and holds the pre-filled bowl sideways into the fire by a neck that, like his own, looks too frail to take the weight. The firelight skips about in the dark centres of his eyes while he sucks noisily to stoke the pipe with a mouth uncluttered by teeth. The tobacco fug is damp and tangy; it mingles with the more reticent curls from the furnace clinging in corners of the riverbank underpass.

Holman completes the question his body started and asks if he can share the fire.

'Not for the night,' the man says. 'I don't like anyone around me when I sleep. But you can linger a while to warm or watch the flames, if you've the mind.'

25

Quigley Regan

'SHE'S A FINE-LOOKING BEAST,' the bookmaker says, looking at the babottweiler.

'Yeah, she is that. But you know what's best about her? I'll tell you: she's my constant companion, my best friend. When I wake in the night with the fears and the doubts, she comes to me and licks my face and for a moment I don't care. See, way I see it, humans and dogs kind of evolved a mutual dependency. Hundreds of thousands of years of marriage. People are supposed to have dogs. If you don't have one, if you've never had one, you don't really realize that. But when you do, well, it's like you're complete in a way that you never knew existed. That's how it feels. Not that she's a full dog, obviously, indeed she's part primate. But the bits they've kept are the bits that count. Like I say, she's my constant companion, she's the light of my life. She breathes my dreams. She stares at the smog-red moon and nuzzles me until I watch it too and realize how beautiful it is. She's still soft and abundant-skinned as the pup I brought home in a brown towel-lined box. When I tickle her, she makes these funny groans, like she's trying to speak, and rolls on her back with her paws all a-tangled.

'But, my friend, make no mistake, if I give the word, she will rip your fucking face off and I'll piss in the mess she leaves. Now give me what you owe us.'

With a roll of notes in his pocket, Quigley makes a stop at the butcher's. Not that he needs money at the butcher's, or anywhere else in The Kross: pretty much everything is gratis for the Regans. Quigley used to try and pay, but found it created more problems and prolonged the transactions, and his brothers didn't like it.

The other thing he didn't say about her – Baskerville, his babott-weiler – is that she's so easy to please. You can give Baskerville a bone and you see ecstasy on her face; she'll lie in sheer unadulterated delight, gripping it in her paws like an otter, seeming to grin while she gnaws. Pleasure at a level Quigley can't remember ever having been able to give to a woman, neither from gifts, nor from jaw and tongue-exertion numb. Pleasure at a level Quigley has never found in life for himself.

The butcher sees Quigley and walks along behind the counter to him, ignoring the line of people already waiting.

'What can I get you, sir?'

'Ah, just a bone for the beast and one of them sourdough sandwiches there, if you will.'

Behind the butcher's glass counter, steel tubs of *in vitro* meat, living, but insentient, bubbling away in some kind of pale honey-like jelly that feeds the cells: porpoise and wilderbuck; peacock and hedgehog, all the meats that were too rare, too small or too hard to farm before. Quigley's tried the peacock; tastes like chicken on the turn. But he can tell this *in vitro* stuff is going to become the norm before long. Just takes people a while to adjust to anything new, that's all. You can already see it's the way of the future, but it takes time for the present to catch up.

Quigley eats his sandwich sitting against a tree shaded from the worst of the afternoon sun, feeling the hard knots of barky muscle against his spine. Moped inner tubes, wrapped in silver foil to protect them from the heat, float in languid dangles from the roofs of roadside stalls, in what little wind is made by passing traffic. In the distance, the pineapple-trunked palm trees that line the Thames. Baskerville lies between his outstretched legs, murmuring into her bone. The black pads of her paws go grey with the dirt and city dust. He watches the tiny shiny hexagons of skin that form her moist muzzle blowing slightly out and then slack as she breathes, like black ship sails on near still seas. Not that he really knows what that would look like. Not that he even knows what the sea looks like. But she puts poetry into his soul.

Before she came along, Quigley knew little contentment. Somehow, though he is genetically identical to all his brothers, he was always different. The things that make them happy – money, power and respect mainly – didn't work for Quigley. He went along, he didn't see that he had a lot of choice, and he didn't want to upset their perma-pregnant mum, but some-thing was always wrong. Having Baskerville has helped give him purpose: she doesn't know that life is futile and redundant, and so keeping her happy keeps him happy.

He smooths his moustache, to make sure there are no crumbs in it, and sets off again on his rounds; last Thursday of the month is protection payday on Quigley's patch. Baskerville trots along beside him, long paws making little slaps on the pavement, proudly carrying the bone in her mouth. He makes her leave it on the street when he has to go into a business, she looks too soppy somehow, carrying the bone like that. Not that he normally even has to raise his voice to get what's owed, never mind threaten with her like he did the bookmaker. Since the riots, people are clamouring for security, and the Regans' rates aren't unreasonable. Quigley can live with that part of his life no problem.

Lately, though, he has started to worry about some of the other things they do. It's not the prostitution, the protection, the drugs. That's just business; someone would be doing it if it weren't the Regans. They manage them well and reduce the harm as low as is possible. Not through morality, it's true, just as a side effect of good practice. But it's the other work that wakes Quigley in the night, needing to know that Baskerville's there; it's the work they do for government intelligence: the black stuff, the spook stuff, the Interfector stuff.

They always used to do a bit, the odd document stolen, bit of evidence planted or journalist intimidated; the Regans occupy a unique position after all: an organized crime family who are genetically speaking all the same individual has no weak links, so nothing will ever be given away. And they carry the ultimate deniability: what law agents would use them when they are not just criminals, but technically they are illegal even as human beings? The brothers are linear twins or identicals – they might have been called clones in less enlightened times – but although the relatively simple process of producing linear twins is illegal, it is not the fault of the children so produced, and that particular genie can't be squeezed back up that peculiar spout.

Even if there was the will to prosecute, the criminal act is perpetrated by the parent, and almost nobody but the brothers has seen their mother in years. She never emerges from a secret home now, living a life like a termite queen, a self-imprisoned monarch whose purpose and desire is solely to give birth. She is in a paradise of her own design, with new babies all the time. People who know about it all call her Red Nell or the Red Queen; she still has a shock of auburn hair and a fiery Irish heart. She carries fewer of the babies herself, now she's getting on a bit; uses broodmares more often. But she's still to be found with a clutch of the younger boys and bairns surrounding her.

A year or so ago Ahab, the eldest Regan brother, got himself elected; he now represents The Kross in parliament. He won more or less fair and square too: no direct vote-rigging or gerry-mandering. It seemed like some combination of *better the devil you know* and *why vote for a weakling* swayed the electorate. But since then the black stuff has escalated, in scale and frequency. There have been assassinations, wet work.

The Regans will always get away with murder, because they all look the same, and even if there is DNA evidence, they all have identical DNA. But most cops are too intimidated even to interview them, and where do they start, who would they call in? There are now twenty-eight Regan brothers over legal majority. But it doesn't sit right with Quigley, the Interfector business: secret-service-sanctioned murder, that's something else. That's down with kiddy fiddling and rape. There are some sorts of crimes that just aren't respectable.

Truth be told, there was one cop who had the baubles to question them. He pulled Quigley in after the taxi biker died in the bar; now that was a rum old business. Wasn't a lot Quigley could have told Detective Günther Bonnet if he'd wanted to: the corpse just more or less appeared locked in the stall of the crapper. Quigley had no more idea than anyone else. But he did tell Frank to get rid of it: you can't just have dead folk sitting on the throne, like they've died of constipation.

Quigley catches a glimpse of his moustache in a shaded shop window. He can't help thinking it looks pretty slick. He's surprised that none of his brothers have adopted one, but pleased to have that little bit of difference in his life.

The cop, Bonnet, seemed to think the taxi biker was linked to Jesus Jackson's murder as well. So Quigley had levelled with him:

'Look, I'm not saying we've never killed anyone, and I'm not saying we ever have; but we all liked Jesus, everyone liked Jesus; his death has nothing to do with us.'

Quigley takes Baskerville for her evening excretion to the usual patch of wasteland behind his flat. No one sees the changes of the season like a dog walker. No farmer nor gardener can have watched exactly the same spot of scrub change like Quigley does, waiting for the babott to do its business. Sees nettles give way to dandelion clocks, smells spring and decay. There doesn't seem to be much else but summer these days, but the plants know there's more to a season than temperature alone.

Quigley knows a bit about flowers; their mum had a garden in those balmy early days. Those were the only times when he was what you'd call happy, before his brothers took over his education.

Not long after they took him away, just weeks past his eleventh birthday, Quigley saw Oliver, just a kid, smashing a lump of bone-pale flint down on another kid's face. Paris' face, his closest brother's face. Oliver's own hand was cut with his grip and the force of the blows. And Paris kept calling out – from a head mangled like road-killed cat – 'but we're brothers', and them maybe the best of friends among them too. But every time he said it, Oliver brought down the flint again. Brother or not, Paris' face was gashed like a stranger's, smashed like the Caliphate, still looks like a fleshly jigsaw puzzle to this day. He can't work normal jobs, Paris, anyone can point Paris out. And that was the start of Quigley's education.

The rest of the Regan brothers seem to all share that propensity – susceptibility to being bullied and proneness to bullying – which means that authority runs more or less in sync with age. Quigley's had to beat younger brothers himself, to keep his place in the hierarchy. Though sometimes he's secretly vomited afterwards, revolted by his own capabilities. He doesn't want it to be like this. But doesn't know what else to do. Doesn't know another life. Doesn't want to be a soldier in this army, but has to keep the line, has to keep marching to avoid being over-taken. The younger Regans seem the worst, more brutalized by their brothers and with less power. And each generational clutch demands of their spawning mother that more be born, deter-mined not to ever be among the youngest.

Evening brings more strange work. The orders come from Ahab, and it's the kind of seemingly pointless act that is almost certainly sinister spook shit. Someone wants the funny dwarf guy found; from the picture, it's definitely the same one. But they've got his name now, Holman Prometheus, and his address – though he won't be found there; he's missing or on the run – and it's a rum thing, you can be certain of that, because he's only the same feller the cop was asking about; like he was linked in to that stuff as well. It all makes Quigley uneasy and queasy. But he doesn't question, just calls Baskerville and gets on with it. Grabs a little bag of the floor sweepings he gets from the barber's shop, in case there's a crime scene that'll need muddying later.

He shuts one eye before he opens the door and then swaps the closed one, so that one eye will be adjusted already. One pupil dilated for whatever the dark will bring. Winking in the distance are the fires of the homeless, and that seems to Quigley like a good enough place to start, when looking for a guy too scared to go home.

26

Holman

THE GIBBOUS MOON LOOKS like the pale sheared ear of that long-dead one. Maybe He once listened to it all, heard every muscle creak and spiralling leaf, but only Holman hears the tramper.

'You're scared,' the elderly, droop-chopped vagabond says. 'I can read it. I'm a good judge of character; good enough to know that I've got none. But you might, maybe you do. Courage, boy. Courage is king of the virtues, because it's how every virtue is proofed. Friendships, faiths, loves, hopes; they can only be tried by courage. I should know: I've failed at every asking.'

He pokes at the brazier with a metal thing, designed for something else but suited just as well perhaps to poking.

Though he had said Holman couldn't stay for long, he proves hospitable, produces bounty from beneath his rancid onion skins of clothing: a bottle each of a liquid made from things not designed for drinking, from which they both drink. A 'blend' the man calls it, and Holman doesn't ask of what. It urges against his gut, but warms the blood that awaited anxiously. The tramper palms a little from his bottle on to his neck like cologne. 'Keeps the mosquitoes off,' he says, sitting frog-legged like a sail mender; more limber than Holman for all his years. He says he was once a ship's captain. His hands are grey like sea fog and criss-cross-lined like fishing nets.

Holman asks if he might sketch the tramper, who says that he may, 'for all the good you'll find in it'. But Holman does find a comfort in doing the familiar in this unfamiliar place. Above him runs a road and beside him mooches the glutinous Thames; so turgid he might almost walk across, it looks. He tries to capture the firelight on the tramper's face and produces some simulacrum of it, though in the soft lead his face is stiller and greyer even than in life.

He's a talker – some people habitually alone go that way – tells two meandering stories, which eventually contradict each other: that he never married because he strived for the best and wouldn't settle for lesser and ended with none; and that he did marry and lost her to a terrorist bomb. And he doesn't seem to notice that they cannot both be true. Perhaps neither is.

Holman hears the strains of salsco – coming from a warehouse party perhaps – across the water. The river seems to diffuse the beat, but he recognizes the lyrics: *Strange fruit hanging from the poplar trees*. Something his mother listened to, or just one of those songs now embedded in the collective consciousness, because Holman knows little of music, but still knows it. *Strange fruit*, the refrain goes, *strange fruit*.

The tramper seems to know the song too: 'Everything wants to survive,' he says, 'even music; and for no better reason than survival itself.'

He cooks snails, prised from the wetted steps by the water's edge, upon a blackened skillet on the brazier. The feminine valances of their undersides curl in, vegetal; then vanish; inutile defence against the spitting skillet. They smell better than the acid tang of Holman's own unwashed self, but still taste like the slimy Thames.

Sometimes he catches fish, the tramper says. 'Even now in that foul water there is food, and nothing in this world is wasted. Even in the deepest oceans in the utter black of void, at temperatures too cold for most life and pressures that implode, nothing is wasted. The ones from the ocean bottoms are like nothing you've ever seen,' he says. 'The fish that live down there are hideous, the ugliest things on the planet.'

Did they move down there in the dark because they were so ugly? Or grow so ugly because down there no one cared?

Perhaps there could yet be a life for Holman, in these depths of London; amidst his own kind, among the tramper and his ilk. Perhaps Holman would be hidden in the shoal.

Nearby on the bank, a dead eel, part rotted, silently calls the rats to itself, tempting them from the shadows to kiss at the open red mouth of its belly. And the splatters of ancient chewing gum on the concrete are as random and endless as the stars in the sky.

The old tramper knows stranger tales. He talks of humanzees, which he claims to have seen as a child; even then the experiments were long banned, he says, but a few of the homo-bonobos not killed by liver failure or fighting still wandered, perpetually torn between trees and alleys. Shunned by the people of father and mother and equally disgusted by each other. Both hairy and clothed, though usually only in rags that even the ragged had discarded. Creatures lynched by mobs at every unsolved murder or missing child, whose dense muscled necks would sometimes allow them to suffer almost until the anger had abated.

Holman doesn't know whether this is true, or the jabberwock of one who sips shoe polish, or if this fable of wretched demi-brothers is intended as a parable, to show that there are lonelier, lowlier states than Holman's.

The old mariner doesn't ask Holman to go, as he had said he would, before he retires to his bed. His 'summer bed' he calls it, an unroofed nest in the rude foliage beside the bridge. He disappears from sight, leaving Holman to curl by the brazier.

Near where the tramper vanished, a section of railings is buckled, where a tree, as its girth expanded, once grew into the fence. Whether or not that iron entombed within the tree's heart dealt the blow, it clearly died; because all that now remains is a torso-shaped rotten husk: rootless below, chopped off above; suspended; crucified on the fence it once enveloped.

An owl wakes Holman up, squawking like a startled deaf child who knows not that it makes noise.

In his still slumbersome state Holman thinks the tramper's words have come true: an eerie half-primate face sniffs about by the brazier light. It is no humanzee though, he sees, but a babottweiler.

'Good girl,' says a man a few paces behind.

Dread seeps through the remnants of sleep as Holman realizes it is one of the Regans. Even moustached there is no mistaking.

'Hello, old son,' he says, like he knows Holman.

And a scene unfurls, like something Holman might have watched at the pictures. A scene in which he is a player and yet spectator:

There is a man, a big man, with a curled moustache like a child's disguise. And he lays his hands upon a small man, a fubsy homunculus, struggling from the floor beside a dying fire. The homunculus resists, he snarls an unexpected oath and tries to free himself. But the big man strikes his face; even open-handed, it is a blow, not a warning. The little fellow struggles on; he has more fight than you would expect, this abridged person. Now a strange hell-black hound, a monkey-dog thing from who knows what foul reach, has grasped the homunculus' leg. It pulls his foot out from beneath him and lands him on his back with an audible crack on the concrete bank. It seems the dance is over for the stubby demi-man. But one last player has yet to take his place. And now he comes, stage left, legs agape, draped in bindweed vines from his shrubbery entry, he leaps upon moustache's back and clings there like the old man of the sea. 'Courage, boy,' he cries. And moustache retreats a step from his foreshortened prey and twirls wildly about, like St Christopher trying to rid himself of a burdensome Christ-child. To no avail, for the old man is clasped as tight as the figurehead to a ship. The homunculus tries to kick at the hellhound with his free foot. But the beast, provoked, lunges instead for his arm. Its teeth pierce through coat and shirt and provoke a shriek. And the still-struggling shrieker feels in his pocket, Holman's pocket, produces Sting. The wasp-knife that was made and ready for just a time such as this.

Inside himself again, Holman stabs at the beast's face and it releases his arm, backs away a pace, blood in its eye. He gets to his feet; knife waving in front of him like a crucifix to keep away this creature of the night.

The Regan stops his struggle to throw the tramper, who grins from his mount, pleased as a lion of Oz to have found courage.

'Leave the hound be,' the Regan says. 'We'll leave you in peace, just leave her be.'

But the babottweiler has other plans, and it leaps, covers the ground to Holman in one simian bound.

The knife is waiting. The knife has been waiting all its life for this moment. It plunges into the beast and a thumb presses the button on its hilt, releasing a burst of gas as big as a pumpkin into the babott's chest. 800psi of pressure explodes into blood, leaves a hole in its ribcage Holman could fit his head in. But the beast's weight and momentum still knock him backwards. If there's one thing he excels at, it's falling. They tumble into the Thames together, entwined. And the river flows faster than it looks because the dead dog keeps pace with Holman a while. Even after he has freed himself from its form. Even though he is swimming, after a fashion. Skills unpractised since childhood physiotherapy pools.

On the bank, St Chris grasps the old man of the sea two-handed and flings him overhead to form a limp bundle in the lee of the bridge. Then St Chris dives into the water, a graceful arc for a big man, and his strokes would catch the homunculus with ease, but he swims only as far as the beast. While Holman drifts away in the black current, the Regan holds the dog's motionless form in his arms, treading water and howling at the moon. And Holman can hear the cries still, when he is long gone from sight.

27

THE ENTRY STEPS OF the Prometheus Building have a long series of large marble balls on marble plinths. They exist solely to show that this is the sort of place that has large marble balls on marble plinths. And together like that, they are not even beautiful, only monotonous. Like a crowd of individually handsome politicians, together they manage to be bland. They annul each other. As with politicians, Ilse – the Leveller – has grown to hate them, but she will not let that hate consume her. She takes her station by the steps; she raises her brittle plywood standard; she stands against the wind.

The Leveller is too small to see, from inside the tower, from where a professor looks down. He isn't in a crowd and – whether or not because of that – he is quite strikingly handsome; perhaps made more so by the flawless newborn baby he cradles. To further accessorize the scene: his wife, his young wife, his perfect wife, stands behind him, soft arms draped about his waist, fingertips gently stroking the expensive cloth of his shirt. She cannot feel the knots of fear that grow daily inside his stomach.

Fear is spreading among the Unimproved as word is spreading, of prostitutes murdered; not eviscerated in Whitechapel, but battered to death in The Kross. A risk of that game, some say, and who would mourn a pimp? But there was a taxi biker too, and others have been found now: a barkeep called Adolf; an old bullfight aficionado in a knitted cloth cap. It seems unlikely they will be the last.

Men of faith need have no fear: God will cover them with His feathers and under His wings they will be safe; His truth will be their shield, as the Prophet said. They need 'not be afraid for the terror by night; nor for the arrow that flies by day; nor for the pestilence that walks in darkness; nor for the destruction that wages at noontime'. The bomb-maker need have no dread of death. But neither does he seek it for himself; his God tells him not to. His God whispers that it is better for one who has learned such skills over such lengthy years to use them with wisdom. Death must be administered wholeheartedly to the lost and the damned; and for that the jihadi must live as long as possible – 'With long life will I satisfy him, and show him My salvation.' The soulless ones passed their laws to make gatherings of the righteous illegal, but the bomb-maker will use their own gatherings against them. Where there is a crowd, there they will find a device. Because God is a God of peace; but those who do not believe that must be annihilated.

A detective looks down at his gun. He habitually lays it on the centre of his desk when he works there. His gun is snub-nosed, because they are easier to use close to, and easier to conceal. It is a revolver, rather than an automatic, because revolvers are simple contraptions, they have few moving parts, and those they have are sturdy. The user of a well-made revolver can whip slits in cheeks and brows with the muzzle and crack black eyes with the butt all day long and still confidently expect it to fire and to fire true. The gun is chromed, because when the detective draws it, usually he wants it to be clearly seen. The handle is combat-gripped, with curved ridges for his fingers, which makes it easier to hold firmly in blunt instrument assault. The grip itself is carved from oak. The tree from which it came was growing long before the detective's parents made him. That thought makes him feel ill.

A once famous lady has not been well of late, but her houseboy ensures that her every need is met. He brushes her hair, knowing that appearance is important to her even when poorly. He makes her favourite meals unasked. His love for her is so strong that he intuits exactly what she wants.

What is loved must sooner or later be lost. A man walks alone who is used to his love walking with him. His love used to trot beside him, paws prancing like the hooves of a Spanish pony at the auroch fights; tail flagging with the joy of being near to him. Now he is friendless, wet and crazed. He doesn't yet know what he will do. But he knows what he won't do. Not any more.

A writer can't go on. There is a scream trapped inside his skull. His hands shake with synth withdrawal and horror of another day ahead. Only bravado makes it bearable – that's why he tells those war stories in the bars – only bravado and the booze. It makes sense in the Loup Hole. The pain is medicated. Not just the pain of his wounds, but the constant internal ache of the unatonable things they've done. He's done. He sits at his Braille typewriter, the chair legs screeching on the floor as he scrapes them down askew. A blank page, another tread of the same stage, a one-man show with no audience. He feels like he could cry, but he can't cry: the tear ducts are singed shut.

A narc slinger slinks his way home, moves still going, music-less. Valentine the boneless. High on his own supply. Nothing left in the belt to sell. No need to be discreet on the street. Dancing down the South Bank.

And the Thames continues on its way, carrying with it a semi-autistic demi-man. The river has seen it all before, has known plague and fire and war. Tonight tidal waters will flow past skeletal scraps of Viking longboats and giant rust-brown wind farms, motionless titans, old monsters whose time is up. And out there in the oceans there will be sharks, which flash their time-sculpted forms – streamlined as fighter jets – designed before the first, pale dinosaur egg was nosed into a prototype nest of aeons-extinct ferns. And out there somewhere, a croc-odile smiles.

28

Detective Günther Charles Bonnet

THE OLD LADY IS slab-laid and still as a sacrificed ewe. Gretchen Gerbi. Unimproved, but not scum. She reminds Gunt of his mother, also dead. Wisps of hair, grey and fine as smoke, lie between thighs of old leather.

Norris puts down the battery hand-fan – with which he has been cooling his pork-fat face – and picks up a circular skull saw, of similar dimensions. It shrieks, like a firework in flight, as he slices into the worriless forehead of Mrs Gerbi.

'It's the dwarf,' Gunt says. 'It has to be. Everything pointed to him from the start. This victim was the concierge of his building. I'm thinking she might even have been the first murder; looks to have been dead a fair while, no? But the door was locked from the inside again. Could he have used some kind of slow-acting poison that looks like a beating? Is that possible?'

'Almost anything's possible,' Norris says, 'but is it likely?'

Norris wears a string vest, which stops his sweat sticking his shirt to him. He's plump enough to have visible tits. You'd almost think he was Unimproved, but that seems staggeringly unlikely. How many Unimproved people get government jobs? None. Pretty much none. They're not allowed to test officially of course, but they have ways to check out people who seem in doubt. No one slips through the net. Pretty much no one.

Being a cop has become almost a family business now. Fathers choose their sons for brawn and reflexes; they sometimes dampen down the genes for fear. In the early days the military tried to remove fear genes altogether, but none of those kids made it to adulthood: dead from falls and fights. Most of the guys on the force now, they're third- and fourth- generation cops. They're bred for it, designed for it. Not Gunt. Gunt looks like a guy who could have been anything. Gunt's as handsome as a politician.

His skin should be scarred by now from all the blows he's taken, but it's too thick for that. His nose should be flattened, but he's too quick for that. Gunt's got the best set of genes on the force and they all know it.

'Just look into it,' Gunt says to Norris. 'There's something rotten, beyond just this victim.'

As Gunt's about to leave, Norris looks up from his bone shearing.

'Detective Bonnet.'

'Yes.'

'I just wanted to say that, look: I know . . . '

'Know what?'

'Nothing,' the path. guy says. 'Sorry, nothing.'

Later, it rains. It rains on the just and the unjust with equanimity. It rains on the cops and the crims. It rains on the Improved and Unimproved. And though the roadside sellers quickly break out their fissile plastic ponchos, everyone walks out in the rain gladly. Everyone wants to feel it falling on them. Because it doesn't rain often after all, and without doubt the truculent sun will be back tomorrow.

The sun's back in The Kross all right; so's Gunt. He watches a sugarcane-juice grinder on a street corner, ice machine whirring away angrily as it tries to fight the heat. The heap of ice it has produced glows a beautiful cold black through the glasses, sucking the surrounding warmth into itself like the obliteration of wayward thoughts.

Gunt's had a call. An anonymous informant wants to talk to him, to him alone. Number 151 Charles Martellus Street. A building under repair. All its windows boarded up. Looking more like windows because of it. Looking like windows that someone wanted to emphasize. Someone who'd never seen windows. Scaffolding fronts it like another line of defence. Green-painted concrete passes for garden in the narrow entry plot.

The door's open, like the caller said it would be. Gunt passes through a small hallway and through another door. He grips his Glaxo – snub-nosed, high-calibre, hand-cannon – but holds it down by his side. One of the Regans is sitting behind a small table. He looks like he hasn't slept. His shiny spiv suit's as dirty as if he'd been keeping goal in it. He's got a moustache like the docked tails of two dogs. Gunt's interviewed him before. Gunt always knew this might be a trap: realized that meeting an unknown in an empty building might not be so smart; but it being a Regan before him raises the stakes. He thumbs back the hammer on the Glaxo.

The Regans, are identicals, all cloned from the same egg. Gunt knows the story: Red Nell – the Red Queen – was there when her husband was gunned down. She cut off his balls as he lay dying. Packed them in ice, so she might keep a part of him. Whatever back-street quack she went to only managed to fertilize one egg from her crude attempt to save her partner's gametes. So they multiplied it infinitely, unaltered, except for the basic immunity charity packs. Now they are a small army of brothers, bred from a dead gangster and his harridan wife. All the same, identical in genes and environment: the clear evidence that we are nothing more than the sum of our parts. And yet this one looks as though he's been crying. This one says:

'Detective. It's about the black stuff. We need to talk.'

'I'm listening.'

'There's a slinger called Valentine. You need to stop him: spooks had us stitch him up with a special package of pills. I don't know what they did to them. But I know it's not good. Someone needs to get to him before he sells them all. I think they've been doctored. I think people are going to die.'

'And you're telling me this why?'

'I don't know, to be perfectly sure. Let's just say I was never like the others to begin with, and I've recently lost the only thing I cared for in this pity-forsaken city. Call it an epiphany, or call it the madness of grief, if you will. But I don't want any part in all this any more.'

'Public-spirited, I'm sure. But why did you call me? Sounds like narcotics terrain.'

'Because of the black stuff: intelligence agents, Interfectors. It seems like it's all mixed up with the wee feller you asked me about before. We picked him, you see. I picked him. They gave us a job and told us the subject had to be Unimproved. I found him dead drunk, asleep on a bench. This would be a few weeks back. I'd never seen anyone so obviously Unimproved as that feller. So I picked him. Like the poor wee guy didn't have enough crap in his life, before whatever it was that we injected him with.'

29

Holman

A MUCK-DRENCHED SHUCK CLAMBERED to land at Deptford. A shivering sluice creature slithered its return to the dry world. It might have been a merman who'd traded soul for legs with a swindling sea hag, for the set it received seemed a trickster's trade. But perhaps it was still breaking them in, as it listed along the foreshore.

The creature slept, as such creatures do perhaps, still wet, nested in a nook of bins, brickbat in hand to swipe the rats. When it woke it found a length of plastic plumber's pipe for a stave, having lost its cane, and pilgrim-like went its way.

Outside Kit's End, a pub of evil esteem, a damp sandwich half consumed, which the creature sniffed as if for poison and then, seemingly satisfied, devoured. It wiped its mouth on its hand and wiped its fingers in its hair and continued on whatever abstract route it was following.

It passed charnel hulks of watercraft, run aground by the wrecker time, in that part of London that was once port. Albion had no more need of them. Only gunboats have sanction to put to sea, so that unsanctioned vessels can be sunk.

Later it rained, and it came shrapnel-fast and the streets were abruptly in an inch of water and the drops, which kept hammering down, left transient craters in the water already fallen. And to the ants it was an air raid, a wet Dresden; to the ants it was Armageddon; but what is an ant worth? And when it stopped, the streets smelled like mould.

He looked like he didn't belong to anybody: the creature; that little man. But he had a family, and he had a mind that on the morrow he might call them.

If the Oedipal view of life is correct, then Holman was cheated from his very genesis: his father died almost upon Holman's birth, robbing him of any possibility of primordial thought-crime. Though perhaps this was in itself success of a sort, perhaps it was his very emergence that struck the death blow. But his brother, or half-brother, was always something of a father figure to Holman, not just for being eighteen years the senior; nor simply because he disseminated the same casual disdain mixed with occasional benevolence as a real father might well have done; but because there was also that other thing. The thing kept in the mind drawer that Holman doesn't look in.

Thoughts of his mother are almost more than Holman can bear. His mother seems to be the only thing for which he has ever been able to summon care. But when he tries to phone her, from a half-cockle call box in New Cross – the coin with which to do so having been raised by a perilous exposed spell spent begging – it is Sebastian who answers.

'She isn't in,' he says; curt, when he is usually courteous.

'Do you know when she'll be back?'

'She won't be back any time soon.'

'Do you mean today, or this week, or what?'

'Any time. Any time soon.'

'Can I leave a message with you?'

'You can, but she won't be back.'

'Well, just say I called then.'

Which leaves only Holman's half-brother: Augustus: scientist; lover; thinker; very much his father's son. Unlike Holman: a last act of vanity; an orgasmic death rattle; an experiment. Fuck Augustus. There must be another way.

The banks of the Thames are smeared with litter from high water. Seen from a distance they are quite pleasing to an artist's eye, straight white lines against the slime.

At a point where he can descend to the level of the river, and is somewhat concealed from the world, Holman strips and washes. Trying to clean the river's filth from himself and his clothes with the filthy river: a task thankless as sweeping a dirt floor. He squats to defecate into the flow and flies buzz amiably around his exposed rear as his body dilates and drops two long bombs of stool into the water. He cleans his unseen hole, pursed like the mouth of an old smoker, in the half-mile-wide bidet, then puts on his wet and battered trousers and sets off again towards civilization, feeling that he has re-established a modicum of respectability. How fast our standards fall. Only a blind man would let Holman in his house right now, only a blind man.

Crick!

Near New Cross station, Holman hocks his watch with a stony, disinterested pawnbroke. Who writes a pink buy-back ticket with professional brevity. Temporarily flush, Holman pays the train fare and then buys a bowl of eggy-rice from a street booth roofed with grey bamboo, still in use beyond its natural life. He spends the last of his watch on a bottle to sip while he waits.

It is a long wait, because the trains run infrequent and late.

Scratchy warnings echo out over the station tannoy. They use multiple voices blended together to do the security announcements, to give the impression of a squad ready for action.

Do not leave luggage unattended. Unattended luggage will be taken to an incendiary area and destroyed.

Beggars operate in this area. Giving to beggars encourages begging and burdens society.

Look out for suspicious behaviour and suspicious persons. If you see suspicious behaviour or suspicious persons report them immediately to a member of the security team.

Holman is a suspicious person – suspicious people are always Unimproved – and people look at him, but seemingly no one reports him; perhaps because swigging synth is generally considered to be incompatible with religious terrorism.

The train, when it finally arrives, squeaks and creaks at its rivets. It sounds almost as if it longs to be peeled apart by the explosion that may just lie in wait for it one day. When Holman was a small child, trains still ran underground; an entire network of tunnels criss-crossed this city. But too many bombs and too little power put paid to that. These tardy, slat-seated surface beasts are all that remains.

For the first ponderous leg of the journey, Holman cannot sit down for the squarm of strangers; nor quite stand up straight, because of a bag stoved behind his legs. But most passengers alight at London Bridge, leaving him to take a bench. Only freight and synth goes to The Kross; and most of the freight is synth.

The bench seat is curved to accommodate rears designed differently to Holman's, but despite that and a cagey agoraphobia, he almost enjoys the journey. He loves all forms of indolent movement. Though the train doesn't run swift, it runs without effort from him.

Opposite him, writing occasionally in a notebook, sits a man who might once have been handsome, but no longer is. Not so much that age has not been kind to him, he'd probably only be mid-thirties. But his features, badly chosen, or possibly even lucky natural, are now lagging behind the place that handsome occupies. By his mannerisms, he seems to take exception to the fact Holman swigs from a bottle. And since Holman doesn't really see this as something to take exception to, it makes him do it more. It riles some obstreperous instinct in him and makes him sup as methodically and noisily as he can. They haven't broken him yet.

He reads the back page of an abandoned newspaper, the 'Duggie' cartoon. Holman remembers Duggie: the lovable loser; always at the bar in his shabby, baggy clothes; hitting on women and failing; never in work. A new artist has taken it over. The character's features are still recognizably Duggie's, but they are sharper, harsher, pointing out that if you were to meet a real

Duggie then he would clearly be Unimproved. And the tone of his escapades has changed: he is more of a bludger; less a lovable loser than a petty criminal and sex pest. When did that happen? When did poor old Duggie become a propaganda piece?

There is a new housing project being built in what Holman remembers was once a park. Space is running out everywhere now. On the site there is a huge artist's impression of the elaborate elegance that is to come. *If you lived here, you'd be home by now*, it says. But Holman's going home.

The banks to either side of the tracks narrow at the approach to The Kross. Shaded from the crushing sun, it is the most verdant scene Holman's seen in days. Plants sprout from clogged gutters. Ivy grows over abandoned sleeper rails. Old tyres are green with mould, which gnaws into their inedible rubber. Even the imperishable plastic bags are brown with age and soon to be covered over by creeping leaf litter. They cannot keep nature out for ever. Nature never gives up. Old fool.

30

Valentine

VALENTINE'S IN THE LOFT crawl space in the common area hall, itchy with fibreglass, sorting what he wants from his supply for tonight, when the cop comes round. Lucky. But then Valentine was born lucky. Through the gap in the ceiling panel, he watches the cop ignore the other doors and go straight for 969: chez Valentine. Which means this is no idle inquiry. The guy doesn't even look like a cop – he's as handsome as a politician – but what else could he be? He's a cop all right; doesn't even knock. He tries the handle of Valentine's door, and because it's unlocked, he walks right in.

Shit!

What to do?

Option 1: slide the panel fully shut and sit it out, hope he doesn't think to look. Why would he? Well, he knows where you live already; who knows what else he knows. You might be safe enough, but even if so, how are you going to know when to come out? Plus you're cornered up here and you've got the stash, so you're totally screwed if he knows or thinks to search.

Option 2: drop down now while he's inside and sneak out, or make a run for it. Take the stash, take the lot. If he hears, gives chase and gets close, you chuck the stash. If he goes for that, you'll get away, if he keeps after you, the stash will be long gone in The Kross and he'll have no evidence. But chances are you'll get clear and keep the drugs too. Even if he hears, no one runs as fast as you.

Valentine lands light on his double arches. Lots of guys cut their laces off, looks cool, but that's no way to treat a shoe. Valentine has his tied tight. Running shoes are Valentine's friends.

There's a noise of movement from inside the flat. Valentine flips plan from stealth to speed straight away. Belts to the banister, flings himself down the first set of stairs. Practically running round the walls, he's cornering so quick.

He can hear the cop coming, though, thundering down the stairs behind. The noise is not getting further away. It's getting closer, if anything. Valentine keeps charging down the drum-roll flights of the stairway.

Valentine collides with a street sweeper as he ploughs through the double doors at the bottom. The force knocks them both over, but Valentine's up in a moment, scrambled to his feet. No way the cop's going to catch him. The cop's a fleet fuck, give him that. But the fox only runs for its dinner; the rabbit runs for its life. Valentine swings the sweeper's little cart behind him at the doors as he starts to accelerate away again. There's a crash and more shouts from behind. Sounds like the cop took a dive too, but Valentine's not going to waste time looking. Eyes on the prize. Eyes ahead.

Valentine's across the road already. Valentine's disappearing into the dusk. Leaving this cop for dust. But no, the swerves and hoots of mopeds say he's still on the trail.

Valentine scales a fence. Has a glance back as he front-drops the top. Hand over fist. Hand over fist, mate. The cop is still coming though, coming quick. The cop's fingers almost touch his through the chain link. For a moment predator and prey, both panting, pause and regard, divided by a mesh of wire. The cop reaches into his jacket. He's not going for a cig. Valentine's already running. Valentine's behind a brick storage shed when the first shot comes. Valentine's off again down the alley. No more shots; the cop must be climbing the fence.

Valentine's out on Colonel Collins Street. Got a lead now. Sees a taxi biker. He's on the back of it before the man's even stopped. Born lucky.

'Drive, now! Fast! Fifty notes, mate! I'll give you fifty.'

Valentine's looking back. Scanning the horizon, hair streaming like a crow's-nested Viking. The cop's still not in view when the biker gets them off the street with a hard left. Which means that you can consider him lost.

Born lucky.

Valentine pays the biker off. And as soon as he's gone, takes another one. Heads south, finds a barber's stripy pole.

It's gutting watching his hair tumbling, lion locks that he's been growing for the best part of forever. But being gutted is not comparable to prison.

Buys some new duds, too. A tank top and a jumbo set of flares. Flares are coming back again, in their latest incarnation; unkillable, but gradually more disfigured, like the nemesis of some superhero. Flares want to thrive and survive just as much as Valentine does.

Well, for that, Valentine, it looks like you're going to need to leave town for a while. Sell the lot first. Get rid of this whole package, take the money and run. They're not going to be after you for ever; it's just a drug thing. They'll forget all about you in a few months. They say there's a good salsco scene in Brighton. Bit of a fucked-up town, but still. Maybe Brighton would be best. For now, though: Fin de Siècle.

The neon light of the club's sign blams the pavement, makes all the other drear night colours even drabber. Neon always evokes that virginal salsco experience for Valentine: that feeling like the first time you saw the dawn: awakened.

There's already a queue outside The Studio, where the Fin de Siècle night is on. A line of ready revellers, some already jiving with expectation. But Valentine doesn't have to queue here; it just takes a moment for the doorman to recognize him with short hair.

The DJ knows what church organists always knew: that God lives in the places that you can't hear but you can sense. Half the salsco beats are hidden from human ears, but you can feel their tremors through your frame. And kick biscuits bring them to life.

Valentine's loaded with kick biscuits tonight: special belt with the little stash pockets full to the gunnels and another bag of two thousand in his pocket.

Even by salsco standards, Fin de Siècle is on the edge. The main room is for dancing, but the themed back rooms are more explicitly orgy: *fin de siècle* Paris; Rome teetering on the brink of its twilight fall. And recreations of favoured fuck-spots from more repressive ages, where the jivers go to re-enact what their forefathers and mothers did: a World War One brothel; a stained, glory-holed subway toilet from 1970s New York; a full-on hump fest, where a tennis-chaired lifeguard invigilates the tangled morass of wall-to-wall mattress to make sure no one drowns.

But that's all for later; most of those rooms will be pretty empty now. People want to dance first. Dance and get their fill of kick biscuits. Though people never really get their fill of kick biscuits: they're like synth; there's always this sense of impending deprivation, this feeling that you will likely need more than there is ever likely to be available. Well, ladies and gents, perhaps tonight there will be plenty for once. Plenty for all. Tonight Valentine's got a sale on. Hand over fist, mates.

31

Detective Günther
Charles Bonnet

GUNT'S NEVER BEEN OUTRUN before. Outrun by scum. Standing, panting like a spaniel, on an empty street. Nothing in view but a solitary parked car, either the colour of street dust or covered in street dust. Probably the latter; it probably hasn't been used in months. No one round here can afford to run a car. Gunt looks it over, just to make sure the perp isn't hiding inside. Writes 'scum' in the window dirt with his finger. But the car's empty, the perp's vanished.

The game's not over, though; the Regan grass told him where the dealer operates. It's the Regans who control the club door staff in The Kross. So the Regans decide who gets permission to deal where.

The neon light of the club's sign blams the pavement, harsh and ugly, but the colours that surround it are beautiful through the glasses; still-hot walls give off raspberry and pumpkin glows: shades like the first time you saw the dawn: awakened.

The bouncer has a face like a potato a kid's taken a spud gun to: pocked and fucked.

A chick in a man's suit jacket, loose so her boob-tubed tits poke from it, has the guest list, seems in charge of fast-tracking. So Gunt walks up to her.

'I don't care how handsome you are, honey.' She smiles. 'If you're not on the list, you queue with everyone else tonight.'

The bouncer comes and stands beside her, chest drawn up to his pie-pecked mug.

Her perfume creates a cold shudder at the back of Gunt's lungs. An old shudder at the back of his mind, the memory of another time.

She had kissed him – a perfumed near-child girl, kissing a near-child boy – he had felt a thrill surfacing, then consciously killed it. And a sneer came to replace it. She was scum. Günther could do better than that lack-gene girl. That lack-gene girl who loved him. Günther wasn't like her. Günther felt nothing for her. Günther felt nothing for the scum.

Gunt floors the bouncer with his first blow. The rage upon him. Punching, smacking it out of him, away from him, smacking out the filth. Showing that he isn't scum like them. Not Gunt. Knuckles bleeding, still smacking. Blood mingling. Different species almost. Blood mingling. Not so different.

The blows glow red on the man's skin where the temperature has been raised by kinetic force. Redder than the blood. The man's nose is flat now.

Noses are our antlers. So far in front of human faces, so easy to break, for just that reason. They stream with blood and they hurt like fuck and they prevent fatal fights. The man holds his flat nose with both hands. Gunt slows. Gunt stops.

'Police,' Gunt says, 'sorry. Police.'

He gets out his badge, shows the trembling guest-list girl and a second bouncer who is even now emerging from inside.

'I thought he was going for a gun. I was mistaken. There's no problem. I'll just go on in.'

Gunt turns and tells the line of people there's no problem. No problem, folks. No problem here. No problem at all.

It's early, but the club's already busy. A crowd out on the vast agora floor. Old church pews line the walls, salvaged by some entrepreneur, so tired jivers have somewhere to sit. But mostly people are dancing. The girls kick up their legs high in tease. Gunt doesn't dance. Gunt has never danced. But you can bet he'd be the best dancer in the room.

There's a remix playing, typical salsco shit: take a great old tune and bat it about so the long-dead original artists wouldn't even recognize it. Bang a hefty salsco bass on it. Music by numbers. *Strange fruit*, the refrain of this one goes, *strange fruit*. A song from a time when prejudice was so entrenched that people could be lynched, just because others believed they were lesser. A song making a comeback.

Gunt's fractured snapshots are back too. Grainy brain Polaroids, impolitely reminding him of what he is and isn't.

She pinned him to the floor once, though he could have thrown her easily. 'Will we marry?' she asked. And though they were just grazed-kneed infants, he meant it when he agreed.

Gunt needs to get some height to have a chance of finding the perp. There's a gantry for the lighting rig, a gangling steel thing lit by demi-moon lamps. Gunt's done a lot of stairs today, but still takes the rattling metal steps three at a time.

Years later, they rode the helter-skelter together, hugged close on hessian mats. Galloping up again to take the next turn, hand in comfortably damp hand.

Valentine – the slinger – is in the crowd. He's had his hair cropped but Gunt still spots him. Looks like he's whistling through his teeth to the music, the prick. Handing out pills like a hospital. Doing who knows what kind of crazy bandy-ass dance. Gunt hammers down to the ground again, stairs clanging like cymbals to the music. Busting through the cursing crowds. Shoving people out of the way as much as he can without causing a fight that will slow him.

She held a bagged goldfish up before her face. 'I won you at the fair,' she said. But she stared through the clear plastic, past the sherbet yellow fish, at Günther. Her eyes wider than the fish's, with refraction of the water and some strange new delight at life. 'I won you at the fair.'

The fuck's disappeared, by the time Gunt gets to the spot he mentally marked. Gunt gets his Glaxo out; people see the pistol, people part from in front of him pretty bloody quick. If only the scum knew: Gunt's trying to save their shitty scum lives.

She lived in his street. They grew up together. Rode bikes. Threw stones. Stole kisses.

Valentine spots Gunt about the same moment as Gunt spots Valentine. Gunt's actively looking, but Gunt's about a head higher than most of the crowd, easy to see. Valentine rips open the plastic bag he's holding, throws it behind his head. Sending an arc of pills into the strobe-lit air. A still photo flash of failure.

'Cops!' the perp shouts. 'Cops! Help yourselves, but don't be holding the prize when the music stops.'

He rips off his belt as well, flings it out there behind him. A big wide thing with pockets, pills spilling from it. People echo Valentine. 'Cops, cops. Don't have the bag when the music stops.' Jivers are scoffing the freebies, troughing. Pills scatter everywhere, to be guzzled by the crowds. The belt itself is tossed good-naturedly about like it's crowd-surfing. Like a flopping flexible stage diver. It's all over, it's all in vain.

A gently bobbing boat in the tunnel of love. A girl from his street. A kiss from France.

Gunt forces his way through the mass, raises the pistol, trains it on Valentine. People spread from around him like water off wax. The two of them in a ring of crowd, like a dance-off.

'Don't take those tablets,' Gunt shouts. 'They'll kill you.'

But only those immediately around can hear. Most of them have already taken pills. One girl starts shrieking, hysterical. Gunt shoots in the air. Trying to get everyone's attention. Brings the gun back on the perp. Repeats what he said. But people are already flooding away from the madman with the gun. And it's the worst thing he could have done, because now it can't even be contained. Now people are pouring out on to the streets, as scattered as the pills on the floor. The belt lies limp, like a dead serpent. Someone has probably pocketed the remains of the bag.

A sideshow trailer. Mirrors distorted them. Showed their bodies as they would be if stretched, squashed, squared. A pain-free peek at disfigurement. Günther's young frame was starting to fill into its predator future. His muscles already gave him performance pleasure when he tensed them. His cheek bones were hard and proud. His jaw was like a graven god's. And her? Less than that. Her body was ripening, daily opening, like a home-grown orchid, but less than that. Günther could do better than her, the lack-gene girl who loved him. Günther wasn't like her. Günther felt nothing for her. Günther felt nothing for the scum.

Now the scum are all he has, and most of them have fled. Only Gunt and Valentine remain, in the centre of the dance floor of an emptying club. *Strange fruit*, the tune still plays, *strange fruit*.

IV
The End

32

Holman

CRICK IS WEARING MIRRORED sunglasses when he comes to the door. As he sometimes does when he is abroad from this flat, to save others the shock of looking into eyes that are not. Holman sees himself reflected in the lenses: bulbous head balanced on small shoulders, like an inelegant tulip. Varicose nose; tumescent purple lips thrusting from his curled black beard like a parody of a woman's sex. His hair, now a fibrous matted ball, reminds him somewhat of the dead pimp Jesus' locks. Holman's trademark bowler hat is long lost; floating out to sea perhaps, to be marooned on some withered Caliphate shore, or to sink to the ocean depths, to nestle with what jitter creatures the ragged ship's captain talked of.

Holman knows he should be concerned for what became of the old tramper; but somewhere in a long refusal to be pitied, he lost the power of pity.

'You don't smell of oils, H,' Crick says. 'Usually you smell of oils.'

'I haven't been working for a little while. I'm in trouble, truth be told.'

Crick doesn't ask of what form; he turns and walks with stiff solemnity back from the doorway into his flat.

'You can have the sofa, as long as you need. I could do with a hand, place probably needs a good clean. And I could do with some company: I get lonely when I haven't got the strength to get to the Loup Hole. I prefer not to drink alone; although I prefer it to not drinking at all. Do you want a drink?'

A *ménage à trois* with the green witch, their shared mistress. Candlelight rebounding from the synth, which swirls in its own world in the sugarcane mixer, like a ghost, not a spirit. Holman watches the moths that fly in through the open window. One after another they dive, deep into the flame of the table candle, to vent their love or their fury at this invulnerable, irresistible lure. Time and again they spiral to the table, their wings singed to stumps; or else still burning as they plunge, to splutter and flap in voiceless agony till he ceases their pain with a palm. The candle has been lit for Holman. Crick has no need of light and thus the flat no longer has lights.

Through insufficient practice or flawed nature, Holman lacks the instinct for when he should look at, or away from, those he converses with; and often his attempts to replicate this, from memory, by volition, appear to make him look less normal still. Like a creature trained to pretend to be a man. With Crick it doesn't matter. With Crick and the witch, none of it matters.

Crick tells about when he lost his eyes. His eyes and all but this night terror of a face. A child, Nordic pale, in a place they thought still beyond the edge of the Caliphate; a boy with a jug of Belgian beer and a phosphorus grenade. Crick tells about the drip-drip dreams of morphine and the caverns measureless to man. He tells about coming home to the girl who was waiting for him. Wanting to tell her not to; not to wait; wanting to persuade her that her happiness was more important than what they had; that her life would be better spent not tethered to a blinded, bark-faced scar. Only to discover that she agreed.

Crick says how it is and will be, without fear or forethought, like a soothsayer or a speaking clock. And so, opened by his openness, Holman tells what he knows of himself.

Holman's grandfather founded Prometheus Industries, borrowing the name of course from the fabled Titan who taunted the gods by stealing fire for mankind. But while its namesake was cursed to have his liver consumed daily for all eternity, Prometheus Industries created the first livers guaranteed to outlive their recipients. The first livers developed in synchronicity with synthetic alcohols.

Holman's father was given the name Prometheus as his own and eventually the company too. It grew and flourished under his management and conspicuous eminence and added to the glory of both. His teams perfected and patented the extra chromosome pair, which enabled so many more genes to be altered so much more efficiently and cheaply.

His destiny so manifest, Prometheus believed his own press. Eventually as an octogenarian he married the country's most famous natural model. He decided that, having created numberless beings as beautiful as gods, stealing their fire; having fathered, craftsman-like, one son, an heir to his own design, almost to his own replication; that his crowning achievement would be to sire a child naturally, and that it too would be perfect. In his delirious dotage with Holman's mother, Prometheus became obsessed with having a 'real' child. It would have been so easy to have selected and improved. But he wanted to show that for all his wealth and power, for all the techniques he himself had helped refine, his natural child with the last 'Miss Natural' would still be a marvel. Old fool.

The thing that emerged was hairy as a beast. A normal stage in the womb, apparently, which even Improved fetuses pass through. But in which Holman, as a few always have, became stuck.

Prometheus, watching the birth from a wheelchair, could not believe that he had fathered the thing. 'Tell me that you mated with a bloody ape!' he shouted, pride finally punctured with the folly of it all.

'He that came forth first was red, and hairy like a skin: and his name was called Esau,' Adele Nicole sobbed through her exhaustion.

'Call him Esau then. No, I know you and your Bible nonsense. You would take that as a message from God. Call him Homunculus instead. Another curse on a bristled back. But he's going to suffer anyway, for my pride. He'll grow to curse me like I've cursed him.'

Perhaps the birth fur was a symbol, of a boy more natural. Or perhaps it was nature's mark of a thing ill-conceived: an outward show of inner frailty; perhaps Holman would have been better dashed from a cliff as the Spartans once did to preserve their race's purity. He lost the hair within weeks. But before then Prometheus had died, his legacy unaltered: leaving all to Augustus, his firstborn. Adele Nicole called her child

Holman, close enough to Homunculus, she thought, to honour an ungrantable last wish.

How does Holman know all this? Because his brother told him. Yet another reason he will never turn to him. Fuck Augustus.

From what little expression Crick's eldritch visage can produce, Holman suspects he must be in mid-speech. But he doesn't know what he was about to say, or even what he was talking about. Holman doesn't even remember coming here, to tell the truth. But the bottles between them on the table suggest that he has already been here for some time.

Tomorrow he will try and reach his mother again.

33

Sebastian

'I'M LOOKING FOR THIS man,' the detective says; he holds up an ID reader with a picture of Holman on the cracked and smeared screen. 'I understand his mother lives here.'

'She does, but she's not here at the moment.'

'And you are?'

'Sebastian, I work for her.'

'When was the last time you saw Mr Prometheus, then?'

'Which one?'

'Holman Prometheus, the picture I just showed you.'

'Not for a couple of weeks, I suppose.'

'There's another Mr Prometheus, then?'

'His brother: Augustus Berkeley Prometheus; the scientist; the renowned scientist . . .'

'Get your mistress to call me when she's back.' The policeman hands over a card, which Sebastian reads.

'I will, Detective Bonnet, though I am afraid that may not be for some time.'

Adele Nicole is waiting for Sebastian inside. Waiting for her bath, hands upon her lap; waiting for Sebastian in his favourite carmine-pink felt dress with the fur collar. It is made with heavy cloth, but she hasn't uttered a word of complaint about the heat.

She has been quite a different person these past few days, strangely compliant. They've made love whenever Sebastian's wanted. She's worn whatever he's wanted. Sometimes they have just sat and held hands for hours.

The salt from her last tears has left marks on the black cotton T-shirt Sebastian still wears. Two tear spots, side-on snakebites, down the blood gutter between his pecs.

'Let's get you ready for your bath,' he says, helping her by unbuttoning her dress. Her bra is a front-fasten, and as he releases it he sucks in momentarily, never readied for the rush of her body. The wan moons over which so many men drooled for so many years are now Sebastian's. Entirely and solely his, to do with what he will. He kisses each nipple solemnly, like a religious observance. The skin of her sweet, fey-chinned face is almost as bone pale as her whitened teeth. Her eyebrows seem dark against it. He wonders whether he should pluck them after he's cleaned her.

She has lost her hair, so he keeps the wig on in the bath, keeps her dignified. She has a vast array of wigs anyway. It doesn't matter if this one gets wet. It opens out in the water like the frond sprays of some near-creature water plant; as if it filters what it needs from the seas.

He dabs her dry, the better to avoid taking too much make-up from the bruises; though some needs reapplying none the less. There is only one bruise on her face. Next to her full lips, as if some brute had hit her. A back-handed fist across the mouth of the sort favoured in the old films. But Sebastian would kill any man who did that.

There are more bruises along the line of her left side, and Sebastian carefully dusts on the cover-up she always uses to hide any slight blemishes, following the lowland undulations of her ribs. It is an expensive preparation, which she has made to order; but because her skin has changed colour, it doesn't match nearly so well now as it once did.

They dine outside, under the shard light thrown by the purple bougainvillea vines, though Adele Nicole doesn't eat; her plate is left entirely untouched on the table.

As a child, Sebastian used to hide under the table when something bad happened; used to tuck himself away beneath the pine dining piece and just pretend that whatever was happening wasn't happening.

They make love after luncheon. He carries her up to her room, cupped in his arms as if crossing the bridal threshold. Tenderly he undresses her on the stiff sheets of the bed he made not two hours before. He had a twinge of guilt as he tucked down the starched cotton, because he knows she always used to insist on silk. But she makes no murmur of complaint as he slips her clothes from her. She makes no murmur at all.

And somewhere Sebastian knows that this can't go on for ever. But it can go on for a little longer. It can last for now. Because she was right; it's like Adele Nicole said: things don't have to be true all the time; sometimes it's enough to be beautiful. And it doesn't hurt anyone if we keep believing, or even just trying to.

Adele Nicole was watering her garden when the attack came. Her eyes bloated bulbous as she staggered back into the waxy begonias. A brittle gurgling the only noise. That and the splashed thrashing of the hosepipe, writhing in a serpent circle on the flagstone floor. Sebastian ran to her and cradled her head as her limbs stiffened and spasmed in a shocking parody of orgasm. Hair came away on his palm, where it supported her skull, and more fell off, as if of its own volition, as she shook her head in clear but near-silent pain. As if blood seeped through gauze, the welt on her face grew before his eyes. Then more rose omens flowered on her bare legs. The whole macabre dance lasted less than two minutes. Before Sebastian could decide between finding help and staying to comfort, she was gone. As he hugged her to his chest, he felt a change. And Adele Nicole was no longer in the Adele Nicole-shaped object he held.

An age ended: the last natural beauty passed into another state. But Sebastian doesn't have to face that for a while. Before the nation need know, he can keep what remains of her to himself just a little longer. For now, for once, Adele Nicole is Sebastian's alone.

34

Detective Günther
Charles Bonnet

VALENTINE DIDN'T KNOW ANYTHING that Gunt didn't already know. But Gunt beat him anyway. Gunt always beats them. Beats the suspect so that he isn't suspect. Gunt hates the Unimproved. Not just because he has to see them all the time. Not just because he's been attacked by them so many times. He has been bitten by dogs and stung by wasps, but he doesn't hate wasps or dogs. He hates the scum.

Gunt is not singular, the ages have known others: slave whippers who cried for their black mammy in the black nights; Nazi men, matured from boys scorned by Hebrew beauties, or who knew that a Jew peered from a far-flung bough of their own family tree; queer-bashers who grew tumescent in their drainpipe trousers at the cries of their prey. Even today Gunt is probably not alone. Though that is precisely what he is, because to find another would mean to be ruined utterly. To find another would mean exposure.

Gunt's at his desk. The phone rings, shrill in the hot silence. The phone was once white, is now brown, like the pages of an aged book. The perforations of the earpiece are waxy yellow, part plugged with the cellular silt of Genus Gunt.

It's Norris on the line, the fat pathology guy. 'Detective Bonnet,' he says, 'this is massive. We need to talk.'

'So talk,' Gunt says.

'OK, to put it simply: the bruising we've seen on the victims is caused, as I said, by extravasations: in other words the leaking of blood into the skin. When there is direct trauma to our largest organ, the skin, it results in bleeding of the blood vessels beneath: bruising. But that doesn't mean to say that all bruising is caused by external trauma. Occasionally there can be other reasons. Your victims die from haemorrhaging of blood consistent with a heavy beating, but . . . '

'But they're really being poisoned, right?'

'Not in so many words, no. It is a bleeding diathesis: your murderer is a disease.'

'What?'

'I know, it would be exciting if it weren't so frightening: a new virus, never recorded, so far as I can tell. A systematic inflammatory disorder causes the bruising and the hair loss, but it's a vasculitide: a kidney disease. It grows rapidly but unnoticed as the virus multiplies, until a tipping point beyond which a devastating cascade of events unfolds: direct blood vessel injury combines with a clotting factor overload. In some victims, this will be accompanied by hair loss, but that is just a side effect of the skin trauma – it probably happens as the virus reaches the tipping point. The final death will be swift: everything collapses at once. So we don't have a serial killer.'

'Good news,' says Gunt.

'Not really: what we have is a massive terrorist attack. Those pills you gave me, it's in them. Still live. They have tiny

225

packets of protein in them. They are in effect a life support for a live virus. Though from what I can see, it is pretty hardy anyway. It may survive quite long periods with no support at all.'

'Like how long?'

'Only time will tell. Hepatitis B can survive for months, maybe six months without a host. HIV can last only minutes, or a couple of hours at really optimal conditions. From what I've already found out, we're not looking at the lowest end of that scale. But if this virus was really long-lived, why would they put it in the host cells in those tablets? Just a precaution perhaps, but it's pretty sophisticated stuff. Though not nearly as sophisticated as the production of the virus itself. It's staggering how they could have created that in the Caliphate or some clandestine lab. Would probably take our top genetic ordinance doctors to come up with something like that. But we'll know more soon enough. I'm pretty sure they are going to throw every resource at this now. I've already sent a message straight to the top. We might have uncovered the biggest terrorist strike ever. Germ warfare; they're trying to wipe us all out. But they've made a serious error: most of the population will have immunity anyway. The disease is completely blocked by the same CCR5 delta 32 genes as block HIV. So anyone with improvements is already immune.'

'Sorry, could you repeat that?'

'Anyone with improvements is already immune.'

'And you think this is terrorists?'

'Who else? I think we can safely say there are going to be commendations and promotions all round for uncovering this.

Don't worry, I made clear your tenacity and vigilance in pursuing it. But look, Gunt, we need to be careful. Have you been directly exposed?'

Gunt puts the phone down. Gunt laughs. Gunt picks up the Glaxo snub-nose from his desk, spins the chamber. Puts it to his temple. Pulls the trigger. Click. Pulls again. Click. Again. Again. The act clears his head. Though not in the same way a bullet would. The bullets are on his desk, from where he was cleaning the gun when Norris rang. Gunt looks around the other cubicles, to make sure no one saw him. No one's looking. The few cops in there tap away two-fingered on typewriters or banter about, telling lack-gene jokes, holster-strapped backs to Gunt. Gunt's cubicle is against the wall at the farthest end of the office. The privilege of his clean-up rate and cojones. The privilege of being the guy that no one wants to sit near.

Why would the fat lab rat think it matters if Gunt's been exposed, if the Improved are immune? That in itself stinks of exposure. Gunt needs to see Norris. Find out what he knows.

Norris is in his office, alone. Norris is lava and maroon, but fades cold at his extremities. Norris' eyes look bulbous and glazed like a frog's, tawny and unblinking. Norris' throat flesh bulges like pie dough above the extension lead ligature from which he is suspended. Norris has funny small feet, Gunt notices, quite out of place on his portly frame. A stool lies on its side beneath Norris' funny small feet. It looks like suicide. It looks unquestionably like suicide. It looks like the sort of suicide someone would come up with if they were trying to imagine what a suicide would look like.

There is a fish on the desk, swimming round in a tiny tank, and Gunt can't see how such a long fish can circle around in there. It takes him a moment to realize it's a screensaver on Norris' computer. Only the science guys have decent technology these days. Gunt watches it: some sort of streamlined predator, pike or barracuda or something, swimming around inside a screen. Probably there is a suicide note typed out by latexed fingertips on the computer. Gunt doesn't much care either way, or on what they're blaming it. Because it's pretty obvious why Norris is dead and it's pretty obvious who's going to be next.

Gunt doesn't even cut the corpse down. He's not waiting around, and leaving prints and more DNA would make it all too easy to stick this on him. He might be the only one not involved who knows about the virus now. Maybe evil is a virus too, a self-perpetuating parasite that needs to thrive for no reason other than its own need to thrive, its own will to live, like flu or ivy or man.

Gunt isn't afraid. Gunt isn't afraid of anything; anything except exposure. The glory wouldn't have made Gunt happy anyway. None of it does: the promotions, the awards, the rewards. The luxury in a world of want. Nothing will. Nothing can. Nothing fills the hole. That's why we had to invent God. And that's why, even though that was perfect, even though that was for our own good, we had to dismantle God. Because we're on the move – we're army ants – it doesn't matter if this place or that place was the best we've ever been, we're going somewhere else and we're going to devour everything in our path and each other if we're too slow. Only forward movement keeps us from disintegration. Only motion masks the emptiness. And Gunt is now in the way. Gunt is blocking the column. Gunt is impeding progress.

35

Holman

CRICK PERSUADES HOLMAN THAT he must go and get his paintings and materials from his flat. On the bus, they sit together on the seats reserved for war veterans. People who pass to go further back accord them a deference there, when they would look away or stare at this auslandish pair if they saw them on the street. Strangers nod, as if they share some understanding of what Holman has lost for their life. Though they can't and he hasn't. Perhaps they think he had both legs shot off and teeters now on knee stumps, strapped to his shoes as in the child's game of dwarfdom.

Crick walks slow, when they dismount the bus, his twitching stick enquiring of the ground ahead. Holman's own drain-plastic cane quivers even more and his shoulder shakes with the fear, though Crick has his hand upon it for guidance. The weight of Crick's hand partly serves to remind Holman how much smaller and weaker he is.

By the bottom of the stairs, he's palsied with what might await him. 'Police Line' tape, drooping as if the vestige of a missed party, runs across Mrs Gerbi's door. When Holman describes this, Crick says it's a good sign: that the one-time pursuers would not stick around where the police have so recently been in force. It doesn't seem like a good sign for Gretchen Gerbi.

It also means Holman can't get the spare key from her, but Crick says they can probably force the door.

As Holman looks up at the stairs, he looks back; to another time; to stairs not dissimilar to these and a tumbling rag doll boy with legs of glass bottles. A boy who screamed for the mother he had just seen through a door crack, naked and oblivious on her bed. So soft and sweet were her nipples, to his child's eyes, they had seemed like berries in cream, ready at any second to sink from view. The hair between her china thighs was shocking, in his innocence of such things, bright red like a burning bush. And also between her legs was Augustus, his half-brother, her stepson.

Holman had turned and fled the frightful sight. The gorgoning assault that his mother seemed to be enjoying. But how could she be? Who could enjoy such a thing?

He wasn't supposed to be up there, on the second floor. His legs were not yet fully healed from their stretching. But Holman had wanted to show her how he'd climbed the stairs alone. It was to have been a surprise. He'd wanted her to hold him and tell him how brave and strong he'd been.

In his fleeing fright, Holman quickly descended the first flight, ungainly clinging to the anchor banister. At the second set of stairs he tripped and pitched. Back bumping in escalating tumble. Landing awry. His legs broke the fall. And his legs broke. His leg bones shattered. Even when healed, they would never grow again. Holman's lower half remains much the height it was that day.

Adele Nicole never knew what he witnessed. Holman told her he fell trying to climb to the first floor. He sensed that to say what he saw would be to change something, and he didn't want anything to change, for fear she'd stop loving him. She was all he knew of the world. But Augustus would never be forgiven, for all he seemed to notice.

Holman will never turn to Augustus for anything. Fuck Augustus.

Even blind, Crick exudes confidence. He is rangy and military. Though at the cheapest end – probably a charity pack – he is Improved, for what good it has done him. It allows him to drink synth to excess without fear of his health; that is perhaps all his parents' savings and scrapings have bequeathed now.

They mount the wooden hill together, as unsteady a pair of cragsmen as ever climbed a kerb. Crick gripping the rail and kicking his boot to feel the front of the next step before trusting his foot is truly on it. Holman long wary of stairs and fresh scared of what he might find in his flat.

There is no need to force the door; it is unlocked. There are no interlopers inside, but it is clear they have been by. It looks as though they were searching for something. Furniture is over-turned, the chair has been smashed, broken glass is everywhere. They have slashed open the great canvas Holman was working on, as if to hunt for something hidden underneath. The figure he had based on Dolly, in her memory, is all but obliterated, dangling in fronds. They have even searched through the paints: pots and tubes, all are empty, squeezed and thrown at the walls. Splashes of paint are now dried into leprous peels like sunburnt skin.

'There's nothing left here,' Holman says, 'nowhere even for you to sit. I'll stuff a bag with what I can, then let's go.'

He finds the black leather bag his mother gave him when he left home. It belonged to his father once; *Prometheus* is stitched into it in gold. The leather is flaking now in places, like scales or scabs working free. Holman fills it with what he can: a couple of sets of clothes and his bank cards, which were still in his table drawer; his books of sketches; his pencils and charcoals and brushes; his telescope and toothbrush. Then he changes, from the washed rags he's in, into his best suit – the trouser hems nonetheless worn, from his uneven gait – and he gets his other walking stick: the timeless half-shepherd handle, single sturdy piece of tree, sawed down to size.

Little is left of his work now. Most of it was destroyed at Charlie Smith's gallery, back in the riot, and now the biggest piece is despoiled as well. If Holman wasn't so scared, he would be heartbroken.

Only the portrait of Dolly that he painted after telling her about Jesus is worth saving from what has been spared. Holman slices it from its frame to rescue it, inflicting pain for its own good, as once they claimed for him.

As a boy he had the voice of an art curator in his head. He used to hear it as he dreamed and painted. A little imaginary monologue, as if an elderly but impassioned man was taking a tour around the Tate, and Holman's work was what the throng he addressed had come to see. He speaks now, the curator, as Holman looks at what he painted, before he rolls it up and consigns it to the bag.

Look at the brush strokes, the curator says, *see how they each curl down at either end, almost as a frown. The subject is unknown, but it would not be a stretch to suggest she is a lady of ill repute. The bed is rumpled and sunken in the centre; is it echoing the sadness we see on her face? Beside her, on the little table – painted so minimally yet so evocative of poverty – we see the shadow of the artist himself. He wants viewers to know he was there and yet he is not depicted. He isn't comforting the woman, he just observes. He always seems detached like this in his paintings; he wanted to create an impression that he didn't care, and yet the sensitivity of his depictions belies this. Is it possible to have empathy like that and really remain so detached? I for one doubt it; I think the detachment was a wall built to protect himself from further hurt. I think the detachment was an illusion.*

36

The Jihadi

REPETITION OF THE WORDS is what is important. It is quantity that pleases God. The meaning of the words scarcely interrupts, nor should it, the flow of them.

The jihadi finishes his prayers and rises from prostration on the floor. There are scuff marks on the lino, where things used to sit but now aren't. The room is large, but its original contents are all at one end: piles of wooden chairs, stacked in a mash like Jacob's Ladder collapsed; and other junk, all worthless so far as he can see. Who knows why someone would pay him to be caretaker of such goods, but the Lord moves in these mysteries. Soon this will all be blown into pieces so tiny that only God could count them. But God has no need to, God already knows how many there will be.

The jihadi feels no pity for those who suffer from his works. Most of them – the so-called 'Improved' – have no souls; therefore they are not truly people. Only God endows the soul, at the moment of conception, natural conception. Creatures made by alchemists are just golems; man-shaped, but not men. One cannot help them; one can only end their evil and alleviate their empty misery. Some real people may be killed, but most of these have turned from God, most of these have been seduced by the siren promises of the soulless ones. And if a true believer were to die, there need be no sadness: God will know His own. God knows every sea-smoothed pebble and grain of sand, and the righteous will be plucked to sit by His red right hand.

The man's own right hand is bandaged. White gauze, grubby from his work, crosses it, to cover the coin-round wound in its palm. A steel rod was blown through it, in his experimental days, and the wound still weeps. A seeping, solo stigmata to remind of the suffering of his Lord. It hurts the wound, this work; long weeks spent lugging sacks of fertilizer and bags of peroxide into this cellar; sometimes more modern explosives, when he can get hold of the materials. But such pains are sent by God to remind of what rewards are reserved for those who ignore Him. God speaks, and God is the word God speaks, and the word is God.

God told the man that his task must be to come not in peace, but bearing the sword, as Matthew taught. God told the man that Luke spoke the truth: for whoever is not for Him is against Him. God told the man that he must be fierce as Christ was when he drove the moneylenders from the temple with a scourge. God told the man that he must be that scourge; he must be the tool of Christ's wrath. God told the man that he must be a jihadi for Jesus.

The man has sympathy with the other jihadis, his brothers from the now cowed Caliphate; they are fellow travellers on the straight and narrow road. All straight and narrow roads lead to God, as once led to Rome, once His seat on earth. And even though the Vatican was taken by the Muslims, such things can be forgiven. Muslim means 'submissive towards God', and submission is the true path. Ours is not to question: knowledge should not be sought. Look at the world distorted by science: soulless creatures soil its face; beautiful succubae, created by Satan, try to tempt at every turn. We must choose obeisance and faith, not thirst for the false promises of sorcerous science. The Caliphate, or what remains of it, is a truer testament to God than this forsaken land of satanic genetic mills.

Once the jihadi thought it was possible for Christ's children and the soulless ones to share this land of Albion, separately but peacefully. In the commune, as a boy and young man, Lazarus had been contented. But such indolence was not the true path. God willed the crushing of the communes because they had strayed into ease, they had drifted from submission. By allowing the soulless government to destroy His children's world, He showed that there could be no coexistence. God showed that the Improved are anathema; they are cursed by God, and must be smitten from the earth. God's children must take back London as once they took Jericho: to utterly destroy all that was in the city, both man and woman, young and old, and ox and sheep and ass, with the edge of the sword. So it will be in the days that come. Such is God's will, as Leviticus wrote: *You will chase your enemies, and they shall fall by the sword before you. Five of you shall chase a hundred, and a hundred of you shall put ten thousand to flight; your enemies shall fall by the sword before you. For this is the day of the Lord God, a day of vengeance, that He may avenge Him of His adversaries: and the sword shall devour, and it shall be satiate and made drunk with their blood.*

Lazarus knows the drunkenness of blood is near, for the Lord God has told him so.

He calms himself, from the adrenalin of anticipation; stacks his chemical crates next to the bonfire piles of furniture. Guido Fawkes, another victimized man of God, once toiled at work such as this, in a cellar such as this one.

The jihadi knows his history, for they were taught well in the commune. They were taught of the sufferings and persecutions the ages have heaped upon the faithful of all sects. And still they were unprepared when persecution arrived.

Big-wheeled lorries churned up the mud. Soil that had been toiled for generations splattered up truck sides. Low gears jeering as they carried screaming children away. Soldiers smashed down doors with metallic phallic rams, designed purely for such violation. And eyes streamed with the agony of tear gas and eyes streamed with the agony of the havoc. And those who resisted were taken away and those who submitted were taken away also. And some elders said that this was the end time. But Lazarus could see that it was only the beginning.

Lazarus has more crates to bring in after his afternoon prayers; he wheels them through the lanes of Malebolge London on his sack cart, surrounded by enemies but protected as if through the valley of the shadow of death. For Lazarus' success is God's will. Did not God see to it that Lazarus was selected by a stranger and offered the job of caretaker to these unused cellar storage rooms? The jihadi would almost have thought it was a trap, so prime a target and so ordinarily secure was the building, and so out of the blue the employment offer. But it was one of the Regans who gave him the job, and though they are unquestionably creatures of Satan, such infamous criminals could never be involved with the forces of law enforcement. No, the Regans could not be in cahoots with the Babylon of Interfector agents. And anyway: neither group would wish for the building to be destroyed. It is just God's will. God has shown Lazarus the way and God protects him. Once he was even taken in by the police and questioned and it seemed as if he must have failed in this entrusted labour; but then God confounded the enemies' eyes, set upon them mists and darkness; blinded them just as St Paul blinded the false prophet Elymas, and Lazarus was suddenly freed without charge. One minute he was in a high-security cell, being sweated and slapped, then his interrogator was called away to take an important call, and when he returned, Lazarus was released back to The Kross. What was that if not a miracle?

Lazarus sees the same Leveller woman who is often outside the building, with her placards and her shouts. She is strong-hearted, but she is a fool, because she wants to join the soulless ones when she should be delighting in their downfall. He will show what it means to be a 'leveller'; Lazarus will level the entire Babel tower. He would like to go to her and tell her the good news about Jesus. But to do so would be to risk the whole enterprise. Though God protects him, he must also try to protect himself. *You shall not put the Lord your God to the test.*

The woman is beautiful in the wholesome, holy way of the natural, and Lazarus cannot entirely suppress a desire to see her naked, to touch her softness. Lazarus cannot help wishing to see another girl naked.

The only girl Lazarus has seen unclothed has been seen near alike by half the nation, on billboards, in magazines. *She hath grievously sinned and all that honoured her despise her, because they have seen her nakedness. Her filthiness is in her skirts. The adversary hath spread out his hand upon all her pleasant things.*

Adele Nicole, the girl who should have been Lazarus' bride, his first and only lover in the commune of his youth, became tempted by the beast. Their shared sin became her door to greater sin. While Lazarus retreated to beg God's forgiveness, she revelled in their transgression; she danced out into the world and became a very flagship for fornication. She copulated with Prometheus himself, one of Satan's great chiefs. In God's eyes she belonged with Lazarus, who knew her first. But in the eyes of the nation she was Mrs Prometheus.

They believe that their genetic enrichments are safe and right, but it is not God's way. Whole nations can be wrong and so often have been. Quantity does not create sense, but only a sense of sense. If something is not real then it must be imagined. The fact that the same delusion is shared by two people or ten or ten million doesn't make it more real, only more dangerous. The truth cannot be revealed by scientific experiment, but only from divine scripture and the voice of God in our heads.

God's Holy Bible has shown Lazarus the true path: *The nation shall become desolate; for she hath rebelled against her God: they shall fall by the sword: their infants shall be dashed in pieces, and their women with child shall be ripped up.*

Like Samson, Lazarus will pull down the pillars of this enemy's palace. Like the psalmist says: *Happy is he who repays you for what you have done to us. He who seizes your infants and dashes them against the rocks.*

Because the Lord God is a God of peace, but before the olive branch and the dove, there must come the flood. And this flood will be of blood. The blood of the soulless ones and the unbelievers. Blood will flow in the gutters amidst all the filth and pus. Blood will run so fast that it purges the dirt. For all things are required by God's law to be cleansed with blood; and without the shedding of blood there can be no forgiveness. This God wrote, through the people to whom God spoke, and God is the word God spoke, and the word is God.

37

Detective Günther
Charles Bonnet

FIND THE DWARF.

Why?

What else is there? Find the dwarf and maybe Gunt can take this to a higher authority. What higher authority? Norris tried that; higher authorities are where this is coming from. This is raining down from up top; they're trying to clean the streets. Albion's sick of the scum. Maybe it's too late anyway. But the dwarf's not dead, the Regan said, so some Unimproved must have immunity to the disease. There is a chance. Something's keeping the dwarf alive anyway. Find the dwarf, and maybe Gunt can find out what. Find the dwarf and maybe Gunt can make himself murder-proof: if he has the whole plot, fact-backed, laid out in letters held with multiple lawyers, ready to go to the press if he should die or disappear. It's not a great plan, but it's as good as Gunt's got. Solve this thing. Find the dwarf.

'Tell me, Professor, where's your brother?'

The professor tries to close his apartment door. Gunt's toe is in it, though, wedging it open. His badge dangles through the gap.

'I don't care if you're police, you have no right to be here, I'm calling security.'

'Security wanted a warrant. Security's cuffed in a cupboard behind the front desk. Security's got his tongue stapled to a shelf. Where do you think I got the key for the lift?'

The professor swallows audibly. 'There are others; this building's full of security.'

'No doubt, but they can't make you feel more secure any more.' Gunt draws his Glaxo and pushes open the door. 'They can only make this worse.'

'I don't know what this is about, but . . . ' The professor moves over in front of a baby-blue crib, as if to shield it from view with his body, but only pointing it out.

Gunt smashes the phone from the wall with his gun butt.

Perhaps the most beautiful woman Gunt has ever seen is motionless, mouth open with shock, on a cream leather sofa.

'Look, I don't know what this is about,' the professor repeats.

Which is a strange thing to say – because why would he? – and moreover, it strikes Gunt that he's lying. His lies look bright red through the glasses; the extra heat in his cheeks shines like a beacon, like a babottweiler's arse. He certainly knows some of what this is about, or he at least knows what it could be about. Norris' words: *Would probably take our top genetic ordinance doctors to come up with something like the virus.* The professor is just such a person: a fucking 'god'; one of the masters of the universe.

The professor's got the imprint of a Glaxo barrel in the side of his head. The girl's finally stopped screaming. The baby's in the microwave.

Gunt knows he's gone way too far this time. These aren't Kross trash; there will be consequences to this. But Gunt knows he's dead anyway. They'll get him like they got Norris. Unless he gets the whole story. Unless he gets insurance. Something to make him murder-proof.

'You wouldn't do it,' the professor says.

'You wouldn't believe half of what I would do,' says Gunt. 'Or maybe you would. You create people, don't you? So tell me, what puts the darkness in some hearts? Because it's there, isn't it, in some of us? Is it born or made? It's in me: coiled oil slicks of possibility, just waiting to rupture out. You know people so well; look into my eyes, you'll see what I'm capable of doing. What I want to know is what you're capable of doing. So you tell me; tell me what you've done, Professor, or I'm going to give your bouncing baby boy twenty seconds of suntan.'

'I can make another,' the professor spurts, trying to steal back possession of the situation. 'I can make another child absolutely identical to him. Nine months' time. He'll be ready before you're executed. I'll hold him up to watch when they do it.'

But Gunt can see right through the bluff. It will be an identical child, but it won't be this child. Maybe Gunt is bluffing too; he's not even sure himself any more, of what he is capable. But he twists the timer dial so numbers flicker upwards on the microwave's digital clock.

'Let me help you get started, Professor: you know about the disease, don't you? Was it made here?'

'Tell him, Augustus,' the girl whispers. Her should-be-beautiful face is drained and crumpled, like a stabbed football. 'If you know what he's talking about, tell him what he wants to know.'

'OK, look, it was a military project. One of our labs had worked on a virus they could use to stop the Caliphate ever growing too strong again, but something our troops would be immune to.'

'Sounds a perfect weapon. And what, you just decided to test it on your own people first?'

'No. I don't know. As far as I knew, the project was parked. A weapon of last resort; never to be used. Interfector agents had a few prototype vials, that was all. There were rumours they might have tested them in the last Caliphate War, but just baseless rumours. Then a few weeks back we got an order to make up some pills with the virus in. A lot of pills. And they wanted them to look like kick biscuits. I don't imagine there are any salsco clubs in the Caliphate, but there are a lot in The Kross. That's when I started to worry. I mean, I didn't think they'd ever do anything. But I was worried. I tried to get Holman out.'

'Your brother, the dwarf. You were right to be worried, but maybe you should have done something to stop this thing: he's got it: got a dose of the bug. They injected him with it.'

This drops the professor to the floor, to his knees, like someone praying, or about to be put to the pistol.

'I tried to get him out,' he whispers, almost to himself. 'I sent men to find him. Good men, ex-military. They must have scared him off; he disappeared, lost them. Then I paid the Regans to find him. But you're saying he got injected with it? I never thought they'd do it. Not really. It was never to be used. But Holman's safe then, safety of an horrific sort ... Those who get a patriarch dose, they're lucky, after a fashion. They're immune vectors of the disease; they're carriers; spreaders. I suppose Holman's the perfect vehicle, with his whoring and drooling. Now he's cursed, like Midas, to kill what he touches, but safe.'

'You really don't get this, do you?' Gunt says. 'We aren't any of us safe. None of us are getting out of this alive. Not a soul who knows a thing about it.'

'Maybe you aren't,' says the professor, 'maybe some others aren't. But me and mine are. I'm Augustus Prometheus. People like me don't just disappear. There is no one like me. My scientists and researchers don't just disappear; there are hundreds of my employees living and working in this building. Plenty will have some knowledge of the virus. They can't kill us all; some people are too big for that.'

'They'll have to. They can't trust you to keep quiet: this is way beyond you. The only way we're getting out of this is to get murder-proof. We're going to have to work together, to make it more embarrassing to kill us than to keep us safe. That's the only chance. You can't be so confident that you don't want insurance?'

Gunt gently takes the baby out of the microwave, its head cupped and haloed by his big hand. The baby already has hair, looks like a little boy. Gunt passes it to its mother, 'I wouldn't really have done it,' he says.

'Let us go now,' she says.

Hate pours from her. She's got strength you can see. She's made of fire and the sky.

'Fine, you go, get somewhere safe. Me and the professor are going to talk about making us all safe.'

'Go to your parents,' Augustus says. 'I'll meet you there.'

'Fuck you,' she says.

And she's already out of the door. Holding what looks to all the world like a baby, as if it is all the world. Cradling the little creature like she hugs her own heart and lungs.

Gunt slumps on the sofa; the Glaxo is still in his hand, but he lets it dangle towards the floor. 'Why did you do it?' he says, 'Why the hell did you do it? It's madness.'

'Just following orders, I suppose,' the professor says with a self-sadist smile, 'but that's what we all do, you know: free will is an illusion; a necessary fraud, because without it society would collapse. We have to punish those who transgress. But the truth is that we are stranded in our fates more authentically than any Calvinist. We act because a particular set of neurons fire. If another set had done so, we would have done something else. But they didn't, they never do, because that was already determined by the prior material state of the brain; which was determined by the prior state, ad infinitum; back to the first time we gurgle. Based on our external environment and our genetic make-up, we can never do other than we do.'

'That it?' Gunt says. 'You're claiming destiny or fucking fate as your excuse?'

'I suppose I am; though in the most pathetic sense, not in the grandest.'

Augustus pulls himself up, shaking, sits down on the sofa too. They are side by side, but staring straight ahead. Like they're strangers at the wake of a mutual friend.

After a while the professor says, 'You're not one of us, are you?'

And Gunt pauses, and a huge weight of air releases from

inside him with a heave. 'No,' he says, 'no, I'm not one of you.' And even though this might well be near the end, there is still some relief in saying that. 'Sometimes nature just gets things right. Sometimes the scum on the surface looks just like cream.'

'Amazing. I'd love to examine your genome, when this is all dealt with. Murder-proof, you say; so how does one go about becoming murder-proof?'

38

THE PROMETHEUS BUILDING CONTINUES its eternal metamorphosis, in the last of the daylight; gradually spiralling its floors around the solid core. A movement powered by nature: wind turbines and solar cells. Architecturally it is singular and symbolic: it has ninety-six storeys; double the forty-eight chromosomes of a gene-enriched person; like a couple, or a parent and child. And the tower was designed so that, when the sun reflects from its Möbius faces, it resembles the double helix of DNA. But, the Leveller thinks, tonight it looks more like twin towers, swirling one about the other.

Ilse is still disturbed by the mental picture of a man she saw entering the building; because, from a distance, he looked like her Günther, the boy's name erased, lasered away from the tattoo on her arm. The boy she loved, in the way back when, who loved her, who she was sure loved her. But who hated them both more, for being what they were. For being normal and human. Who turned from her and disappeared into a world of dissemblement, to a place she could not follow.

She is watching the doors, in case the man comes out again; of course it wasn't him, but just in case.

No one leaves, except a woman clutching a baby; running

out as if she'd stolen it. No one is chasing the woman, but she keeps running. She's in trouble, Ilse thinks, and drops her placard to the floor to give chase. Not knowing how she might help, only that she must. And for once the reward of the virtuous is instantaneous, because this single impulse of kindness saves Ilse's life.

The bottom floors of the building burst outwards like flowers. Fiery yellow narcissi flash first, then the petals lick back and up like burgundy roses. Smoke cloaks the floors above and hangs there in a scrunch of taffeta, like a black garter. The streets are a sandstorm. A shard squall of broken glass.

Inside, the fire blast violates the lift shafts; the lifts hang motionless, like hand-stopped pendulums. And the flames find the staircases and find the people on them. The fire is alive and thus must feed, the fire is leviathan, the fire wants to survive, whatever that requires.

And people trapped in rooms by the flames grow so hot that for a moment the cooling rush of air, of falling, seems preferable to such heat. And for a moment it is. Their clothes are blown tight with descent. Too tight to move limbs. Too tight to flap. Too late to evolve. Only falling. Just screaming. People falling. People.

Fire crews rush towards the blaze. Plated in protection they think sufficient. But the firemen will soon be forgiven all their simple sins and petty cruelties; because no one speaks ill of the dead.

***

A helicopter appears. Those who have made it up to the strange green Eden of the rooftop garden wave frantically. But the helicopter has no rescue line and the helicopter will not land. The helicopter just takes pictures. Pictures of people waving for help. Pictures of people falling. Charred-oil people. Dusty-ash people. Bomb-blast half-people.

It is a microcosm of life in the tower: because some give in and some struggle; some strive to help others and some claw them aside and clamber over; some are hale and muscled and some are frail and brittle; some were among the enriched elite, some scrubbed floors on knees scabbed by solvent eczema. And it's a microcosm of life in the tower, because no one leaves alive.

Black smoke flags out into the sky. A watching child thinks he sees an evil face in the smoke. He points it out to his crouching mother with a small, pale, clean finger.

Figures tumble, spinning in the air, like sticks thrown for a pet. But no one's going to fetch, no one's going to retrieve. Stuff flies everywhere. Everything flies. Everything's blurry. Everything's made of glass. Everything can shatter.

In The Kross, people feel the judder of the explosion. And the cynical say The Kross will feel the aftermath. And grey dust drifts through the streets like mist from an old horror film.

The bomber is arrested immediately, almost as if the Interfector who apprehends him knew precisely what he was up to and where he would be found. And the Interfector's eyes look dead already. All the stone-cold killers the bomber has known before, he realizes they were scamps next to this spook. The Interfector doesn't care enough even to kill for kicks. The bomber is just something that needs a decision. But all that's already decided.

Augustus Prometheus, whose tower this is, is inside. He watches from his top-floor window; static, as befits the captain of this *Titanic*. With the lifts dead and the fire now consuming the lower half of the building, there is no way he could make it out. But because the lifts were high speed. Because several minutes had passed before the blast. Because Tabby was scared and running, Augustus is able to believe that she made it in time, that she and his child are safe. And that's not nothing. That's something.

A detective murmurs that there's no such thing as murder-proof; not kings nor presidents nor popes were ever murder-proof. He should have known better. He leaves this other man's apartment to go and find his own place to die: a corridor corner to sit in, near a smashed window, where it is still a bit cooler. A breeze made by the oxygen being sucked in to feed the fire. Through the glasses he can see the air moving, flowing like cold ghosts in the heat. Life seems to have been getting hotter every day since childhood. Since acing the seven-plus SATS and going to a school apart. Günther wonders if the professor was right: whether we could ever have done anything other than we did. Günther thinks about Ilse, wishes that once, just once, a different set of neurons had fired. It could all have been so different, but in the event it wasn't; in the event it never is. Then he thinks of Dolly. A more terminal error. Possibly he's been dying ever since that day. Maybe even this is better than the bug: waiting on its arrival. He flicks the chamber of his revolver. It clicks just like the ticking of a clock; and like clock hands, it only moves in one direction. No sense in dwelling; there's only ever the future, and there's little enough of that. There is still a way to be murder-proof. Gunt puts the Glaxo to his head.

Outside in the gathering mass, those watching think there is a second explosion. Or even a string of near simultaneous explosions, which sink the tower down in on itself, as if it was done by controlled demolition. The people who think that think it came from the seventh floor, not from the basement where the original blast was. But all of those people must be mistaken. They must be confused, or be conspiracy theorists, or they must not know much about building structures or ferrous melting points, because the government-appointed experts and investigators will say that there was no second explosion. The reinforced-steel building concertinas down so impossibly neatly into mangled metal, rubble and dust because its internal structure has been weakened by the first blast; the only blast, rather. To sow seeds of suspicion when your nation has just suffered such an attack is to be a traitor. And newspapers don't talk to traitors. Not in Albion.

39

Holman

IN THE TWO WEEKS since the bombing, safe in Crick's flat, Holman has been working on a new painting, *The Refugees*. An historical picture, set long before his birth, in the days when the waves of escapees fled to Britain from the Islamic incursions and insurrections in Europe that led to the First Caliphate War. An androgynous child sits in the foreground, chest shrunk over its ribs like a street dog. The child has only a loincloth and a toy: a wooden clown that raises up on its arms when a string is pulled from below. The clown resembles a crucified man fighting for breath. This is a new level of ugliness, below and beyond the hardened stares of whores and the broken spirits of the synth drinkers Holman's captured before. But the picture would be blacker if only he could find blacker paint, because refugees are coming to The Kross anew now.

Reprisals were inevitable – or so the papers say – in the shadow of the bomb's horror and so soon after the riots. Those who wish to remain in power cannot do other than retaliate with shock and awe. Not when the Unimproved terrorist was captured red-handed; by the bloodied, bandaged right hand. Not when the 'natural' spawned scumbag babbles at press conferences about sleepers across the land. Not when the unen-riched filth tells that the end time is near and the streets will be swamped with blood. Not when the womb-rat says the Improved have no souls and his people will soon rise as one and strike them from the earth. The slaughterous Kross scum is proud of his actions and happy to spout to an audience. Happy to be the fall-guy figurehead for all his knuckleped kind.

The hate that had been slowly growing, like mould inside a bin lid, can now be tasted on the air.

A wall is being erected across the wasteland, blocking out the sign that read *Everything Will Be All Right In The End*. The finished sections of the wall are eight metres high. In front, military engineers in armoured bulldozers – cages over the windows like late-night synth shops – have dug a trench, four metres wide and four metres deep, and between the pit and the barrier laid a stretch of sand, to show the footprints of anyone who comes too close.

The wall is rising fast. Lorries arrive suspension-sunk with prefabricated sections.

'Prefabricated when?' Crick asks.

Because there is an unmistakable sense that this has all been planned ahead. In the last days, Holman and Crick have walked parts of the partition's route, and it is remarkable how much of it includes already existent walls and vacant buildings with bricked-up windows. It is remarkable how few streets need to be blocked by barbed-wire entanglements and soldiers. A perfect ring around The Kross seems already drawn up. As if the forces of order were only waiting for an excuse to execute their plan.

The authorities say this is a temporary but necessary internment, until the malevolent elements can be identified. Until the enemy within is withouted. The wall on the wasteland does not look temporary.

The soldiers who guard the building works and man the barricades are from the sixth army. The battle-hardened 'Butchers of Bilbao'. At the razor-wire road gates they wear rebreathing masks; which make their smoke-lensed eyes look long and alien. Their faces grey. Heavy machine guns – burly one-eyed beasts – poke from sandbag hides, snouts sniffing the horizon, handlers hidden from view. They serve to say that there will be no more riots now. The days of throwing bottles and bricks are gone. Welcome to the future, feel free to stay.

Those who want to leave The Kross must queue to be scanned. It is an open secret what the yellow digital script of the chip readers must say if you are to be permitted: you need only have a little list, just the basic immunities that any Improved person would have. The watershed is that sharp now. The apartheid is precise.

But they keep the synth flowing. They keep the party going. Twenty-four hours. Hand over fist. These days may go down in history; people who fear the future hit it hard: falling Rome; *fin de siècle* Paris; Weimar Berlin; 1970s New York; pre-Caliphate Madrid. The Kross' residents are made for synth and self-destruction: animals that grow in conditions of deprivation addict easily; the dopamine rewards of oblivion are the only rewards they know. So on with the show. Roll out the barrel. Like it or not, it's a lock-in.

Crick could leave if he wanted. Because Crick is Improved, though his face is burnt away. Though his mouth is a slashed tyre slit and his eyes streaked cicatrices. But why would he, and where would he go?

Crick's fingernails have grown long and pointed, untended like wolf claws. He's stopped biting them since internment. His writing's flowing. They wander together in the mornings. Holman describes and Crick absorbs. The afternoons they both work. In documenting these events, Crick has rediscovered purpose.

Holman holds his muse in the inner pocket of his suit, imbibing his own feral smell. The picture of Adele Nicole is from a newspaper in the days after the blast. She is believed to be among the martyrs. Her houseboy told the press that she went to see Augustus that fateful afternoon. She is once again newsworthy now: 'The Unimproved Terrorists Even Murdered Their Own Queen'. Holman can't call Sebastian; there are now no phone lines out of The Kross, for fear extremist cells could send orders. Or so they say.

So he paints them instead, his mother and brother, holding each other against a wash of red. Holman's glad they had each other at the end, if that's how it had to end. Why shouldn't they have sought a little comfort with each other when they were alive as well? Augustus must have seemed to her like the younger version of the man she loved. A version better suited even. It is all too easy to forgive when it is all too late.

Holman can't make sense of it. He can't grieve when he doesn't know for sure. And yet life of recent weeks leaves him little reason for optimism. Is he filtering his grief through art, does he lack that capability entirely, or is it just coming like a train delayed? Is it going to hit his track-tied self soon?

Presumably Holman will eventually inherit his mother's estate, but only once the law decides if she is really dead. Thousands must be in the same situation.

His brother's fortune will go to his wife and new child. Holman didn't even know they had a child. *Ozzy*, the papers say. Brave baby Ozzy, the last person to make it out alive. The symbol of new hope. Prometheus lives on.

There is no mention of the other Prometheus: the unenriched brother warrants no column space, even though the papers are filled with the horrors of his ilk.

This morning on their walk, Holman saw a group praying together in the ghetto. Outside, in the open, as if internment had given them pride. They seemed happy. The happiest people he's seen in weeks.

Does it matter if religion's a lie, if it's a good lie? If it's a lie we evolved to believe so we could bear to live, like we evolved lungs so we could breathe? As he looked at the praying circle, Holman stepped on a lump of wood in the gutter and a fungus or something exploded and coated his trousers in a spray of green. Nature always finds a way. That's all you can say in the end: nature finds a way.

40

De Castillo

D E CASTILLO KNOWS THESE woods like the way to the pisser. He used to play soldiers here, in those days when he used to play. Then he used to bunk school in them, smoke fags and drink synth in them, banged his first few girlfriends in them. They should be full of sweet memories, these woods. But they're not tonight. They're pretty bloody creepy, in fact. Make him almost glad he's got the guy with him. Though the guy still hasn't said anything, and it's not like De Castillo wants to get to know him. But De Castillo wouldn't want to be alone in these woods tonight. Even if – by the nature of the job – on the way back he will be.

The cobwebs disquiet him. Invisible to his torch's beam, they drape across his face with the dark's foulness, leave him feeling invaded. Like he woke to find a cockroach crawling around his mouth. As if he ever sleeps well enough for that to happen. He's wiping his cheeks constantly as he brushes between the trees. His companion doesn't seem to be affected by this hindrance, but then he doesn't have use of his hands anyway, and maybe the blindfold that covers half his face makes the webs less disgusting. His skin looks real waxy whenever the torch shines on him. They must have sweated him a lot before it came to this. De Castillo suspects he's Unimproved. They didn't say either way, but the Unimproved are all being interned now; maybe they had to get him quick while they could. The guy's wearing a cheap shirt, in which he shivers in the chill of the woods, and his hair is black and plasticky, now covered in a shredded nest of twigs and leaves that have stuck to it from branches and falls. He's as blind as old Crick, the last man injured from De Castillo's platoon, who took the phosphorus grenade that time. Crick missed the end of the war. Missed the mushrooms and the searing lights; missed it being all over for those Caliphate fucks.

The guy keeps falling over – because his legs have gone weak or because he can't see – but since his hands are tied behind his back and to the tail of rope that De Castillo holds, every time he goes down, De Castillo has to grab under his dank armpit and yank him up. It's tiring work. De Castillo didn't sleep again last night, just stared at the ceiling and his life through his own eyelids until grey daylight slunk through the stained curtains. He could have done without this – slogging round the woods with a dead man in tow – and he can't help feeling he's messed up the route somewhere, because he's pretty sure he should have been at the shaft by now. It's not that these woods are even that big, and he knows them well, or once he did; it's not like it's something to worry about; but it'll all just take even longer now.

He must be going round in sodding circles. He sees a tree that looks familiar, like he's seen it already tonight. Though it's also anything but familiar, it's bloody freaky-looking. It's only got one bough – thick as a babottweiler's throat – lurching sideways from its trunk a few feet above his head. Set just high enough from the floor for someone to be hanged from it. If the guy was to be left as a message, it would be perfect. But he's not, he's got to disappear, and De Castillo knows he'll be screwed with forensics if the body's found. De Castillo hates the man for that. Hates him for what he represents: that De Castillo has to do what other people say he has to do, however risky and shitty. And because of this hatred, he knows that he'll have no problem killing the guy and slinging him down the shaft. When he eventually bloody gets there.

De Castillo keeps moving, shoving his prisoner onward, and jerking him up when he stumbles. A weary, trudging race against the dawn. De Castillo'd be pleased about the light coming, if it didn't represent failure and danger. He's sick of the dark, and the torch-cast spastic shadows of the trees. Shadows as black as your shit turns after you swallow too much of your own blood. He strokes unconsciously the scarred and flattened jut-bump that remains of his nose. He's not the sort of man that's scared of shadows. He's the sort of man that likes them, lurks in them. He's the sort of man unlikely to come across anyone more to be feared than himself; whether in a rough pub or a dark alley or a sodding wood. He's the one with the torch and the rope-end in his hands and the .22 piece in his belt and the unmasked eyes and the untied wrists and the woollen hat and the leather coat on. So why is he shivering as much as the guy?

Now he's at the edge of the ring road again. Strands of long-ago wind-shredded plastic bags hang like flayed skin from the barbed wire on top of the mesh fence. He doesn't know who that fence is supposed to be stopping from going where. And he doesn't know what the hell's going on, how he's ended up back here. He used to know where he was going, once upon a time. These days he feels like he's sitting in a tyre and rolling down the hill. No control, no way of stopping, just dizzying sickness and the certainty that it can't go on for much longer and it's going to end with a juddering crunch that he won't get up from. Not this time.

Pull yourself together, De Castillo.

You're not the sort of man that loses it.

Focus on the job.

Find the shaft, get it done, and get out of here.

He grabs the guy, who has fallen again. Pulls him steady and pushes him in the new direction. The once proud Parachute Regiment tattoo on De Castillo's hand seems like it's crumbled in on itself. The fractured torchlight and his drooping flesh make it look more like an old broken umbrella tonight.

The guy's doing his best to stay upright, to head where De Castillo prods or leads him. He must know there's no way out, but he still struggles on, hoping that something or someone will come along. Or just not knowing what else to do. Just wanting it to be over.

De Castillo wonders what he would do, in the man's place. A thought that has a sickening, ball-shrinking edge to it, because that is not just some hypothetical. That is a situation that might just come around sooner or later, if De Castillo can't figure out how to get out of this business. And he can't figure that out. His every waking moment – and he gets fuck-all sleep – is spent not figuring that out.

Would he try and fight back, if he were the prisoner? How, with blindfold and bound hands against an armed hardman in an unknown place? That's a path that can only lead to the executioner's one threat left: to do this a more primitive way, like they used to do in the Caliphate; to turn those final moments into moments of unimaginable agony and to make those moments long. No, he would act just like his prisoner is, staggering on and hoping it will be quick, eventually. A rivulet runs down the leg of the man's suit trousers, like the streak De Castillo's leaky fridge leaves daily on his shitty rug. He can only hope he wouldn't piss himself. That's about all he can hope. But right now De Castillo just needs to hope he can finish this before dawn.

Everything seems to happen at dawn; it's the meeting place of the old enemies – where the light hasn't won and the dark hasn't fled – and De Castillo knows he is in it over his shaved and scarred charity-pack head if he doesn't have this dusted by then. This area has gentrified since he grew up here. There will be dog walkers. There will be witnesses. There will be people with handsome faces, and beautiful bodies and assertive intelligence and unshakeable, unscareable senses of self-worth. Wankers, in other words. People who won't even be tired at that time of day, because they slept so bloody well.

De Castillo kicks sideways at the tree, the blighted one-armed bandit that's stealing away his time. How can he be back at the bloody tree again?

He's been fighting halfway round the world, to end up back here. To end up where he started, in these woods he grew up in. Working for guys he grew up with; who've never been anywhere, who've never done anything, except grow dirtier and danger-ouser and get hooked up with the Regans.

They told De Castillo that everyone has forgotten about the shaft now. Though it was local news, for a short while, when they were kids. When that other kid rag-dolled down it. There was a campaign, led by the sniffling parents still paying the instalments on him, to have it filled in with concrete. But it fizzled out, like everything did round here, back then. Too expensive probably, or needed too many trees cut down to get the cement trucks in. It just had metal doors fixed over it. Stainless steel, to replace the rotted wood. Padlocked shut and left to it. Overgrown and out of mind. The padlock has been bolt-cut off, though. They did it. Or rather some other fool who has to do what they say did it. De Castillo's got the key to the new lock in his pocket.

'Flawless,' they said.

De Castillo is the flaw. Him and the first parrot-crap-grey streaks of daylight that are now oozing through the tree canopy.

He hears a wolf howl, unmistakable. But these are not the sort of woods that have wolves in them. So it must have been a dog, or some dog chimera, whatever it sounded like. Wolves are just dogs with empty stomachs and full seed bags; we can all be wolves given the right set of circumstances. De Castillo knows that better than anyone. But he fears dogs more anyway, at the moment, given this predicament. Because dogs mean dog walkers. Dogs are part of daylight's threat. The failure that will mean going on the run, or death, or both. De Castillo's not afraid of death, but he's afraid of dying afraid.

He punches the guy in the back of the neck, only because he doesn't know what else to do. The man makes a noise like air from a dropped kitbag, no grunt of pain. Then De Castillo has to help him up again and push him forwards, because he can't stop moving.

On the next try he doesn't even get as far as the ring road's fence, because as he nears it he can already hear the low growl of military lorries, taking ever more prefab wall sections into London. The guy slumps down on to his knees and then his arse and starts to laugh. Even sightless, he seems to know they've been here before. He laughs a mucky Irish laugh. And it's the laugh of a man so far past despair or hope that absurdity is suddenly funny again. A noose-necked murderer whose trapdoor won't open. In other circumstances De Castillo might like him for that. De Castillo's the sort of man who admires bravado. But right now he can't remember the last time he liked anyone or anything, except sleep. He grabs where the man's ears bulge from the blindfold and uses them to force him up to his feet. Then De Castillo butts his thick-skulled forehead into the guy's nose. It makes that satisfying crunch as the bone breaks. He stops laughing then.

The light of a sunny morning mocks from the lens of the switched-off torch, which De Castillo still holds only because it won't fit in any of his pockets.

He used to play soldiers in these woods, in those days when he used to play. They should be full of sweet memories, these woods. He once knew these woods like he once knew his family.

Sporadically he hears the bark of dogs now, him with a man, not a mutt, on a rope lead. A dead man, not yet dead. The top half of his head covered in a thick black cloth, the lower in the congealing blood that swamps his dumb moustache. De Castillo is not the sort of man who would go unidentified, if spotted in circumstances such as these.

De Castillo has made the guy kneel on the leaf-litter floor. It's all too late now. This is the only way.

De Castillo unties the man. Who moves his newly released hands minutely slowly, either through cramp or fear, to rest on the floor by his heels.

De Castillo repeats his words, more or less exactly as before: 'Count to ten thousand before you take off the blindfold, then get out of here. Piss off far away. Disappear, for ever!'

The man says, 'Thank you, feller,' in a placid whisper, but is still expectant, body instinctively braced against a shock it couldn't possibly counter. Like he thinks this hope De Castillo's given him is just a final kindness, or final cruelty, before a bullet pulps his brain.

De Castillo pushes the pistol down the back belt of his trousers; chucks the torch; bandoliers the rope across his chest, in what he hopes will look like a workman's carry to anyone he encounters. It seems almost certain he will meet people before he gets out of here. It seems unlikely they will think he is a workman.

It's only as he's leaving the guy – who is counting quietly, but still tensed against a death that is not now going to come – that De Castillo realizes where he's seen that chin before. He's seen a few of them, of different ages, but all identical. All on men you definitely don't want to kill. So maybe De Castillo was screwed from the start.

He knows his petty despot bosses will find out about his failure sooner or later. He just doesn't know whether to try and bluff it out till he can get some money together; or to get as far away from here as he can, while he can. He should never have come back. Of course not. But the memories made him. He used to play here once.

41

QUIGLEY REGAN PULLS OFF the night-damp blindfold and wipes the mucus of blood from his moustache. Looks about him, blinking in the sun, bursting with the vernal feeling of resurrection. He's never been anywhere as crammed with chlorophylled life as this wood. Not since Red Nell's garden and his early years. But he'll never see his mother again. However they discovered that he grassed, he's dead to his brothers now. Maybe he was never their brother to begin with; there's more to a man than a collection of chromosomes. There are dog chimeras barking in the distance and the noise stirs his spirit, pulls him to his feet. First get moving, then get a dog. Maybe get a real one. Something that took thousands of generations of breeding; there's a certain artistry to such animal husbandry as that: a dedication to something grander than yourself.

The jihadi, Lazarus, becomes animated in front of the gathered journalists; he thumps his handcuffed wrists down on the table.

'You call us *credules* and *cretins*,' he sings, 'but you don't even know where "cretin" comes from. From *Chretiens*: *Christians*; it was not an insult, but a reminder: that those who appeared less fortunate were men, not beasts. You hate us, you seek to destroy us. But it is you who are the beasts; we have what you lack: souls. For the soul is endowed by God at the moment of conception, and those who are not conceived have none. It is you who will be extinguished when the Lord's people rise from their slumber. Your attempts at genocide will fail.'

'Ugly word, *genocide*,' the suited spook who watches murmurs. 'I prefer *evolution*.'

Sebastian kneels and plants a kiss on the soil, like a worshipping animist. Nothing lasts for ever, but she'll be happy here, under the purple bougainvilleas. And his mistress will be remembered as she deserves: as Britain's last natural beauty.

Valentine's not made for prison life. It's dull and it stinks. How do guys who do sod-all get so sweaty? The rumours change every day, in this post-Promethean world. But the one that keeps on coming back is that those Unimproved guilty of minor crimes are going to be released, into The Kross. Now they have internment anyway, it makes economic sense. Valentine can only hope the rumours are true. Can only hope his crimes are minor enough; because he will wither and fade in here, and Valentine's a man made for dancing.

Tabby holds up little Ozzy. Only he makes the going-on possible. Only the will to stop anything ever hurting him again in his life.

'You will do whatever you want, my prince,' she whispers into his soft hair. 'The greatest men in the country will look to you and the things you will do, my Ozymandias.'

Though all exhausted from unpaid overtime, it is a surprisingly large crowd of enforcement officers who have gathered to salute the new plaque. *Even until the end*, it reads, *He feared nothing. He gave all. He was the best of us.*

And Gunt would have been fine with that.

Holman's flabby tongue licks the synth-rotted hollow in the centre of his teeth. Whenever he does so, the hole seems to be extended. Like it is decaying appreciably hourly. Holman feels mortality upon him at every moment. What would he give to be a squirrel, a rag-tailed rat, with ever-growing incisors, whose only thought is to survive. Humans have to survive and simultaneously know that they cannot. What would he give to believe in heaven, like the folk he sees pleading passers-by to prayer on the street corners?

Internment conditions in The Kross descend daily. There are bodies lying, unburied and unmourned, in the litter-clogged gutters. Da Vinci used to attend executions to sketch the faces of the dead; Holman need only take these walks outside.

Yesterday he saw a corpse that looked familiar: the pencil stub guy who mocked him at the bullfight, lying there bloated, blue and hairless against a wall. An unwished-for revenge, out of all proportion to the sin.

Crick holds Holman's arm, not just to let himself be guided, but for the human contact in the horror. Holman has become Crick's eyes now, and he describes what he sees so vividly – with an artist's attention to detail – that Crick feels almost as if he's regained his vision. But pictures such things he's glad he has not. Later they'll chronicle it, both after their fashion. They will glaze the moments, like scenes on Grecian urns. Someone has to. Someone must document times like these. Even if the paintings and writing will only be hidden for now.

42

Crick

CRICK TYPES:

A would-be escapee pokes head-wise, helpless, through a hole in the bottom of a room-less building, part of the barricade not yet reinforced. Soldiers smoking on the other side see him. They crack his skull open with the bricks he pushed out. Who gives a shit if you kill the odd still-born? The hole is blocked from the guard's side. The body – shoved back, now on no-man's-land sand – is left for flies to pock, and to rot.

All the bodies would be left where they were, if it weren't that committees have been set up. Superimposed from the world outside the walls. Certain individuals have been elevated to run things inside. They get paid and they get extra rations and offices. They probably get promises as well. There were no elections; they have been selected. Some were party members, some were gangsters.

Even the dead are no longer allowed to leave The Kross. The crematoriums have been vamped up, to deal with the collateral of concentration. Corpses are incinerated in paper shrouds and cardboard coffins. A few are suicides, many are victims of 'the Flowers': a sudden disease they say takes more each day, with blood-burst blooms.

Some people have taken to wearing masks, surgical lints and biker bandannas. They think that by this, and by avoiding touching others ungloved, they may evade whatever eerie illness this is. But they can't hide in their homes; those who do, starve. There are two ways you can die of the Flowers: fast through the fact or slow through the fear.

Newspapers – mostly wall-thrown or windblown; they are no longer sold in here – allege that if there is such a disease, then it is quite certain that it is linked to the bestial way the Unimproved live: 'Like the cannibals of old suffered from prion disease, humans must leave the dark past if they are not to suffer from Dark Age illnesses.' Rumours of contagion only increase calls from the press to prolong the internment, to protect the general populace.

It appears that the power to shut people up indefinitely is still on the statute books anyway; no new law even required: the 1603 Act for the Ordering of Infected Persons.

Inside, some people begin to wonder if they see bruises on themselves, even when there are none, or even when they know the cause. Others ignore the Flowers entirely. As if they're in a salsco club, and though more and more people are being quietly taken outside and murdered, they carry on dancing, because what else is there?

Yesterday some of the soldiers made a group of girls dance all day long, until they dropped from exhaustion. Then they beat them anyway.

Food rations are brought in daily. People have to have their arm ID chips scanned to pick them up. Fifteen hundred calories per day. Mostly potatoes. 'Scan your chips to get your chips,' one ration doler jokes, like he's trying to get trade at a market, when the rations are almost the only show in town. The lines are long; the wait itself can occupy several hours.

Earlier a woman tried to flee the ration queue and escape when a gate was opened. A guard broke her nose with his rifle butt and then he broke her teeth with his rifle butt and then he broke the rifle butt itself. No one else tried to escape.

But there aren't even rations for everyone; some are arbitrarily excluded, perhaps only to create gratitude and fear in those who aren't. Sometimes people are declined when their scans have always entitled them before.

A declined man snatched a hunk of bread from a ration doler. The doler beat him about the head and back with a closed-fist thump. The man seemed oblivious; he just tried to stuff as much of the bread into his mouth as he could. His hunger more urgent than the pain.

Some beggars have started to hold up pictures of what they once looked like: showing themselves as healthy, hearty people. Apparently it is a popular strategy, as it does elicit sympathy to see whence they have come to this.

The water is only on intermittently. People are getting lice. The papers say that the Unimproved are dirty, and for once they are right.

Broodmares who are pregnant with an enriched child and have papers to prove it were released and taken to a separate camp, where nutrition and conditions are supposed to be optimum. The man who told me this said it means we can expect internment to last at least nine months. I think him an absurd optimist.

In spite of the Flowers, the brothels and the strip clubs do better than ever. There is end-of-age abandon. With the food ration, money is bizarrely unimportant, those who have it mostly throw it around, though some hide it away in the hope that it may help them in the uncertain future.

People are hungry for news; rumour and misinformation spring like mushrooms after rain. There has still been no rain.

There is a stink in the streets; it's said sections of the sewers have been blocked to prevent escape.

A man in a home-made hang-glider was shot from the sky, spiralling down like a lamp-singed moth. Parts of his hang-glider still dangle from a wall. From the old broken glass set in shark-fin triangles in the concrete of its top and the sun-slicing bright new razor wire above that.

The wall's erection has been seamless and sudden. Holman and I have the feeling that this partition has long been discussed as a solution to the quandary of the Unimproved.

I tried to talk to the soldiers at a gate, told them I had served my country; I showed my Parachute Regiment tattoo; I got a sense of shame, but that was all.

Holman is holding up well, from his bereavements and this new world. We drink less now; we have our work and we have each other.

We may yet extend the sanctuary of our flat, because it's more crowded than ever in The Kross. They say that identity checks are being performed across Britain. In Croxteth and Govan, Moss Side and Maryhill, soldiers, police and Interfectors scan on suss. And on the screens of chip readers, the numbers come, from where they are indelibly inked inside all of our arms. When the condemning words 'no immunities' appear, the digital script tells all the authorities need to know: human worth defined by yellow stars.

And every day now, more trembling specimens of 'sub-men' arrive on the trains. With one suitcase apiece they come, to find what future they can ferret on the streets of The Kross. There wouldn't be space for all the new arrivals, except that mortality is so high. But they say there will be more trains soon, to this ghetto of plague; that long-silent lines are being readied. And they say the trains will run on time.

43

FOOTPRINTS ARE ON THE sand in front of the barrier that constricts The Kross. But they are up above the ground, like three-dimensional negatives, like police plaster-casts of footprints. Where the pressure of human weight was placed, the sand must have been compacted and made stronger. And now the wind has stripped a layer away, the footprints remain, raised like altars.

Someone tried to get out, the footprints say; by the way they disappear at the wall. It is impossible to tell if their maker succeeded. But perhaps he did: the footprints are double-arched, so perhaps their maker was fast.

Far to the north, a heavy-set man with a pale upper lip eats in the shade of a tree. Though he gives away almost as much as he consumes, to the dog in the crook of his legs. It's a stump-muzzled pup, can't be long weaned, but it eats all it's presented and licks even the scents from its master's fingers. It could be a pedigree or it could be a mutt; at that age they all look the same. But the man knows, better than most, that not all things that look the same are.

And there's a woman, with a ragged green ribbon still tied around her arm, above a vacant tattoo that once held a name. Fine sea spray is leaving her face powdered with scales of salt as she stands on the prow of a boat that ploughs proud into the waves.

The craft is piloted by an ancient mariner, as brave as the west wind. An old man of the sea, once a broken wino, who found his nerve again. None on board are short of courage; they strike out for some new somewhere, on a boat salvaged and patched; a pilgrim crew, of misfits and maybes. So that's what they called her, their ship of scrap: *The Maybe Flower*.

And out there in the oceans, there remain places where crocodiles and sharks share the same waters. At times their lamp-pale undersides flash one another as they curve away, like polite drivers ceding priority. But that's just an illusion. The sort of thing a writer or artist or unbalanced detective might imagine. The sharks and the crocodiles – though they crossed paths for millions of years before either ever tasted naked ape – show no professional courtesy. They but rarely even register their rivalry. And it will be millions of years yet before they know which of them has won.

Acknowledgements

Thanks to: James Gurbutt; Amanda Preston; Tally Garner; The Monkey; Grendel; Mum and Dad; Camelia Liparoti; Anna Davis, my professor; Nick Connold; Kevin Ellis; Zavier Ellis (no relation); John Chambers; Tim Hiscuit; Tony Keating; Nigel McGuire; Jim Hinks; Jo Stansall; Charlotte Macdonald; Emily Burns.